JJ RICHARDS

The Dunes

DCI Walker Crime Thrillers (Book 4)

Simulacrum Press Publishers

First published by Simulacrum Press Publishers 2025

Copyright © 2025 by JJ Richards

All rights reserved. No part of this publication may be reproduced, stored or transmitted in any form or by any means, electronic, mechanical, photocopying, recording, scanning, or otherwise without written permission from the publisher. It is illegal to copy this book, post it to a website, or distribute it by any other means without permission.

This novel is entirely a work of fiction. The names, characters and incidents portrayed in it are the work of the author's imagination. Any resemblance to actual persons, living or dead, events or localities is entirely coincidental.

JJ Richards asserts the moral right to be identified as the author of this work.

JJ Richards has no responsibility for the persistence or accuracy of URLs for external or third-party Internet Websites referred to in this publication and does not guarantee that any content on such Websites is, or will remain, accurate or appropriate.

Designations used by companies to distinguish their products are often claimed as trademarks. All brand names and product names used in this book and on its cover are trade names, service marks, trademarks and registered trademarks of their respective owners. The publishers and the book are not associated with any product or vendor mentioned in this book. None of the companies referenced within the book have endorsed the book.

First edition

ISBN: 9798307236185

Editing by Hal Duncan
Cover art by Tom Sanderson

This book was professionally typeset on Reedsy.
Find out more at reedsy.com

Contents

PROLOGUE	1
CHAPTER ONE	12
CHAPTER TWO	22
CHAPTER THREE	27
CHAPTER FOUR	32
CHAPTER FIVE	39
CHAPTER SIX	42
CHAPTER SEVEN	48
CHAPTER EIGHT	55
CHAPTER NINE	59
CHAPTER TEN	65
CHAPTER ELEVEN	72
CHAPTER TWELVE	76
CHAPTER THIRTEEN	81
CHAPTER FOURTEEN	83
CHAPTER FIFTEEN	88
CHAPTER SIXTEEN	94
CHAPTER SEVENTEEN	101
CHAPTER EIGHTEEN	111
CHAPTER NINETEEN	118
CHAPTER TWENTY	123
CHAPTER TWENTY-ONE	129
CHAPTER TWENTY-TWO	132
CHAPTER TWENTY-THREE	136

CHAPTER TWENTY-FOUR	141
CHAPTER TWENTY-FIVE	145
CHAPTER TWENTY-SIX	148
CHAPTER TWENTY-SEVEN	156
CHAPTER TWENTY-EIGHT	159
CHAPTER TWENTY-NINE	165
CHAPTER THIRTY	170
CHAPTER THIRTY-ONE	175
CHAPTER THIRTY-TWO	185
CHAPTER THIRTY-THREE	189
CHAPTER THIRTY-FOUR	197
CHAPTER THIRTY-FIVE	202
CHAPTER THIRTY-SIX	206
CHAPTER THIRTY-SEVEN	210
CHAPTER THIRTY-EIGHT	214
CHAPTER THIRTY-NINE	217
CHAPTER FORTY	221
CHAPTER FORTY-ONE	226
CHAPTER FORTY-TWO	235
CHAPTER FORTY-THREE	240
CHAPTER FORTY-FOUR	257
CHAPTER FORTY-FIVE	267
EPILOGUE	271
A Note From the Author	275

"We shall not cease from exploration, and the end of all our exploring will be to arrive where we started and know the place for the first time." **T.S. Eliot**

PROLOGUE

July 4th, 2011

'Why are you doing this to me?' asked Sally, pleading for her life. His face red and sweaty, her abductor looked down at her, straddling her on the bed, holding a rusty old chef's knife. 'Look, you don't have to do this. I won't tell anyone. I swear.'

'It really is nothing personal, my dear,' he replied as they struggled, his legs squeezing her tight, showing her who was boss. 'I just... have to. I've no choice in the matter. It's time. But if you scream, I *will* cut you, and it *will* hurt.'

'What are you... doing?' she said, stalling for time, her thoughts racing frantically. She never should have gone away, not alone. It was stupid, dangerous. And she'd not even told anyone where she was going or what she was doing. She'd just wanted to be alone, be somewhere else, to start over after everything that happened—the unplanned pregnancy, the abortion, the break-up and all that. She'd gone off the rails a bit in her late teens and early twenties, she knew it, had been partying hard—probably because she'd never really dealt with what had happened to her when she'd been younger. She'd been hanging round with a bad crowd, drinking and taking drugs, met the wrong guy, but she wanted to turn over a new leaf now, stop all that, start fresh. To do that, though, she'd needed some money, so she'd rolled the dice, took a gamble, had threatened to go to the police about what happened all those years ago—had toughened up and demanded the bastard gave her some money. It wasn't blackmail. She didn't see it like that at all. It was compensation. And by God, she deserved it.

She'd arranged to pick up the money on some old industrial estate just outside of Birmingham. He'd said some guy called Steve owed him money there. She thought it was perfect, as she was heading south to London anyway—she'd always wanted to try living in the capital, where it was all happening. She thought she might be able to make something of herself there, *if* she had the funds to get started; it was incredibly expensive to live in London. She wasn't stupid though. She'd brought a knife with her, just in case there was any trouble, for protection, and she wasn't even going to get out of the car, would keep it locked, just roll the window down a little to get the package. But it had all gone terribly wrong, and now she didn't know where the hell she was, trapped, confused, and alone. It was all so messed up. She mustn't have been thinking straight. It was reckless. She could see that now.

'Just, hold still, will you?' said the man, who'd confirmed his name was Steve when they met—but she doubted that was his real name now. He'd been the one who'd shown up at the industrial estate, said he had the money for her. She had no idea what happened after that. The last thing she remembered was being in her car, window down, talking to him, and then she came to on this bed, realised she'd been abducted. He must have drugged her, somehow. She felt her neck—it was a little sore, like she'd been injected there. 'This will go a lot easier if you cooperate,' he said.

'What will?' she asked, terror welling up, spiralling, making her feel like she'd already died. Was that what he was going to do—*kill* her? Was that why he'd brought her here, in this...? It was a motorhome—she could see the steering wheel up front. No, she thought, he was just trying to scare her... she hoped.

'I just need to... I just need you to be her for a while first,' he said. 'I can't help it.'

He wasn't making any sense at all. He was a complete madman.

'Be *who?*' she asked. 'I can be anyone you want. Just... don't hurt me,' she said. 'I'm sorry.'

The man pointed the knife at her, even more threateningly than before, his expression stern, austere, telling her she'd better not disappoint him. He slowly clambered off, keeping the knife pointed right at her. 'Don't even think about moving,' he said. 'Or else. I *will* use this. I have before.' She believed him too.

He took some items from a nearby cupboard—a summer dress, some glasses, and a scrunchy—and put them on the bed.

'Put these on,' he said.

'But...'

'Just put them on!' he insisted, raising his voice. So, she did, stripping off the jeans she wore with a hole in one of the knees, followed by her lavender fields pastel coloured fluffy-knit top, and pulled on the dress. She never once took her eyes off him, but her vision was blurred first by the tears in her eyes, and then by the glasses she put on—which were prescription, and not a good match for her eyesight.

When she was done, she could just about see him looking

her up and down as he said, 'Good. Now, lie back down on the bed.' She did as instructed, not wanting to anger him further.

Next, he opened another cupboard—below the one he'd got the previous items from—and took out several large glass jars containing… something. She peered over the top of the glasses frame and saw that the something in question was moving, crawling, squirming around, some flying. It looked like a variety of bugs and insects, real nasties.

'What the hell is that?' asked Sally, horrified, her imagination running riot. She hated bugs. She couldn't even get a spider out of the bath by herself. Her second-worst nightmare was unfolding right in front of her—her first, well, that's what had got her into this mess in the first place. She felt like she had "victim" painted on her goddamned forehead for freaks like this. She felt cursed. 'What are you going to do to me?" She was starting to cry now, really losing it, her thoughts frantic.

'My babies are hungry,' said the man. 'It's feeding time.'

With that, Sally sat up on the double bed he'd forced her on, instinctively retreating towards the headboard and pulling her legs up into the foetal position, her body telling her to protect herself.

'Look, if there's something I've done wrong, just tell me? I was told to come and pick up the money. Can we just forget about it? It was a bad idea. I can see that now. I won't say anything. You can keep it. All of it.'

'It's too late for that now,' he said. 'You're mine.'

'You're not well,' she said—it was all she could do to stop herself screaming for fear he would attack her, stab her to death in a bloodthirsty frenzy.

The man looked at her, dead in the eyes. 'I'm not crazy,' he said. 'I'm just doing what I need to do, like everyone does. We can't control what we need. It's the longing you see. I must feed that too. It's insatiable.'

'You don't have to do this,' Sally begged, her bottom lip quivering. 'I really won't tell anyone, about this, or anything else, I swear. And you really can keep the money.' It was all so unreal, all of it. She'd never been in any real life-threatening danger before—had only ever seen this kind of thing on TV. Sure, she *felt* like she was dying all those years ago, when she went through what she went through as a teenager, but she knew she'd get past it, somehow. But this was different: her life was in danger. Her parents had given her so much love, especially her mum. It made up for everything, all that bad stuff she'd not told them about. She never should have run away, out into the world all by herself. She should have talked to them, told them, all of it. At twenty-six now, she was a woman in every way possible, but she'd never been independent, had never taken care of herself. She'd still been living in the family home up until a couple of days ago for Christ's sake. She didn't know what she was doing. More tears streamed from her eyes as she wondered if she'd ever see her mum and dad again. They'd be worried sick. She felt for them, and then for herself, the reality of the situation now fully hitting her.

'No, you won't tell anyone,' said the man. 'I already know that. That would be impossible, where you're going. Now... tell me that you love me.'

He *was* crazy. 'You want me to tell you... *what?*" asked Sally, unable to comprehend, unable to do what he asked, her body rebelling in revulsion.

'I want... I *need* you to tell me that you love me, and that you're so grateful for our lovely day at the beach together,' said the man. 'Do it, now.'

'But... We never went to the beach,' said Sally, getting hysterical.

The man got closer again, raising the knife up once more. 'Say it,' he said.

She hesitated. 'I... l-l-love you. And I'm so grateful for...'

'Our lovely day at the beach together.'

'I'm so grateful for our lovely day at the beach together,' repeated Sally, trying to appease him, hoping he'd back off.

'Good,' said the man, seeming satisfied. 'Good girl. That's smart.'

Sally looked at the curtains in the motorhome they were in. They were closed, so she couldn't see outside, but she could smell the sea air—probably parked just off the beach somewhere in a remote spot.

If someone was out nearby, perhaps a dog walker, she could bang on the glass, scream, and maybe, just maybe, she could fight him off until they got in, helped her. But that knife was big, and scary, and he looked like he could handle it. She couldn't risk it. It was too dangerous. And there probably weren't any people around anyway. She was on her own with this, with *him*. And it was up to her to get herself out of it. Perhaps this was her chance at redemption, to empower herself once and for all. It might even change her life for the better if she could turn the tables somehow, hurt him instead. She had to find a way.

'Don't even think about opening those curtains,' he said, reading her mind. 'I've blacked out the windows anyway. Nobody will see you.'

But they might hear her, she thought. 'Can I just go now? I'm begging you. I did what you said—I put these clothes on and said what you wanted me to say. I understand, whatever it is. You needed to feel better. But you can stop now. I won't tell anyone, really. I promise.'

The man exhaled through his nostrils in a controlled, steady fashion.

'Are you sure you're not going to tell anyone?' he said, regarding her, scrutinising her expression.

'No, of course not,' she said, and she wasn't lying, either. She wouldn't tell a soul. She'd go far, far away and never look back, never get involved with anyone like this ever again.

'Alright then,' said the man. 'I'm a bit too tired for this anyway. Let's call it a day then. Be on your way, lassie.'

She wasn't really expecting that at all. Hope flooded back in, rejuvenating every cell. Sally got up off the bed, tentatively, still not quite believing him, thinking it might be some kind of cruel trick. 'I'm going then,' she said, hesitating. She looked at her own clothes for just a split second, the ones he'd made her take off, considered grabbing them, but thought better of it. She needed to get out of there quick smart, while she had the chance. 'I really won't tell anyone, I promise. You don't have to worry about that.'

'Go then,' said the man, nonchalantly. 'Go, go, go!'

She squeezed past him, getting more and more terrified the closer she got to him—his proximity making her skin crawl—then finally getting near the door. 'You didn't have to do this,' she said, thinking it was over. 'You didn't have to go this far. You're not well, do you know that? You should use that money to get yourself some real help. Whatever happened to you, you need to deal with it. Trust me, I know.' She tried the door, but it wouldn't budge. She felt like her heart was jumping out of her chest, so close to freedom, but so far. She shouldn't have said anything, should have kept her stupid mouth shut.

'Locked,' he said.

She started to pull and rattle it, panicking again, keeping her eyes firmly on him and that knife.

'Easy,' said the man, putting the knife down on the kitchen worktop and picking up one of the glass jars filled with insects instead, looking at them, inspecting them with something like pride in his eyes. 'Use your brain. Just turn the lock. It's time for you to leave.'

She turned around, found the locking mechanism, but had to take her eyes off him for a second to find it. She turned the lock, and it opened, relief washing over her, ready to exit; but before she could, the man brought the glass jar down, fast and hard, on her head. It fully connected, but didn't break. It was solid. She fell to the floor, stunned, but still just about conscious. There was nothing she could have done—there was no space to manoeuvre, no time to react. He had her.

'You... You said you'd let me go,' whispered Sally, not having the strength for any more than that, the attack leaving her in a severely weakened state. She felt her head, felt the wetness of blood before it started dripping down onto the floor.

'Oh. I'm good to my word, dear. That's exactly what I'm doing—letting you go. There'll be no more pain after this. You'll end up as fertilizer, and the cycle shall begin again. It is God's way, after all,' he said. 'It's kind of beautiful, when you think about it. There's nothing to be afraid of.'

'Please,' she begged, but she'd almost given up hope now.

'I love you, mummy,' said the man, getting down on his knees, fixing her hair and glasses, brushing her face. 'We'll be together again soon.'

PROLOGUE

'I'm not your—'

There was an abrupt bang on the door, cutting her off mid-sentence. Somebody was outside. There was still some hope. It was a miracle. Sally was clinging on to consciousness now, tried to shout, tried to say anything, but the man covered her mouth with his hand, suffocating her, preventing her from breathing properly.

'Hello?' said the voice from outside—a male one. 'I know there's someone in there. Just heard you talking to someone. Could I have a word, please?'

Her attacker hesitated, just for a second. 'Just a moment. I need to get dressed,' shouted the man. He stretched and grabbed a nearby remote with his free hand, turned some music on, and cranked up the volume, something orchestral. Then he dragged Sally back up onto the bed, still covering her mouth, got some gaffer tape and taped her mouth shut with a rag stuffed inside; then hurriedly bound her hands and feet too. She was still conscious, but only just, couldn't struggle much. She was dizzy, disoriented, but still clinging on to life and hope with everything she had. She saw the man pull a doormat over her blood on the carpeted floor, then he threw a heavy blanket over her, so she was fully covered and could no longer see. With the music on, and her gagged and tied under the blanket, there was little she could do to make whoever it was hear her.

She did hear what sounded like the door opening though. 'What is it?' he asked, voice raised over the music. 'I'm a little busy here. I've been waiting for this live music performance on the radio all day.'

'Parking regulations, I'm afraid,' said the person outside, also talking above the music. 'You need a permit to park here.

You'll have to move on.'

'Fine,' said the man. 'I'll get ready and move soon. Is that all?'

She heard the door close again and she tried one last time to scream, but it came out as little more than a whimper—not enough to challenge the noise of the music.

The man removed the blanket once more, so she could see again. Blood was dripping down her face now, restricting vision even more in one of her eyes—which already wasn't good with the prescription glasses still on—but she could still just about see with the other, and she soon wished she couldn't. The man took out a syringe and filled it with something. That's how he must have got her there in the first place. She tried to move, tried to do anything, but her body wasn't working properly, and she was still bound even if it was, so he injected it into her arm with little fuss.

He watched her for a minute or so, and she looked back at him, wondering what could possibly make a person do such abhorrent things, wondering what kind of a monster he was, what trauma he might have had to endure himself to bring him to this. She was expecting to lose consciousness— like she had when he'd brought her here—guessed it was an anaesthetic. But she was still lucid. He removed the tape from her hands and feet with some scissors and pulled the tape from her mouth. She tried to move again, but she was completely paralysed. She couldn't move a muscle, not even her index finger. *What had he done to her this time? And what was he about to do?* Panic started to rise again, coming in waves. She wasn't just going to die; she was going to suffer too, more than she could possibly imagine. He got several of the bug-filled jars closer to her and started opening them, one by one, pouring out the various nasties—the bugs and insects—onto her body, with her powerless to do anything about it. They crawled and bit her, but thankfully she was numb now, her fear also receding when it should be at its height. She was slipping away—she could feel it—and this she was grateful for.

'Feed, my babies,' said the man. 'Feed.'

Sally closed her eyes, prayed she was dreaming, that she'd wake up from this nightmare soon, that she'd be back home with her mum and dad. She felt some of the bugs find the orifices on her face—her ears, nostrils, and mouth, crawl in there, her disgust diluted, her physical senses diminishing. She closed her eyes, wishing for a quick death, to escape it all. She'd submitted to it now, had accepted it, and that helped. There was nothing she could do. And then she felt the man crawl on top of her too, like one of his bugs, and she prayed to a God she didn't believe in to let her go.

'I love you,' said the man. 'I'm so sorry.'

And then, to her great relief, her mind and body fell away, and it was all, finally, over.

CHAPTER ONE

'Why are we here?' asked Walker. He was with DC Briggs in a small office inside a mortuary called D Hollowell & Sons, just off the South Promenade on Alexandria Drive in Lytham St Annes. They'd been sent there to start their investigation into a thirteen-year-old cold case involving one Sally Fielding, who just happened to be the first cousin of former Deputy Chief Constable Harry Potts—now retired.

'Detective Walker, DC Briggs, it's good to see you both again.' They were talking to the coroner assigned to the case, the familiar face of one Mr Park, a Korean-Lancastrian they'd worked successfully with a couple of times before, the last being just over a couple of months ago in neighbouring Blackpool. That case had been a proper shitshow, and Walker was hoping for something a bit more straightforward this time after a two-month suspension and a review of his leadership of it, investigating any wrongdoings or neglect of duty—a review he was ultimately cleared by, but a case which he nevertheless still felt the need to redeem himself from.

Walker nodded to Mr Park, appreciating his greeting. 'So? I really need to get to the crime scene first, look around. What's so urgent here?'

CHAPTER ONE

'I'm afraid they're sending in the big guns for this one. We've got Chief Constable Sarah Harriet coming along,' said Mr Park. 'She asked that you be here too, *before* attending the crime scene. Said she tried to call you herself, but you never picked up, asked me to let you know if I spoke to you.'

'I see,' said Walker. He already knew the case had the added importance of the alleged victim being who she was, but he'd never have expected the Chief Constable herself to come in person, not for a cold case. 'Who found the body?'

'Some dog walker,' said Mr Park. 'Apparently the dog started digging, frantically, and the owner thought it funny, so they just let it dig, until it picked up an antebrachial bone—a forearm—one that belonged to Sally Fielding. They've already been interviewed. You'll get the transcripts, I'm sure.'

There was a knock on the door.

'Come in,' said Mr Park.

The slightly familiar face of the middle-aged Chief Constable Sarah Harriet—who Walker had met a few times before—entered along with an older male with a pot belly and a balding head. Walker recognised him too. It was Harry Potts.

'Chief, and Deputy Chief,' said Walker, addressing both, not quite sure what to call Harry Potts now he was off the force. DC Briggs nodded and bowed her head, courteously.

'It's just plain old Harry now,' he clarified, his face gloomy, serious. 'Takes some getting used to though, must admit.'

Walker nodded his understanding. 'So, what are we all doing here?'

'Detective Walker,' said Chief Constable Harriet. She had short mousy hair, appeared strict, like a school headteacher of days gone by, not to be messed with. 'I believe Superintendent Hughes already gave you a brief rundown on this.'

'Yes. I understand human remains have been found in the sand dunes at Lytham St. Annes, right by the coast somewhere?' said Walker. 'Estimated to be deceased by more than ten years, I believe.'

'Thirteen,' said Harry. 'Almost to the day. It's our Sally.'

'Yes. I heard the DNA test linked the remains to your family. I'm so sorry,' said Walker. 'Please give my condolences to the rest of your family.'

'Will do. But it's okay. We already knew she was dead,' said Harry.

Walker opened his eyes up, asking for more.

'She'd have been in touch, otherwise,' Harry went on. 'She wasn't the type to just disappear like that. She loved her folks—poor Ken and Sheila. They've never been the same since. Sheila's my auntie, my mum's younger sister, God rest her soul. She's been taking all sorts since her Sally went missing, anti-depressants and that. My mum had been trying to help her through it, for years, before she passed—heart attack, very sudden. I'm concerned this case might tip Sheila over the edge if the media gets hold of it.'

'We're going to do everything we can to keep this one away from the media, do everything possible,' said Chief Constable Harriet. 'And that's an order.'

Walker nodded. 'I promise we'll do everything in our power to—'

'I know the sodding speech,' said Harry. 'I did forty years in the job. Just catch the bastard that did this, give my Uncle Ken and Auntie Sheila some peace, will you? Give us all some.' He glanced at Chief Constable Harriet, communicating something with his eyes.

'Look,' said Walker, 'you know how it is with these cold

cases, Harry. With all due respect, these things are tricky. It was such a long time ago. So much evidence will already have been lost.'

'I'm afraid there's more,' said Chief Constable Harriet. She looked at Mr Park. 'Much more. You haven't seen the half of it yet. Show them.'

Mr Park nodded. 'Come with me.' He led them all down a long corridor, into another room in the mortuary, a larger, much cooler room containing three gurneys, each with some human remains on in various stages of decomposition.

DC Briggs was the first to react, letting out a breath. 'Damn,' she said, before seemingly realising who she was in the company of. 'I mean...'

'We know what you mean, Constable,' said Chief Constable Harriet. 'As you can see, three bodies have been found in the sand dunes at Lytham St. Annes, not just one as we first thought, and we're still looking for more.'

'Superintendent Hughes mentioned you were using ground-penetrating radar to search for evidence,' said Walker. 'All found in the same location?'

'There or thereabouts,' said Chief Constable Harriet. 'All neatly laid out, arms by their sides, as far as we could tell. We have pictures of the graves, prior to extraction. We informed Harry once we had the DNA results confirmed from the first body—one of the officers ran a check on our database of missing persons—and then I contacted Superintendent Hughes, who recommended that yourself and your chosen team be put forward for the investigation. We since found the two other bodies, making this a serial murder case.'

'Good God. Another one? Why me?' asked Walker. 'I've only just come back.'

After his recent review and suspension, what with him being out of action for a while, Walker hadn't been expecting to be assigned to such a big case so soon. His leadership of the Blackpool case had come under considerable scrutiny both internally and by the media—something he felt unfair given the complexities of that case. But this was hardly surprising given the body count and the international riots it had inspired. He was pleased his colleagues had all been very supportive during this time though. They tended to stick together when the going got tough, something he liked about the job.

'Apparently, you have a great track record with such cold cases, a much better success rate than anyone else currently on duty in the area,' said Chief Constable Harriet. 'And with catching serial murderers in general. The work you did over in Rufford was exemplary—now that you've been cleared of those allegations—the case in Rivington too. The more recent case over in Blackpool we're all well aware of too, of course, but not every hit can be a winner, I suppose.' She was right, it was a stain on his record; but it was all over now, time to move on and forget about it. He appreciated the trust she was putting in him, although he wasn't quite sure he deserved it.

Everything else she said was true as well, though—he did generally have a good record of catching such killers over his long career—all except the one that really mattered: that of his dead sister. He'd never really made a dent in that case, had never made any real progress at all, never got anywhere near close, despite his efforts both on and off duty. His obsession with finding her killer had ruined his marriage and his health, so he well knew how Harry Potts and his family might be feeling, and he desperately wanted to help. No, he *needed* to help. Although his record with cold cases was also up there, compared to his peers, he knew the real chances of success with such cases was still relatively low, and she would know that too. His record was just slightly less low than others, in reality.

'I'll do everything I can,' said Walker. 'But I can't make any promises, as you know. It's part process, part luck, at the end of the day. The killer might not even be alive anymore, and the evidence trail could easily hit a dead end at any point, if we can even get started, that is.'

There was a pause in proceedings while they all took a few seconds to take it all in.

'Doesn't matter if he's dead or alive,' said Harry. 'We just need to know who did it, hold them accountable, officially, close this thing off once and for all.' He glanced at Chief Constable Harriet again. 'It's been going on for too long, now, hasn't it? We all need some closure.'

'It would have been better if I'd been able to inspect the crime scene, with the bodies in situ,' said Walker. 'But I understand you only thought to bring me in on this once you'd exhumed and identified the first victim. Can I see the photos of the graves?'

Chief Constable Harriet handed Walker a brown A4 envelope, already open. Inside were several macabre-looking photographs of the type Walker had seen too many times before. The depths of human cruelty never ceased to amaze him. He looked through them, one by one, with DC Briggs looking over his shoulder. 'The other two bodies look more far gone,' he said, comparing the photos to the remains on the gurneys. 'Have we been able to date these?'

'The time of death of the first body was estimated at ten to fifteen years ago using a combination of taphonomic analysis and environmental data,' said Mr. Park. 'The DNA test matched to Sally Fielding, who went missing in 2011, thirteen years ago. This was consistent with the condition of the remains, including the mineralization of the bones and the degree of collagen degradation. We're still awaiting dental records for confirmation, though this is complicated by the fact that Sally's dentist went out of business years ago and subsequently passed away. The second body has an estimated decomposition timeline of twenty-four to twenty-eight years. This was calculated by comparing the degradation of proteins, such as amino acid racemization, to the first body and adjusting for environmental conditions specific to this burial site. The third body is estimated to have been buried thirty-six to forty years ago, based on more advanced weathering of skeletal surfaces and evidence of soil interaction consistent with a longer burial period. All victims have been confirmed as female.'

'That's pretty eerily regular,' said Walker. 'Could be every twelve or thirteen years or so then. When exactly did Sally go missing? In the summer of 2011?'

'It was early July, 2011,' said Harry. 'Her folks said she went missing on July 1st, and they never heard from her again. Her car turned up just outside Birmingham on July 6th. She was just twenty-six years old—too young. It should never have happened.'

'I'm afraid the remains and condition of the teeth of this body are also consistent with a female who was around twenty-six years old at the time of death,' said Mr. Park. 'Dental analysis revealed wear patterns typical of someone in their mid-twenties, along with incomplete closure of the root apices of the third molars, which aligns with this age estimate. As for the other two bodies, skeletal examination suggests an age of around thirty, with a variance of plus or minus seven years, depending on their lifestyle and environmental factors—which can impact on biological age. The pelvis morphology and cranial suture closure patterns were consistent with individuals in this age range, placing the likely age at about thirty.'

'Well, our first job is to try to ID these other two victims then,' said Walker. 'We find that out, and we might be able to find some kind of a connection between them, take it from there. And in the meantime, I want to see that crime scene.'

'I'll hand things over to you from here on in then, Detective Walker,' said Chief Constable Harriet. 'I just wanted to look over things myself first and impress upon you the importance of this case. Mr Potts will now be going home, won't you, Mr Potts, and leaving this in the good hands of our DCI and his team?'

Harry Potts looked like he didn't want to leave, probably wanted to remain in the area, get involved in the case, do some digging of his own. But he would also know that any evidence found in this way, by an ex-cop, would not be admissible in court. He'd be interfering in a criminal investigation, which was a serious crime itself.

'Indeed,' said Harry. 'But please, keep me in the loop and let us know what's going on.'

'We'll do our best,' said Walker. 'Is there anything else you found with the autopsy?' he asked Mr Park.

'There was. Front upper left central incisors missing on each of the bodies, pulled out post-mortem in a crude fashion, possibly with a pair of pliers. As I said, we've not been able to obtain the dental records of Sally Fielding as of yet, but her family have stated that she didn't have a missing tooth when they last saw her,' he said.

'Interesting,' said Walker. 'Probably souvenirs. Serial killers often take jewellery, clothing, hair, fingernails, teeth, or even larger body parts as personal mementos, unfortunately. It also adds weight to the argument that the same person did this, if there's any doubt—I'm not sure there is. Let me know if you find anything else.'

'Will do,' said Mr Park. 'We'll be going through everything today, so should have a full report for you at the end of the day.'

'Sounds great,' said Walker. 'Let's get over to the site then, DC Briggs, see what's what. We'll start making some calls on the way, get our team mobilised.' He already had it in mind who he wanted on this. It just depended on whether they were all available.

'Aren't you going to show them the other thing?' asked Mr Park, looking at Chief Constable Harriet.

'Of course. There is one more thing, Detective Walker,' said Chief Constable Harriet. 'Although this is where it gets a little weird, if it isn't already.' She opened a drawer and removed a wooden box. 'Each of the victims was wearing a necklace when we found them—almost identical.' She opened the box. Inside sat three necklaces of the type Walker had never seen before. Each one consisted of a black leather string holding a particular species of scorpion encased in a transparent teardrop pendant, possibly glass. 'Observe. The craftmanship is not of a particularly high quality, perhaps homemade.'

'Interesting. And do we know what species this is?' asked Walker.

Chief Constable Harriet nodded. 'We do. *Leiurus quinquestriatus*,' she said. 'Also known more informally as… "the deathstalker scorpion".'

CHAPTER TWO

'DI Hogarth, DC Ainscough, it's good to see you both again,' said Walker. 'And thanks for agreeing to do this. I understand you had to give up some holiday time, DC Ainscough, to work on this with us. That's much appreciated.'

They were sat in the appropriately named Beach Café on the South Promenade in Lytham St Annes. DI Hogarth had half-jokingly said he'd agree to come and join the team as long as they had some lunch first, but Walker knew the voracious Detective was not completely joking, so he reluctantly agreed. The man liked his food, that was for sure, and Walker knew he wouldn't be at his best on an empty stomach, needed him firing on all cylinders for this one—as they did for every case, of course, but this had the added importance of the victim being a family member of one of their own.

'Not a problem,' said DC Ainscough. 'It's good to work with you again. Any time.'

After the fiasco that had taken place in Blackpool, the case involving the killer calling himself 'The Defender', and the widescale social unrest and disorder that followed, Walker was a little surprised the young Detective had given up his holiday time to work with him again. But Walker had been

CHAPTER TWO

impressed with his diligence during that case and wanted him back on his team, gave it a shot. It'd paid off. They needed someone on this exactly like him, someone who was prepared to sift through a mountain of documents, if necessary, or go the extra mile somehow, without complaint, to find that one clue that might get them a foothold on a decades old cold case. Plus, he had DI Hogarth, his trusty colleague, also on board, for his expertise in computer analysis and digital data accumulation. Walker never ceased to be amazed at what he could find.

'Nice place,' said DI Hogarth. 'Didn't think much of the last location—Blackpool. I know some people love it, and it has its quirky charms, but it's not really my cup of tea. Bit more refined here, isn't it? Upmarket.'

'Yes, our killer has been very considerate this time,' said Walker with as much sarcasm as he could muster, while viewing the menu, all of them sat at one of the café tables inside amongst a mannered and well-dressed clientele. 'Enjoy the holiday.'

'Some of these girls might have been on holiday too,' said DC Briggs. 'Enjoying the sea air, maybe getting some sun. Lots of people come up here in the summertime. There's Lytham Festival too—it's a music festival that's attracting some big names these days. I got tickets to see Noel Gallagher's High Flying Birds a few years back but couldn't make it. Got the damned flu. Shame. Plenty of folks come up here for that festival in the summertime, though, so that's something to consider.'

DI Hogarth had already ordered his meal before they arrived and was tucking into some sausage and chips with gravy, with more than a little enthusiasm.

'Mm. It's good,' he said. 'I already checked Lytham Festival, actually. Only started in 2009, so could only have been a possible factor for our last vic. And it was in August back then too, so probably not a factor at all. Hey... this is *really* good. Can we come here again?'

On cold cases like this, there tended to naturally be a slightly more relaxed attitude, due to so much time passing by already, and a few hours here or there not seeming to be of much further significance—unlike on fresh cases, where the first 24-48 hours was vital. But in this particular investigation, with the Chief Constable breathing down Walker's neck, and the victim being someone well connected with the force, he didn't want to hang around too much.

'Maybe we can return when this is all over,' said Walker. '*If* we get a positive result. Nice work checking the festival, though. Can't say I've really heard of it.'

'Well, you're not exactly the alt rock type, are you, Chief?' said DC Briggs with a mischievous tone and a little smirk. 'Not really the music type at all, are you?'

'I wouldn't say that', Walker snapped. 'Used to listen to a bit of Guns N' Roses when I was young, some Poison and Mötley Crüe too.' He immediately regretted this confession, probably trying too hard to make himself sound hip and edgy, but likely doing the opposite, he thought.

'I stand corrected,' she said, with a hint of sarcasm, that smirk now turning into a broad smile.

'Never mind,' said Walker, shaking his head. 'Let's get back to the case. If the festival isn't a factor, then the most likely scenario is that the other two victims are local, or they were here on a holiday or something similar.'

'Well, it's not a holiday if you don't come home though, is

CHAPTER TWO

it?' said DC Briggs.

'What's that?' asked Walker, now getting distracted with choosing his own menu after DI Hogarth's endorsement of the food; also, being guilty, it seemed, of not feeling quite the same urgency with an emerging cold case, even if he did have the Chief Constable up his arse.

'I mean, if these girls did come here for a holiday, and that's a big *if* at this stage, as they could be local—like you said—then it wasn't much of a holiday for them, was it,' she said. 'It would have been an absolute nightmare, no doubt. Poor girls.'

'Well, that's why we're here, Detective, to catch whoever did this to these poor women,' said Walker. 'DC Ainscough. Did you manage to make any headway with the missing person's report? Our first task here is to try to ID those victims. That's our way in to this thing.'

DC Ainscough pulled his tan leather briefcase up onto the table, opened it, took out a file. He handed it to Walker with a little satisfied smile in the corner of his mouth. It was a good sign: *he'd got something.*

'We already know the ID of the first victim is one Sally Fielding, of course, as DNA evidence was able to be taken from the remains and matched to the Potts Family, which we already had on file. They have not had any other family members go missing, so we can be fairly certain it's her,' said DC Ainscough. 'And here's the good news: I think I might have leads on the other two victims as well.'

'Well, that's great!' said Walker, putting the menu back down, flipping through the file he'd been given. 'Can you give me the highlights and I'll read the manuscript later?'

'Of course,' said DC Ainscough. 'I searched for missing persons in Lytham St Annes during the dates provided for the estimated time of death of the other two victims. I narrowed it down to a shortlist, and the ones that popped out with a similar age and gender to the first victim were a Tracy White, aged thirty-one, reported missing on 12th July 1998, never found. Her sister reported she came up to Lytham St Annes on 3rd July in the same year, alone, apparently taking a four-day break there, staying in a hotel. Never came back. And then the next one, which was more difficult to find—found it in the newspaper archives at the local library—was a Jackie Wakefield, twenty-eight, the daughter of a local politician, who went missing in early July 1985. Again, due to the longevity of the cases, it's been problematic getting hold of dental records to confirm this, just like with Sally Fielding, but I have a couple of officers back at Blackpool HQ digging around, so hopefully we'll get something positive back in due course.'

Walker gave it some thought, crunched the numbers. 'Same time of year, with thirteen-year gaps between each victim,' he said. 'And the ages of these missing persons also match the gender and age of our Jane Does.'

DC Briggs whistled. 'That's something,' she said.

'It certainly seems that way,' said Walker. 'But what that *something* is, is for us to find out. Hey, hang on a minute.'

'The dates...' said DC Briggs, her eyes going wide, evidently also realising what Walker just had.

'Oh, no,' said DI Hogarth, putting his knife and fork down. 'It's time to go, isn't it?'

'It's almost thirteen years to the day,' said Walker. 'He's due to kill again, right here, in Lytham. And it's up to us to stop him.'

CHAPTER THREE

'Get them all out of here, now!' said Walker. They were at the site where the bodies had been found, the three deceased young women, up on the blustery sand dunes on the North Promenade at Lytham St Annes. There were several officers still up there, along with a couple of crime scene investigators finishing off their work. Three empty open graves in close proximity were surrounded with police tape on metal poles stuck in the sand. 'And get all of this shit out of here, pronto.'

'Sir?' said one of the officers, as a strong gust of wind shook them. 'Is there a problem?'

'Are we all done with processing the site?' said Walker, raising his voice, but not too much. 'Is there anything else that can be done here?'

'No, I think we have everything we need,' said one of the CSIs. 'We were just finishing up.'

'Then get these holes filled in too. I want it like no one was ever here,' said Walker.

The CSI took a double take. 'You sure about that? What if—'

'Yes, I'm sodding sure,' said Walker, now getting very annoyed with the whole thing. They had a murderer out there who was killing in this area every thirteen years, almost to the day, for God only knows what reason, and by some wild coincidence—or perhaps not—that thirteen-year cycle was almost up once more. He wondered whether the killer might have returned to the graves, disturbed them or dug them up for some reason, before burying them again—something that would be very difficult to verify forensically, but it was a theory. Perhaps that was why the remains had been found now of all times. He could be out there now—the killer—stalking his next kill as they spoke. And Walker also knew that if they missed him this time, they might not have another chance for another thirteen years, if he even lived that long. Given the timeline, Walker thought, if he wasn't dead already, he must be somewhere in the range of fifty to seventy plus years old now already. It could be their very last chance to get him if he was still out there. 'This is all on a need-to-know basis,' he added. 'And all you lot need to know is that we need this back to how it was as soon as humanly possible. Is that clear?'

They all nodded and got to work, despite some looks of confusion, filling the holes back in and removing the police tape.

'And try to leave without being seen, if you can,' said Walker. 'Go a bit further up and walk around if you must. We need to keep all this hush-hush. Don't mention it to anyone, not even your colleagues, or you'll have me to answer to. Got that?'

'Got it, Chief,' said one of the officers. 'Everyone get that?' All the men, and the one female officer who was with them nodded and slowly began to leave once everything had been tidied up. Once they were gone, only Walker, DC Briggs, DC Ainscough, and DI Hogarth remained, the latter of who was still out of breath after having climbed up the sand dunes,

CHAPTER THREE

what with him being not the fittest officers of officers—and that was putting it mildly. He was usually confined to a desk, eating himself into an early grave, so it was good to get him out and about for once, get him some fresh air and exercise.

Walker looked out at the sea just as he had at Blackpool a couple of months earlier, during his last case. There was definitely something in the sea area on the west coast at the moment, he thought. Someone had been coming here, every thirteen years, at least, burying these bodies, breathing the same salty sea air as he was now. It made him feel sick. And it was his job and responsibility to catch that person, bring them to justice, hold them accountable.

'Come on, let's get out of here. And tuck your lanyards inside your shirts. I want us looking like members of the public from here on in. We're just friends out for a walk as far as anyone else is concerned. I don't want to spook whoever it is doing this. This could be our only chance to get them, as we all know,' said Walker, 'And as cliché as it is, killers often come back to their burial sites for whatever twisted reason, so we need to move before our perpetrator potentially spots us.'

They all nodded their complaisance and understanding, did as he requested, headed out of there.

Walker had a thought as they were leaving, though. 'DI Hogarth, any chance of setting up a hidden camera here—one of those motion activated ones with infrared that can see at night—like those that are used in nature documentaries?'

'It's possible. I could arrange that,' said DI Hogarth. 'I'll look into it.'

It wouldn't prove anything, of course, not unless another body was being buried. Anyone could go up there, for any reason—just like that dog walker had, the one who'd found the body. But it might give them a lead to work with, at least, a person of interest to investigate.

They were back down on the beach now, off the dunes, walking further down the coast, heading south, away from the burial site. Walker had parked further down the road on purpose, anticipating a much-needed inconspicuous exit—something which DI Hogarth had grumbled a little about at the time as Walker hadn't revealed why until now.

'We need to get set up somewhere nearby,' said Walker. 'But there's no station at Lytham anymore, is there? They relocated to the new station over in Blackpool as I remember.' He gave it some thought. They didn't want to be wasting time travelling around, not when the clock was ticking as it was. If he was right, their killer was about to strike again any day now. They needed to get on their tail, and fast. But they needed a proper lead to do that, and he knew they might have to get creative to find it—although he wasn't quite sure how yet.

'How about we hire a room somewhere?' said DI Hogarth. He was on Walker's wavelength, understanding the urgency of the situation. That was good. They all needed to be on the same page, and he was confident they would be. That was why he'd chosen them for this team in the first place. Hiring a room for surveillance purposes was well within operational protocol, provided it was justifiable and pre-approved by command. It would be a modest expense logged as part of the investigation, ensuring they had a discreet base near the scene while maintaining operational effectiveness.

'I'd be happy to write it up, get any expenses for the case reimbursed,' said DC Ainscough.

'That's not important now. We can do that later,' said Walker. 'Let's focus on the case for the time being. Time

CHAPTER THREE

is of the essence now we know, roughly, when and where this bastard strikes. If he is a "he" that is. We shouldn't make any assumptions. But chances are he is. They almost always are. Let's find somewhere.'

'Where we gonna go then, Chief?' asked DC Briggs. 'A hotel?'

'Somewhere like that. We can get a room each, and hopefully there'll be a proper business meeting space we can use to conduct our meetings. Let's try to find somewhere like that,' said Walker. 'We can put a "Do Not Disturb" sign on the door, keep the staff out.'

'And then what?' asked DI Hogarth. 'Plant a camera looking like a rock and hope he turns up at the burial site?"

'And then,' said Walker, 'we do what we always do: put all available evidence up on the board and get our thinking caps on, work the case, stay objective.'

'Roger that,' said DI Hogarth, still out of breath, struggling to keep up as they upped the pace down the beach. 'I'm definitely getting room service though. This is going to be a day and night job, I take it, so we need to keep our energy levels up.'

'You can get whatever you like, Detective. As long as we get this freak before he kills again,' said Walker. 'Do that, and I'll buy you all a slap-up meal when this is all over—same place—and you can even finish this time. You have my word on that.'

CHAPTER FOUR

Walker sat with his team inside of the Inn On the Prom hotel on the North Promenade at Lytham St Annes, a 3-Star affair with an indoor swimming pool and live entertainment.

'Are you sure this was the only one available?' asked Walker. 'Couldn't we have got something a bit cheaper, with less eyes on us?'

'It's high season, Chief,' said DI Hogarth. 'Everything's booked up.'

'Well, we better had get reimbursed for this then,' he replied, looking at DC Ainscough, who'd promised to do the paperwork on that. With the alimony money he was paying to his wife and kids, there wasn't much of his wages left over at the end of the month; and managing his finances had never really been one of Walker's strong points to begin with.

'Shouldn't be a problem, sir,' said DC Ainscough. 'As I said. It is vital to the investigation, after all—all necessary expenses.'

'And how's your room, DC Briggs?' asked Walker. 'Are we all comfortable?'

Her expression made *him* feel a bit uncomfortable, like he was being too concerned, or too considerate, or something.

'We are,' she said, smiling.

CHAPTER FOUR

He'd missed working with her over the past couple of months while he'd been on suspension. He'd not seen her at all during that time, despite her calling a couple of times and offering to go out to lunch or grab a coffee and a bagel or something to catch up. He'd been trying to make some headway with getting back with his wife, who he'd separated from some time ago, and he didn't think going out for lunch with his much younger colleague would be a good look if she found out, even if it was all innocent. But despite his efforts, his wife hadn't been much interested in spending any time with him anyway, as it happened. Said he was only ever interested whenever he didn't have any work to do—and sadly she was probably right. She usually was. What really got to him was that his now teenaged children also hadn't been much interested in seeing him either, and on the couple of occasions they'd met up the kids spent most of their time looking at their goddamned devices, doing God knows what.

'Mine's good too,' said DC Ainscough. 'If anyone's interested. This is the closest thing I've had to a holiday in quite some time.'

'Well, it's not,' said Walker, firmly. 'And don't you all forget it. I shouldn't need to remind you that we're here to locate and catch a very dangerous criminal, and the only reason we're here, in this hotel, is so we all keep in as good a condition as possible, and not waste any time, so we can do what needs to be done. The clock is ticking here. Somebody's life could be at stake. This is serious business. We can take turns sleeping as need be, but we're doing this round the clock until we find whoever did this, *if* they return here again. And that's an order. There's always the possibility that they're already deceased themselves, of course, or incapacitated in some way meaning their killing days are over. But for now, until we know otherwise, let's assume not—at least until this window, this period they do their killing in, is closed. Now, let's see what we have so far and get started. Understood?'

'Understood, sir,' said DC Ainscough. 'Sorry. I didn't mean anything...'

The young Detective wasn't the best speaker, was a bit socially inept really, often said the wrong thing, so Walker knew he'd probably just made another typical faux pas, and let it go. He wouldn't have chosen them for the team if he didn't trust them, and knew they'd do whatever needed to be done, go that extra mile, and then some more. They had a track record of it.

In the absence of an available business conference room at the hotel at such short notice, Walker had set up his customary, probably now quite old fashioned, Evidence Board on a wall adjacent to the TV, one with plenty of space for their investigation to grow into. On it, he already had the photos of the three victims: Sally Fielding, twenty-six, Jackie Wakefield, twenty-eight, and Tracy White, thirty-one—the latter two of which had now also been confirmed via a combination of some old dental records and DNA testing, informing their remaining families of their discovery. Underneath each photo, he also had pictures of the three corresponding pendants they were wearing, the ones with the deathstalker scorpion encased in what looked like a glass teardrop on a leather string—but which Walker had now found out was a type of resin, and not glass at all. The macabre adornments were near identical. It was a ritual, as was the pulling of the teeth. Below those photos, he had pictures of their remains in the sand dunes where they'd been found.

'The immediate thing of interest is obviously these scorpion pendants and the missing incisors. Seems the pendants can be made easily enough by drying out the insects and setting them in resin. Since these are quite an exotic species, found in warmer, drier climates, there's a good shout these were bought abroad somewhere, carried in as souvenirs, as it would be much more difficult to get these back into the UK if they were still alive,' said Walker. 'Or they could have been imported in, I suppose, maybe even bought in a car boot sale in bulk, or something similar.'

'Actually, scorpions are not insects at all,' said DC Ainscough. 'They are…' He looked at his notes. 'Here we are. They are animals in the order of Scorpiones, under the class Arachnida, a distant cousin of the spider.'

'Lovely,' said DC Briggs, shivers visibly going up her spine as her body convulsed.

Walker rolled his eyes. 'So, we could be looking at someone with an interest in entomology here then,' he said. 'That's the first thing we have to go on. The next is the dates of the kills: early July 2011, early July 1998, and early July 1985. Every thirteen years, almost to the day, with the next date coming up sometime in the next few days—hence the urgency of the situation and the need for quick thinking here and us being on site. Next, we have the appearance of these women: all wore glasses, at least in some capacity, all were known to typically tie their long hair back in a ponytail, and two of them were found in summer dresses, made of polyester—which meant the garments didn't decompose. The other one, Jackie Wakefield, was found without any clothing garments, but anything made from cotton would have completely decomposed in this timeframe, so it's possible she was clothed in a similar dress too. Her family stated she was last seen... wearing a summer dress. So, that means they were all looking very similar in appearance. All with blonde hair, too, perhaps with the exception of Sally, if we're being precise, whose hair might be said to be a little more mousy than blonde—but still light. Our perpetrator is therefore looking for a particular type of victim—women, aged mid-twenties to early thirties, glasses, long blonde or light-coloured hair tied back, summer dress. That's pretty darned specific. The question is, why? And then there's the missing teeth. But they were apparently pulled after death. Most likely some macabre souvenirs.'

'Well, he definitely has a type there,' said DC Briggs, running her fingers through her long hair, mulling something over.

'Could be acting out violent fantasies against a similar looking woman who perhaps he felt did him wrong in some way?' offered DI Hogarth. 'An unfaithful wife or girlfriend, perhaps.'

'Mummy issues?' added DC Ainscough. 'That's often a factor in the profile and personality disorders of serial killers as well. Too obvious?'

'Possibly. But whatever it is, it seems he's drawn to exactly this type of woman, stalks them, lures them somewhere or abducts them, somehow, and then...' Without any witnesses, persons of interest, or CCTV footage, they really didn't have much to go off. Normally, with recently committed crimes, they'd already be canvassing the area, getting all of these things, and more, collecting data ASAP, ready to collate and analyse. But in this cold case, their data points were going to be very limited. People's long-term memories were just not that good or reliable—and this wasn't just Walker's humble opinion, it was proven by science: *memories are malleable and shift and change over time.* This didn't mean they weren't going to do any canvassing, ask around, interview some people who might know something, but Walker wouldn't be surprised if this didn't turn anything reliable up. Cold cases like this were notoriously difficult to get forward momentum, but he needed something, anything, to get them started. 'What about the car? The one belonging to Sally Fielding, the one found in Birmingham?'

DC Ainscough looked through his files again. 'Found just *outside* of Birmingham. Was impounded at the time it was found, then returned to the family later who I'm told sold it on after a few years of it sitting on the driveway. As it wasn't a murder investigation, just a missing person, it was never checked for forensic evidence.'

Perhaps not officially, Walker thought, but he wondered whether Harry Potts might have processed it, off the record.

'Can we track it?' asked Walker. 'Perhaps there's something still there—blood, DNA?'

'I'll get on it,' said DC Ainscough. 'The new owners aren't going to be very pleased, though, if it hasn't gone off to the scrapyard yet, that is.'

'Oh, poor them,' said Walker, with absolutely no sympathy in his voice whatsoever, this being used up through years of seeing people go through *actual* traumatic hardships. 'Right. Let's get things moving then. We'll make some lists and split up the workload. We need to contact the relatives and last known contacts of the victims, see if anyone noticed anything unusual. As these women have all been treated as missing person's cases until now, it's possible the right questions weren't asked the first time around, so let's put that right. Maybe we'll get lucky, someone will remember an odd interaction with some creepy guy, and we'll get a rough description, or we'll find some seemingly inconsequential detail that connects the three cases. Who knows, maybe they all went to the same sodding hairdresser a few days before they disappeared. It's a long shot, but we must try. It's time to do the donkey work on this, people, scour the files, look for any commonalities, and we will chase up every interviewee we can. We owe it to those women to do our very best to find out who did this. You got that?'

Everyone agreed. Walker was haunted by cold cases like this one, the ones that went unsolved—they kept him awake at night. And he was damned if this was going to be another one.

CHAPTER FIVE

Walker sat on a well-worn sofa in the Fieldings' front room, inside their modest house on the outskirts of Chester, the place they'd been since Sally's disappearance over a decade ago. His gaze moved over the photographs displayed on the mantelpiece. Most of them featured Sally, smiling in various stages of life. In one, she was a toddler on a tricycle, full of energy and joy. Another captured her in the early stages of adolescence, beaming alongside her cousin, Harry Potts. The two of them seemed to share a connection, their arms casually slung around each other's shoulders. The age difference was clear—Harry seemed more like an older brother—but the closeness they shared was undeniable.

'That was her twelfth birthday,' Mrs. Fielding said quietly, her eyes tracing the photo. 'Harry took her and some of her friends to MacDonald's. They were so close.'

Walker nodded, now thinking he understood better why Harry Potts had been so eager to get involved in the investigation.

Mrs. Fielding wiped a tear away and then glanced at her husband before returning her gaze to Walker. 'Do you think you'll find him? Whoever did this to our Sally and those other poor women?' Her voice was shaky.

'We're still in the early stages of the investigation,' Walker answered, keeping his tone steady, though his thoughts were far from positive, having got nowhere so far after days of interviews.

Mr. Fielding stared at the floor, his face tense with worry. 'We just need to put this to bed. After all this time... we just need some closure.'

Walker felt the heaviness of their grief weigh down on the room, a reminder that this wasn't just a case—it was their life, their loss. And yet, as much as he wanted to offer them some answers, he had nothing more than platitudes. The investigation already felt like a never-ending spiral, offering nothing of real substance.

The room fell quiet. 'I can't promise you any explanation,' said Walker. 'But what I can do is give you my word that we'll do our very best to find out who was responsible for this. We won't give up.'

'That's all we want,' said Mrs. Fielding. 'Thank you, Detective.'

* * *

The drive back to Lytham St Anne's was quiet, with only the hum of the engine and the occasional shift of DC Briggs in the passenger seat. Walker stared out of the window, the passing streets offering little more than a blur of suburban life. The final interview had given him nothing he hadn't already known: the parents were still living in the same house,

CHAPTER FIVE

surrounded by memories that hadn't softened with time.

He sighed, tapping his fingers on the steering wheel. 'It's like we're going round in circles with this,' he muttered, frustration creeping into his voice. 'Every lead we've followed has brought us right back to where we started.'

Briggs didn't say anything for a moment, keeping her eyes on the road.

Walker looked out the window again, watching the landscape change as they left Chester behind. 'We need something solid. We're just grasping at sodding straws here.'

They drove on in silence, each of them lost in their thoughts. The cold cases still held too many unknowns, too many unsolved mysteries. But there was no turning back now. They had to push forward—no matter how slim the chance of success was. They had to find something.

DC Briggs finally broke the silence, having been quiet for a few minutes. 'There's only one realistic way we're going to catch this guy now,' she said, looking across at Walker. He had an idea what she might be talking about but hadn't wanted to say, hadn't wanted to put the idea out there in the universe for fear of what it might mean. 'Well, aren't you going to ask me how?' she said.

Walker sighed, knowing that there was no stopping her now. 'How?' he reluctantly asked.

'We're going to have to set a trap,' she said. 'We're going to have to lure him in, provide some bait. And since you, DI Hogarth, and DC Ainscough don't have long hair, I think that bait is going to have to be me.'

CHAPTER SIX

Walker was now alone with DC Briggs in her hotel room. They were still discussing her idea to use herself as bait, to try to get the killer to reveal himself. If they had no leads to find him, then they could, in theory, make him come to them—especially since there was a good chance, based upon what they'd found, that he'd be out there right now, looking for someone of the same appearance as those other victims.

'I won't allow it,' said Walker. 'It's too risky. Are you crazy? He could try to kill you.'

'Well, if it's not me, it's likely to be someone else isn't it, someone less equipped to deal with him, someone without a team in law enforcement on standby ready to incapacitate him,' she said. 'Think about it—it makes sense. There's less chance of him fatally hurting someone if that someone is me. We're trained for this.'

Logically, she was right, of course. They had a far better chance of nobody being seriously hurt by putting her plan into action than if they didn't. And it wasn't as if they had anything like a plan-B at the moment, with time very much ticking down—if they were right about the timeline. But Walker had grown very fond of Shelly Briggs in the relatively short time

CHAPTER SIX

he'd known her, and he was starting to think this fondness might even be a little bit more than just the run-of-the-mill affection one holds for their friends and colleagues. He wasn't quite sure. All he knew was that he felt extremely protective of her, and he didn't want to put her, of all people, in the firing line of this dangerous weirdo psycho.

'Do you have a better idea?' she asked.

Walker was at a loss. He had nothing to say, little else to offer. They had the possibility of finding Sally Fielding's old car, of course, and maybe finding some DNA or some fingerprints that could lead them to their killer, but it was a long shot, and it would take time—too much time—and time was a commodity they didn't have much of until their perpetrator potentially struck again. DC Briggs knew all this too, hence her pushing for this undercover operation with her out there in the field. Walker had the foresight to request an undercover operative of that description be put on his team, of course, so it wouldn't come to this, but that had been denied due to there being only a couple of active officers matching that description in the area, and these already being deep into investigative projects, and ones they couldn't pull out of—not even for a short time. Unfortunately, this was not the only big, important case that was currently in operation. So, it was all down to them.

'Look. I can dye my hair blonde, get some glasses, tie my hair back, get a summer dress. It'll be just what he's looking for. And I'm around the right age too,' she said. 'He won't be able to resist.'

'Aren't you a bit old?' asked Walker.

'Er, I'm only thirty-two,' said DC Briggs, looking insulted, huffing. 'How old do you think I am?'

'Well... I mean... the oldest victim was thirty-one at the time of death, so perhaps you're a little out of his age range, that's all,' said Walker, grasping at straws now.

'So, you mean I couldn't pass for a thirty-one-year-old,' she said, looking herself up and down. 'Is that what you mean?'

He looked her up and down as well, then realised perhaps he shouldn't be. She looked good. And since she was two decades younger than he was, he felt a bit of a creep himself for thinking so—in *that* way, just for a microsecond, anyhow. It had been a while since he'd been with a woman, and this enforced celibacy was starting to take its toll.

'No, I... Look, Shel, I just don't want you going out there, baiting this guy. Something might go wrong. You could get hurt. Or worse,' said Walker, almost begging now. 'I don't know what I'd do if...'

She regarded him, Walker having no sodding clue what she was thinking, which was usually the case whenever he formed any sort of a relationship with a member of the opposite sex. '*Shel* now, is it?'

'Look, *Detective*, I can't be responsible for anything happening to you,' said Walker. 'I couldn't live with myself. I have too many of those burdens already.'

'Oh, so I'm a burden now, am I?' said DC Briggs in an exasperated tone.

'No. Of course not. I didn't mean...'

'Look, could you live with yourself if another woman dies in the next few days, and we know we could have done something about it but didn't?' she said. She had a point—a big one. That would also be unacceptable.

There was a knock on the door, and she opened it. It was, predictably, DI Hogarth and DC Ainscough.

'So?' asked DI Hogarth.

CHAPTER SIX

'I think we're almost there,' said DC Briggs. 'He's coming around.'

'No, he's not,' said Walker.

She let them in, and they joined Walker and DC Briggs—who were stood in the middle of the room, having it out. DI Hogarth and DC Ainscough perched on the end of the bed, like a watching audience, waiting. But nothing happened. They'd reached a dead end, as the case would too if they didn't decide soon.

'I think we need to try this, Chief,' said DI Hogarth. 'We don't have much else to go on right now, and, as you know, time is very much against us. We'll be careful.'

Walker shook his head. If they were going to do this, then they needed to do it properly, monitor things as closely as possible. The problem was they didn't have a wealth of resources to use, what with this being a cold case they were working on, so they needed to be resourceful, get creative.

'It's not like DC Ainscough here can put a blonde wig on and some glasses, lure him in,' said DI Hogarth. He was trying to lighten the mood a little. It worked. They all seemed to exhale in unison and smile a tad, all except for Walker, that is.

'In theory then, and I mean, *in theory*, what would be our options for keeping tabs on DC Briggs if she went undercover?' asked Walker.

DI Hogarth stood up, got a little closer. 'GSM listening equipment is fairly easy to use these days for listening in real-time. We could just use mobile phones to listen and record audio data from the device's surroundings. This is legal to do in public places and wouldn't require any paperwork to set up. Covert listening devices are more specialist spy equipment, but that might take longer to organise. I can set up a mobile phone connection in a few minutes, and we can test it and get started right away.'

'I could just put it in my bra,' said DC Briggs. Walker felt his face going red. That wasn't like him. He was ruffled by the sudden feelings he had for her now that she was potentially stepping into danger. 'Don't worry, I won't do it in front of you three.'

'That might muffle the microphone too much,' said DI Hogarth, also going a tad red. 'We'll need to find a summer dress with a thin pocket.'

'Well, I'm sure that won't be a problem,' said DC Briggs. 'I just need a quick shopping trip to get the dress, glasses, and some hair dye. So? Are we good? Are we doing this?'

'I'm not happy about it,' said Walker, still shaking his head. 'We'll have to stick pretty close by in case anything happens. We don't know what this guy is capable of. But we know he's dangerous. We need to expect the unexpected.'

'We'll need whoever it is to incriminate themselves somehow first though, before we move in, or we won't have enough to hold him,' said DC Ainscough, looking at Walker. 'Sorry, but we will. We can't jump in all gung-ho.'

Walker knew all of this too, which was exactly why he didn't want to take the investigation in this direction. He was still reluctant but didn't really see any other way.

'Chief, I'll be careful,' said DC Briggs, looking deep into his eyes. 'I promise.'

'Well, you'd better be,' said Walker. 'There'll be a mountain of paperwork if anything goes wrong.' He wasn't concerned about any desk work, of course, but wanted to deflect his concerns for her, now feeling emotionally exposed.

'Do we have a plan then?' asked DI Hogarth.

CHAPTER SIX

Walker took a deep breath. 'It seems we do,' he said, still not sure if it was the right thing to do. 'But I want everything checked and double checked, several times, before we action this.'

'Got it,' said DI Hogarth.

'DC Ainscough, you take DC Briggs shopping and get back here as soon as you can. And DC Briggs, do not wear any of that crap before we get you all set up here, do you understand?' said Walker.

'I do,' said DC Briggs. 'You'll be the first to see me in that dress, sir, I promise.'

He felt his face going red again, so he headed for the exit before the others might notice. 'DI Hogarth. Follow me. Let's get on this, pronto,' he shouted back.

CHAPTER SEVEN

This would be the very last time Kevin Lawson went to Lytham St Annes. And he would never leave. He knew that. When you have cancer, and it's terminal, the volume on everything gets turned down. There's nothing else to worry about, nothing to lose. In a way, he felt free, freer than he ever had, without fear of being caught and incarcerated. He could do whatever he wanted now—not that he'd succumbed to fear in the past, but it had always been there, in the background, beneath the surface, urging him to be more scrupulous.

Having parked up, he opened the door to his motorhome and felt the warm sun on his face. He hadn't been out for a while. It felt good. It brought memories of his childhood, of being here with his mother, at a better time, when everything was right with the world. It must have been over seventy years ago when his dad had left them, when he was little—he'd only been about eight at the time—run off with another woman according to his mum; and he had no brothers or sisters, so it had been just him and his mum. But that was exactly how he liked it. It was the best time of his life—the *only* good time.

'I miss you, mum,' he said, almost habitually, before taking a breath of the sea air. Although it had been over six decades since his mother had died right with him, at their home, it remained very much fresh in his mind, like it happened only yesterday. Something had been etched into his synaptic pathways at a young age—her death, his experience of it—had been branded there. It would never go away. The emotions were as raw as ever, and his need to feel close to her, to reconstruct what he experienced, remained constant. It drove him. He needed that one last hit before bowing out, to recreate it one final time, to feel her again. It was his drug, this, his vice, and although he'd learned to fight it for long stretches, he never could resist when this anniversary came around once more; and he didn't want to. 'I'll see you soon.'

His mum had got pregnant with him young—at the age of just nineteen—as many women typically did in those days. The year was 1946, and she'd met some handsome man who'd come back from the war, and they hit it off. They'd got together for a while, as a couple, and when she fell pregnant, he'd married her. It was the "done thing" back then. But he didn't last long with them—said the crying baby reminded him of the screams of dying soldiers on the battlefield, couldn't handle it, and he ran off with someone else, apparently, some floozy, leaving his mum to bring up a child, *him*, all by herself. He'd never met his dad, but had seen a picture of him in uniform, during the war. He'd seemed troubled, traumatised, his eyes giving it away; Kevin had seen the same look in his own eyes after his mother died. He was just thirteen at the time, and she'd been only thirty-two. It was a tragedy that shaped his entire life. He'd loved her so much that he knew immediately, when it happened, that he'd never get over it, and he was right: he didn't.

He sat down in a deck chair just in front of his motorhome in a car park near the beach on the North Promenade at Lytham St Annes and winced in pain. The cancer was in his pancreas; it was giving him belly pain again. He couldn't see much, just a few sand dunes, but he could hear some kids horsing around on the beach, laughing and screaming.

'Won't be long now, mum,' he said. 'Let's have one more day at the beach together.'

She'd known she was dying—he'd found letters from the hospital later, detailing her appointments and treatment. She'd had a brain tumour, and it had been terminal. Ironic that he too was dying of cancer. Perhaps it was genetic, he thought. Perhaps they were connected in ways he couldn't even imagine.

One day, when he'd been thirteen, she'd took him to the beach at Lytham St Annes. It had been gloriously sunny, and they played on the beach, ate ice-creams, dipped in the cool salty sea—remembered how it gave him goosebumps—but had a wonderful time together. She'd kissed and cuddled him more than ever, got him warm after their swim, told him she loved him countless times, and that he should never forget, that he'd always be with her, no matter what. He hadn't realised at the time, but she'd been saying 'goodbye'.

She'd been wearing a beautiful summer dress that day, with her usual dark-rimmed glasses and blonde hair tied back in a ponytail. He loved her, wanted to marry her himself when he grew up, but he was just a little boy, immature, fantasising about a perfect life. It was the best day of his life, that, and then his worst. Shortly after they got home, he found his mother lying on the kitchen floor, still with bits of sand on her clothes and feet. She was dead. He later found out she'd had a brain aneurysm and learned what that was. She'd just wanted one last good day with him before dying, that's all, and she'd got it, timed it to absolute perfection.

Down on the beach, the children's laughter turned to cries and shouting, and a child hopped over one of the sand dunes, sulking, tears rolling down their pale face, before disappearing again.

When he'd found his mother like that, when he'd been just a kid, he knew he should have gone and got a neighbour, got some help. Old Bill at number forty-six had a landline, the only person on their street who did at the time. He could have called an ambulance. But Kevin knew she was already dead, could sense she was no longer there. Plus, she wasn't breathing, and he checked her heart: there was nothing. She was gone. He just wanted to spend a little more time with her before they took her away, sent him off somewhere, all alone. He was scared, needed some time to think, to be with her, to adjust to what his new life might be, and what it wouldn't be.

He'd lain down next to her, pretended she was just sleeping. He spent three nights like that, going to school as usual, to maintain the charade, sleeping with her, pretending to feed her, nurse her back to health. She became his doll. But it was a warm summer and once she inevitably started to decompose and attract insects and bugs, instead of swatting them away the young Kevin became fascinated with the little things. He'd watched them for hours, feeding, going about their business, and his love for her had been, somehow, in some twisted way, slowly, rerouted to them.

The kid was back on the sand dune again, covering their eyes with their hands this time. They didn't look upset anymore—looked more like a game of hide and seek was in motion. He was right. After a few seconds, they shouted, '*Coming! Ready or not!'*

On the fourth day, social services unexpectedly called at their home after his school alerted them to a possible problem—his teachers must have noticed him acting strangely or smelling funny or something. His memory of it all was blurry now. But what he did remember was that when they came inside, they found Kevin with his dead mother, cradling her. They took him away, kicking and screaming, and he was put into care as he had no other family to look after him; none that wanted him, anyhow. And that was the end of his life as he knew it, the end of his innocence.

Kevin lifted a jar full of bugs from an open bag he had on the floor and put it on a small table next to his deck chair, smiled at them. 'It will be feeding time soon,' he said. 'I promise.'

It was after being institutionalised that the young Kevin began studying about bugs and insects, found it becoming a single-minded obsession, fervently throwing himself into such research, voraciously devouring any material he could get his hands on, memorising it all, writing about what he found. It was fascinating. The other kids at the home he was put in thought he was strange, picked on him, bullied him, hurt him— tortured him. And in the wake of his grief and his frustrations with the other children, he'd also experienced some emotional dysregulation and exhibited violent tendencies. He'd been put on medication and given some grief counselling, as they call it now, because of this... when he wasn't being physically punished for his behaviour. It was the early nineteen sixties, after all. He hated it there, couldn't wait to grow up and get out. But get out of there he did, eventually.

By the age of twenty-six, Kevin was living alone in a basement flat in Southport. He was making some money here and there writing about insects, rarely coming out and seeing daylight. But the age of twenty-six started to seem significant to him as it was the thirteen-year anniversary of his mother's death, and she'd died when he'd been thirteen. Plus, he'd been studying and writing a lot about the 13-year periodical cicada, insects that, like him living in the basement, spend most of their lives underground, before emerging to transform and mate. In his mind, everything was coming together at one cosmic, nexus point. It seemed like fate, or his destiny, or something.

The kid who'd been playing hide and seek now appeared around the side of the sand dunes with several other children, along with a couple of adults at the back who seemed to be in charge. They headed to their car in the car park, barely noticing Kevin as they passed, chattering about something or other, a couple of the kids giggling and jumping. They didn't know how lucky they were, growing up like that.

It was at that time, in Southport, that Kevin had begun to relive what happened to his mother, started to descend into something like a frenzy. And he'd begun to feel those same old violent thoughts again, of wanting to hurt someone, even more vividly than before; and he was no longer on the medication he'd been given to temper such thoughts, couldn't fight them off this time. He didn't want to control it anymore though; he'd wanted to let it out. His craving for violence somehow merged with his longing to see his mother again, and he'd started to fantasise about killing a woman who looked just like his mother, about lying next to her, pretending it was her. But they were just fantasies. He never intended to do it. That seemed like a long time ago now.

Kevin felt the necklace he always wore around his neck,

pulled it out from under his T-shirt and shirt, felt it. There were five incisors strung on it—which he'd achieved by carefully drilling holes into each tooth and threading a leather string through. His mother had been missing her front middle-left incisor ever since he could remember; hadn't had the money to get a false one, and one of these teeth was hers. She'd kept it in her jewellery box. He knew which it was because he'd marked each of the teeth on the back, by etching a letter into them. Hers was marked with an 'M' for 'mother'. The others: 'C' for 'Cynthia', 'T' for 'Tracy', 'J' for 'Jackie', and 'S' for 'Sally'. They were all, in some way, very close to his heart, and so that's why he kept them there—near his heart. They warmed him, made him feel loved, important. Also on the necklace was a key to a safety deposit box, should he ever need it—a little insurance policy. But it seemed his time was almost up, so he probably wouldn't be needing that anymore. But he'd left it on there anyway, just in case.

'Just one more,' he said. The number six had become almost magical to him—the number of legs his beloved insects had. He'd like to have collected eight, just like the deathstalker scorpion, but he was out of time, so six would have to do. 'And then we'll all be together forever.'

He tucked the necklace back under his T-shirt and stood back up, stretching.

'It's time,' he said, steeling himself, licking his lips, feeling that deliciously salty sea air again, a taste that always brought him back to his childhood. 'It's time.'

CHAPTER EIGHT

'How do I look then?' asked DC Briggs, who'd just entered the hotel room they'd made into a makeshift Incident Room, where Walker, DI Hogarth, and DC Ainscough all waited for her. She'd done as planned—dyed her hair blonde and tied it back into a ponytail, got some glasses and wore them, and put on a summer dress that wasn't too short, but not too long either. It was tasteful.

Walker wouldn't be going along with it if they hadn't exhausted all other avenues of inquiry already, but they'd done everything they could in the past few days—re-interviewed family members and friends of the deceased, gone through all the old case files of the missing persons reports, re-examined the forensic evidence, tried to locate any existing CCTV footage from nearby hotels and cafes, and more—and much to Walker's frustration they'd turned up bugger all. So, they had to be more proactive now before this guy killed again, take a few risks. Time was running out.

'You look... great,' said Walker. He'd never seen her in a dress before, of any description. She looked different—like a woman, attractive.

'No, I mean, do I look the part?' asked DC Briggs. 'For the gig?'

'I know,' said Walker, lying. 'You have the same description as the other victims—blonde, ponytail, glasses, and summer dress—so yeah, you look perfect. *Great,*' he added, for clarity.

DI Hogarth put four mobile phones on the bed, neatly lines up in a row. 'We're all set up. This one is yours, DC Briggs.' He pointed to the phone on the far left. It was pink.

'Really? You're giving me the pink one? Could this be any more sexist?' she said, seeming like she wasn't completely joking, if at all.

'It was... just easier to remember that way,' said DI Hogarth, looking a touch embarrassed, wiping his forehead as a few beads of sweat formed. 'Anyway, if you put that in your pocket, as is now, we'll all be able to hear you, and anything that's going on around you. And if you want to hear us, you simply pop this earbud in your ear.' He presented it to her, also pink. 'Shall we give it a try?'

DC Briggs grabbed the pink phone and earbud, shaking her head and smiling. 'Shall I go back to my room to test it?' she asked, popping in the earbud, wiggling it a bit until she seemed comfortable.

DI Hogarth nodded and she left, gently closing the door as she went.

'She looks *really* different,' said DC Ainscough. 'Hardly recognised her.'

'Here,' said DI Hogarth, passing Walker and DC Ainscough a phone each, and keeping one to himself. Then he gave them an earbud each too—all *black.*

'I can hear something, some shuffling around,' said Walker. 'DC Briggs. Can you hear us?'

'Loud and clear,' she said.

'DC Briggs. It's DI Hogarth. Can you move to the lobby

of the hotel next, so I can test the tracking app I'm using, to monitor your location?'

There was a pause. 'I could have just done that in the first place, but will do,' she said.

DI Hogarth showed Walker and DC Ainscough the screen of his phone. 'See,' he said. 'She's moving. We can see exactly where she's going, track her, zoom in if need be. You can stay within close proximity at all times, if you wish, be just a few steps behind, monitor her whereabouts.' He zoomed in and out on the map of the app with his index finger and thumb, to demonstrate.

'Jesus, I feel like her damned father,' muttered Walker, 'spying on her like this.' He forgot for a second that she could hear, wanted to put his whole fist in his mouth when he realised, right up to his watch.

'Er, I heard that, Detective. Are you going to give me a good smack if I'm naughty too?' she asked, with some playfulness in her voice.

'That's enough, DC Briggs,' said Walker, trying to keep it professional. 'I'll take you out of there in a heartbeat if you don't focus and do everything by the book. This is serious stuff.'

There was a pause on the line. 'Sorry, Chief. Didn't mean anything by it. I get a little mouthy when I'm nervous, that's all.'

So, she *was* nervous, and so she should be. She was putting herself in the crosshairs of a very dangerous killer, and Walker didn't like it one bit. He felt the hairs on the back of his neck prick up, as was often the case when he sensed danger. But there was no other choice. Someone's life was potentially in danger, and they had to do something.

'As soon as you identify a person of interest, get their name, or a registration plate, and get out of there,' said Walker. 'Tell them you have an appointment, and that you'll meet them in a few hours, or something like that, while we look into them.'

'Got it,' said DC Briggs. 'So, I'm just gonna walk around town and the beach area for a bit, do some fishing, see if we can catch anything.'

'That's it,' said Walker. 'Do some fishing. You tread carefully now. We don't know what we're dealing with here, what might be lurking in the water.'

'Will do, Chief,' she said.

'Oh, and DC Briggs,' said Walker.

'Yes, Chief?'

Walker paused, feeling the walls closing in, time standing still, like it was a potentially fateful, life-changing moment in his life if he didn't get it right.

'Just, be *damned* careful, okay?' was all he was able to say.

'I'll see you soon, Jon,' said DC Briggs. She never called him that, not really. But he hoped she would again, and soon.

CHAPTER NINE

Kevin took a Rice Krispies cereal bar out from his pocket, opened it with his teeth, spitting out a piece of the wrapping, before taking a bite. He felt like his blood sugar was getting low as he'd been there a while. That would do for now, though—he'd keep the rest of it for later. He stuffed it back in his pocket. Flat on his belly, he lay atop one of the seemingly lesser-used sand dunes according to its lack of footprints there—probably due to its steep embankments at all sides—at Lytham St Annes, one fronting the panorama of the beach. His old body wasn't what it once was, he had aches and pains everywhere, and that was nothing to do with the cancer either; he was just aged. He was seventy-eight years old now. The last time he'd done this, stalking his prey like an assassin bug (the *rhynocoris iracundus*, one of his favourites), he'd been just sixty-five, and had still felt pretty fit and strong then. But not now. And with his terminal illness, this weakened him further, so he'd have to be extra diligent this time, the *last* time, use his experience rather than his strength to pull it off. He'd have to be smart to get things done. What the hell, though, he thought. It wasn't like he had anything to lose. He was practically dead.

'Come on. Where are you?' he said, a little grumpily, the

sand whipping up in his face but thankfully not going in his eyes as he held some binoculars up over those, looking down at the beach below. The tide was out—way out. That was good. There could be a mile of beach between high and low tide here, and this was low tide. People walked by all the time when the tide was this far out—some with family, some couples, others alone, and some with dogs. But if he waited long enough, and was patient enough, he'd find exactly what he wanted. And if he didn't, well… then he'd just have to improvise, like last time. He carried a few items in his backpack for just such eventualities: one summer dress, medium size, one pair of spectacles, and one scrunchy for hair tying. That meant all he needed to do was find a blonde woman around the same age his mother had been when she'd died. He'd never had to use such accessories before the last one, though, before Sally, despite carrying them. It was always better to find what he wanted from the get-go, more meaningful somehow if their appearance was genuine. Most women in Lytham St Annes wore summer dresses at this time of year if the weather was good, which it was, so that wasn't much of an issue, and a good percentage of those were blonde too. So, to find one of these women with hair tied back in the typically windy seaside conditions here, and wearing glasses, was not that much of a stretch either. It was just a matter of bedding in, spending some time watching and waiting.

A woman appeared at the top end of the beach, alone, youngish by the looks of it. He could see her dress blowing in the wind and he waited for her to get closer, excitement rising. For a second, he thought it *was* his mother, come back from the dead, to take him with her. The sun shone off her blonde hair, like a mirage, but it didn't blow in the wind—it was tied

CHAPTER NINE

back. And she was wearing glasses. That didn't take long, he thought, which was good, as he didn't have long. It seemed it was his lucky day after all.

'There you are,' he said, lowering the binoculars from his eyes for a second, and then fine-tuning the adjustment ring further, before looking again. 'Beautiful.'

The woman was carrying her shoes in one hand, just like his mother had when they'd come to the beach, *that* day. It was uncanny. It couldn't have been better even if he'd set it up himself, if he'd been saving the best 'til last.

'We'll be together soon,' he said, touching the ring of teeth around his neck. 'We'll all be together, complete.'

Kevin got up, with some effort and straining, put the binoculars in his bag, prepared to climb back down off the sand dune. He didn't mind if he looked frail, looked weak. That would only work to his advantage. He just needed to get her inside his motorhome, and then he'd inject her, incapacitate her, tie her up. It would be easy—she'd feel sorry for him. He was an ill-looking old man, after all. He'd just make up some excuse, like he needed help injecting himself with his medication, or something. Maybe he'd tell her he was diabetic, and that his blood sugar was low, and that he was scared he was about to pass out, all alone. That should do it. Who could say 'no' to that?

He was down on the beach now, looking right at her as she walked past. She glanced at him and smiled, walked on. He began to follow, but she wasn't walking very fast—ambling really—so it wasn't that difficult, even at his age and in his condition.

'Excuse me, miss,' he said once he was within a few feet of her. She turned around and pointed at herself, looking around to see if anybody was behind her.

'Me?' she asked. She was cute, a little ditzy.

'I'm afraid I need some help,' said Kevin. 'I'm so sorry. I'm in a bit of trouble.'

'You are?' she said, pushing a stray bit of hair behind her ear, unsuccessfully. 'What seems to be the problem?'

'I'm afraid I'm feeling a little woozy,' said Kevin. 'Need to get back to my motorhome, take my injection. I think I might faint if I don't get my medication soon.'

The woman moved in, looking concerned, ready to help. 'It's okay,' she said. 'I've got you.' She put her arm around him, took a bit of his weight—which wasn't much now, because of his illness and the chemotherapy they'd been giving him.

'Thank you,' said Kevin. 'It's just up here, just a little further.'

'We'll get you there,' said the woman, meaning that *she* would.

It wasn't too long before they made it to his motorhome, and she helped him up the steps and inside.

'There. Is there anything else I can do for you?' asked the woman. 'Do you need some water or anything?'

Kevin opened a drawer and took out a plastic folder that contained a syringe and some medicine. 'I just need to take this,' he said. 'Do you mind? My hands are shaking.'

The woman hesitated. 'I... I've never...'

'What's your name, luv?' asked Kevin.

'It's Shannon,' said the woman.

'Okay, Shannon. It's easy. You just open the medicine, pop the needle in it and draw back the syringe until it's all inside, and then you give it to me.'

Shannon breathed a sigh of relief. 'Oh. Is that all? I thought you were going to ask me to inject you! I don't think I could

CHAPTER NINE

do that. I've never really liked needles.'

Kevin smiled. 'No. I just need you to help me set it up, that's all.'

She did as asked, got the medicine inside the syringe, and then handed it to him. 'There you go,' she said.

The label on the vial said 'Succinylcholine', something most people weren't familiar with, and Kevin had been banking on that or he'd have removed the label. He knew exactly what it was: a neuromuscular blocking agent that paralyzes a person while allowing them to remain conscious. The injection wasn't for him, of course. It was for her. He wanted her immobilised, but conscious of what was about to happen. He needed to look in her lucid eyes while he did what he was about to do, to see that spark go out.

'You've made me a very happy man,' said Kevin.

'What?' said Shannon, looking a bit confused. 'It really is no problem. Anyone would have helped.'

Kevin got the syringe ready, put some downward pressure on it. 'No. Really. You're very kind.' He put his hand on her arm, gently at first, but then he increased the pressure until he was holding her firmly.

'Hey, what are you doing? Get off me!' said Shannon.

He went to inject her, but he wasn't as strong as he used to be, and she jerked her arm away just as he was about to land the needle. *Damn it.* She wriggled free, got to the door.

'Wait. Don't go. I'm sorry,' said Kevin. 'I get a little confused when I'm having one of my turns.'

'You need help alright!' snapped the woman. 'What the hell is wrong with you? This is the thanks I get for helping a complete stranger? I won't bother next time.'

She opened the door and left. Kevin got up to get after

her—he just needed to get that needle in and drag her back inside—but he really wasn't in the best shape, couldn't move fast at all. By the time he got to the door, she was running up the beach at a speed he could no long handle, so he never even tried. He'd have to find someone else, and fast, hope she didn't report it. And he'd have to be more careful next time. He knew it could be his very last chance.

CHAPTER TEN

DC Briggs was out and about in Lytham St Annes, undercover—dressed in a summer dress, bleached blonde hair tied back, glasses on; just like those poor women: the *victims*—looking for someone who might fit the profile of their killer. She was wearing some Shokz wireless bone conducting headphones instead of the pink Bluetooth earbuds DI Hogarth had given her, which were gaining popularity these days for folks wanting to exercise and listen to something while also being able to hear the ambient sounds around them. It was a change she'd suggested to DI Hogarth at the last minute. It would aid in bolstering their communication efforts and help her blend in better. A woman of her age would never choose pink earbuds like that. It just looked off—like they'd been chosen by a man, which they had. This was better: more natural, more fashionable. Plus, she already had some and knew how to use them.

She'd take off the headphones if anyone approached her, or if she located a person of interest—just casually popping them around her neck like she had nothing to hide. It was all in the details. Plus, the headphones had a mic embedded, which would provide a much clearer signal than just the phone itself. DI Hogarth agreed, actioned the swap with little fuss, showing an interest in the tech, asking her where she got them. In the end, it was more important that her colleagues could hear her than she could hear them, and for possible suspects to be comfortable talking to her—and they might be more cautious if she kept an earbud in. So, they all agreed this was better, more practical, more day-to-day and natural looking. People didn't tend to wear earbuds when they were having a conversation. It was an important detail they'd initially overlooked.

Right now, she was using the headphones to keep in close contact with DCI Walker and the team, just like he wanted—although perhaps a little too much for her liking, as it was all a little distracting to the task in hand.

'How's the fishing going?' It was Walker, *again*. He was making her feel like a teenager being monitored by a nosy parent. It had only been about sixty seconds since he'd last asked.

'Plenty of fish still, but no bites as yet,' she said.

'You on the beach now?' he asked. 'Where are you, exactly? This map tracking thing isn't as accurate as I'd hoped. You're out of my line of sight again.'

'I've come to this row of beach huts,' said DC Briggs. 'Perfect place for hiding out while stalking a victim. I'll take a look around. I'm taking the headphones off now, but you'll still be able to hear me. Over.'

She took the headphone off and put them around her neck, her phone still in the side pocket of her dress, wirelessly connected to it via Bluetooth. She looked around. There must have been thirty to forty huts in a row on the beachfront, small units, not even big enough to sleep in, she thought. A few of them were open, with people sitting outside, so she could see inside some, see what they contained: some basic amenities included seats, kettles, bottles of water—nothing much. There was a long straight path that the huts were on, with the beach out front and a MiniLinks golf course out back.

'Anyone could rent one of these things,' she said. 'I'll hang out here for a while, see if I can spot anything suspicious.'

She walked the length of the path, passed all of the huts, one by one, and sat on one of the rocks at the end, looking back.

'Doing a bit more fishing,' she said.

Some time passed, along with a bunch of people, and dogs, before a guy approached DC Briggs, who was going under the name of 'Kelly Hutton' for this, her first undercover role.

'How you doing?' asked a semi-bald, sweaty man with a sunburned face. He looked to be in his fifties, ogling her a bit, but probably not realising.

'I'm good, luv. How's yourself?' She wanted to be friendly, but not overly so, not so as to raise any suspicion.

'You got a hut?' he asked.

'What? One of these?' she said. 'No. Can't afford it. Bit posh for me. I'm just sitting here, looking at the view. At least that's free.'

'Well, that rock doesn't look too comfy. Why don't you join me? I have one of the huts, it has some comfy seats,' said the man. 'A good-looking girl like yourself shouldn't be sat here alone, anyway. I have some snacks and drinks, if you're interested?'

She paused, feigning uncertainty. 'What's your name?'

'Daniel,' said the man.

'Daniel?'

He smiled, or at least that's what she interpreted the change in his expression to be intended as, but his dead eyes gave something away. It was too cold to be friendly, even if that's what he was shooting for. 'Daniel Brown. But you can call me Danny.'

'Look, Danny. I appreciate the interest, or whatever this is, but I don't usually hang out, or whatever, with older men,' she said. 'I'm thirty-one. How old are you, exactly?'

'Hey, I just thought you'd like to hang out and sit somewhere more comfortable, have some drinks, that's all,' said Danny.

'Danny, I'm a woman. I know what this is. How old are you?' she asked again.

'I'm fifty-six,' said Danny, going even redder.

She looked at him, eyeing him, suspiciously. 'Prove it then,' she said.

Danny smiled again, or leered, she wasn't sure, and took out some ID, showed it to her.

She read it: 'Danny Brown, DOB 2/2/1968,' she said, so her team could hear it. It checked out.

DC Briggs did the math. If he was their killer, he'd have been just seventeen when the first known victim was killed in 1985—not impossible by any means, so she wanted to investigate more. Not that he seemed like much of a killer; but then again, they never did.

'Fine. I guess I could make an exception just this once,' she said. 'I wouldn't mind a drink in this weather, I suppose. But just a drink, you understand?'

Danny held up his hands, palms out. 'Course. Just a drink it is then,' he said, looking clearly delighted with this turn of events. 'Follow me.'

She walked next to Danny, just a step or so behind him, while he led her to his hut.

'It's the end one,' he said. 'Right at the far side. The one next door is empty too, so it's nice and private.'

'Great,' she said, wondering if he might have rented two huts, to get a little more privacy on purpose.

'Here we are,' he said, getting a key out. 'We can sit inside if you like, cool down a bit. It's quite sunny today, isn't it?'

'I like the sun,' said DC Briggs, not seeing any reason to go inside with him. She just wanted to keep him talking, see if there was anything suspicious about the guy other than him being lonely, or horny, or both.

'Oh, come on,' said Danny. 'I'm melting out here. I won't bite.'

She hesitated. Her team were listening in, and she had the defensive skills to fight him off, or even incapacitate him if he tried anything, at least until her team showed up. She wasn't in any immediate danger, even if he was their guy. 'Fine. Let's go inside then, cool down,' she said, making sure to raise her voice a tad so her team heard her, clearly. 'I'm Kelly, by the way.'

'Come in and take a seat then, Kelly,' said Danny. 'What can I get for you? Some vodka and orange?'

'Sure,' she said. 'Are you trying to get me drunk, Danny?'

'Maybe,' he said, playfully, 'if you want to.'

He was enjoying himself now, relaxing into it. There were a few flies inside the hut, along with a large-ish spider on one of the walls.

'Oh, my God. I hate spiders,' she said, standing up, feigning fear, wanting to see what his reaction might be to the creepy crawly.

Danny smiled, put his hand next to the spider, and let it climb on him. 'They're more scared of you than you are of them,' he said. 'Especially when you shout like that.' He took the spider outside and let it go free. 'Do you know spiders have 48 knees! Isn't that incredible—six on each leg.'

'You seem to know a lot about spiders,' she said, her scrutiny of him, as a possible person of interest, increasing.

Danny shrugged his shoulders. 'I know some stuff,' he said. 'Sit down, get comfy.'

She did as he suggested and watched him like a hawk as he poured the drinks, making sure he didn't add anything extra in her drink—like a roofie. It wasn't long before he put a vodka and orange in her hand. His was a vodka and coke; he took a sip.

'Now...' he said. He went over to the doors of the hut and began to close them. She didn't regret going in there though. If he was their guy, it was better to catch him red handed doing something illegal, and then they could hold him while they investigated him further, got the evidence they needed to bang him up. She was confident she could handle the situation—she was a professional—and Walker and the team were close by to provide support.

'Danny, why are you closing the doors?' she said, voice raised, making damned sure Walker and the others heard her this time.

'I want to show you something,' he said. 'In private.' The doors slammed shut, leaving very little light in the hut.'

There was the sound of the doors locking.

'Danny, what was that?' She stood up, got herself ready. Her eyes were already adjusting, and she could just about see he was still a few metres away from her.

'Just thought I'd lock the doors, so we won't be disturbed,' he said, nonchalantly, flicking a small light on. 'You are up for it, aren't you?' He unbuttoned his pants and started to pull the

CHAPTER TEN

zipper down.

'Yeah, no, mate. That's not happening. I'm a police officer, you idiot,' she said. 'And my colleagues are on the way as we speak.'

He did a double take, then smiled. 'Oh... role play, you kinky bitch. I like it—the old angry police officer routine. I can work with that. Come here then,' he said. 'You won't be sitting on any more rocks today when I'm finished with you.'

CHAPTER ELEVEN

Walker kicked the door in to the first hut on the beachfront at Lytham St Annes, DC Ainscough right behind him. DC Briggs had the guy on the ground, his arm twisted behind his back. They were having a heated exchange, Danny's eyes wide and fearful.

'What is this? I swear, I didn't do anything wrong,' said the man. 'You made out you wanted it. This is entrapment!'

Walker took his ID badge out, showed it to the man. 'DCI Walker, and my colleague, DC Ainscough,' he said. 'Daniel Brown?'

'Yes,' said Danny. 'What's going on?'

'When I resisted, he offered me money, for sex. Quite a bit of it, actually.' She didn't seem completely displeased about that last part. It must have been quite a lot for her to react like that.

'I didn't think you were a hooker or anything. You... you just said you didn't have much money, so I thought we could help each other out.'

'By making me into a prostitute? Oh, thanks, Danny,' said DC Briggs. She glared at Walker. 'And what the hell took *you* so long?'

'We were close by but... our connection wasn't great. We

CHAPTER ELEVEN

couldn't hear everything,' he said. 'Sorry. You okay?'

'I'm fine,' said DC Briggs, pulling her dress down a bit lower. 'Now, let's not make a scene, get out of here, and hope my cover isn't already blown. I'll head back down the beach, and how about you take this guy in, DC Ainscough, check him out properly. Detective Walker, will you stick a bit closer by this time? Quite a bit closer?'

'I will,' said Walker. 'Won't let you out of my sight this time, I promise. And if we lose contact, I'll move in immediately, as a precaution. Are you sure you can't just wear the headphones all the time, so we can keep in closer comms?' He didn't like her taking the headphones off in case they spotted some danger, needed to relay something to her immediately.

'It wouldn't look right,' said DC Briggs. 'Trust me. It'll just make them clam up.'

Walker nodded, in agreement. 'Well, just put them on for now then, and only take them off again under my order, once it's confirmed we have you well and truly in our sights.

DC Briggs also nodded and got on her way.

'Am I in trouble?' asked Danny.

'Not yet,' said Walker. 'But my colleague will need to ask you a few questions. DC Ainscough?'

DC Briggs would later realise she'd stepped over a line a little bit there, making orders to DC Ainscough ahead of him. He'd have a word with her about it, but now was not the time. Plus, she was right—they did need to take the guy in for questioning. It just needed to come from him, that's all.

'Come with me,' said DC Ainscough, but Daniel bolted, right past them, making it out of the hut.

'*Get him!*' shouted Walker, and DC Ainscough got after him. It was a shitshow. If this wasn't their guy, and it was unlikely that it was, he hoped damned well their killer wasn't watching all this, or their operation would be over before it had begun.

'Hold fire on the op, DC Briggs. Don't go anywhere,' said Walker, before he got moving too.

Walker soon caught up to DC Ainscough, chasing the man along the promenade, dodging around pedestrians, almost knocking one of them over, apologising on the way. It took a minute or two, but they eventually caught up to Danny, pulled him back by his shirt, wrestled him to the ground.

'It's just a bit of coke, that's all,' said the man. 'Here, I'll show you.'

He took a small sachet of cocaine out of his trouser pocket. 'That's it. That's all I have. All the traders at my firm use it. I don't even take it that often. I just thought, I'm on holiday, so why not? Am I in trouble?' His eyes were pleading, probably worried he might lose his job, or worse.

Walker snatched the sachet off him. 'Damn it. Get some PCs down here to take him back to the station in Blackpool. Get one of the DCs back there to interview him, see what they can find out. If there's anything suspicious that might link him to this case, I want him held there for 24 hours. And I want you here with me, in case we have any more incidents.'

'Roger that,' said DC Ainscough. 'Get up, Mr Brown,' he said. 'You're going to need to take a little break from your holiday, I'm afraid.'

'DC Briggs? You there?' asked Walker.

'Yes, sir. Still here. You got him?' she asked.

'We have,' said Walker. 'He just had some coke on him, that's all, panicked. Just wait a minute and I'll come back. I'll let you know when you're back in my line of sight. Until then, you stay put, understand?'

CHAPTER ELEVEN

'I do,' said DC Briggs. 'Roger that, sir.'

CHAPTER TWELVE

Back down on the beach at Lytham St Annes, DC Briggs was hoping to catch some more attention now that Walker had her back in his sights, and hopefully from their killer this time. If their guy was here, he'd surely see her at some point—and if she looked like those other women, as was intended, there was a good chance she'd be able to reel him in, if he hadn't found someone else already, that was.

The sun was starting to go down now, and the place had quietened some. She came to a stretch of beach that was deserted, apart from one woman who was running towards her. When she got closer, it transpired the woman looked scared, or angry, or both, and said, 'Don't go that way, luv, there's some nutter down there in a motorhome.' She wore glasses, mid-length hair tied back, and a long summer dress—exactly the type of woman their killer might be looking for.

'Wait!' said DC Briggs, but the woman kept running, off to her right, heading between some sand dunes toward the main road in a hurry. 'Hold on a minute. Police! I'm Detective…' The wind had whipped up, masking her words. The woman glanced back but kept running, probably not having heard her properly. DC Briggs hesitated. She didn't know if to follow the woman, try to question her more about who this

CHAPTER TWELVE

'nutter' was, or go the other way—the way the woman had come from—try to find out who she was talking about, find this motorhome, check it out before it left. It could be their killer, she thought, perhaps a failed attack, and it might be their one and only chance to find him. If she followed the woman, questioned her, they might lose their opportunity, let him slip through their fingers. They could be able to track the woman down later for an interview. It was better to go after the motorhome first, she thought.

She popped on her Shokz bone conducting earphones again, which were already turned on.

'Can you hear?' she asked.

'Loud and clear,' said Walker.

'Possible suspect, been harassing some woman, I think, in a motorhome. She was dressed just like me. Heading north on the North Promenade beach to check it out. Over,' she said. They'd already tried looking through some historical harassment claims in the years they thought their killer to be active, to see if anything stood out from the bog-standard indecent exposure or assault—but nothing had resonated with their case. But this was different. This was something potentially significant, what with the woman's appearance and all.

'Roger that,' said Walker. 'We're right behind you. Be careful, Detective Briggs. You may remove the headphones now if you feel they might spook the suspect. We've got you. Over.'

DC Briggs looked behind her, saw Walker following a good distance back on the beach; but it was him, alright. At least someone had her back, if she needed it. She *was* scared—there was no doubt about it—had seen how those poor women ended up, and didn't want to join them. But she also knew that someone else could die if they didn't stop him, and this spurred her on to do what needed to be done, risk her own safety.

She disconnected the headphones, took them back off and put them in her bag, phone still in her pocket, connected—using the mic from that instead. If she found their suspect, she didn't want to spook him, as Walker said, have him run, and wearing a headset might do that. It was better to be approachable, see if he incriminated himself further first. She had back-up if need be.

'Headset removed. I'm using the phone's monitoring application now. If you can't hear me, or if you need to tell me anything, just call with a regular call as discussed. That'll look less suspicious. I'm following the woman's footprints, see where she's been,' said DC Briggs, loud enough so Walker would hear above the seaside wind.

She walked further down the beach, following the same set of footprints, having to pause once or twice while the prints crisscrossed with some others, making sure she was following the right trail. The footprints ended at a sizable car park, mostly empty, called the 'The North Promenade Car Park', which contained a toilet block at the far end. And next to that toilet block, away from the few cars that were parked there, was one motorhome.

'I can see a motorhome here, just like that woman said. Must be the one. There aren't any others. I'm approaching now. Can't see the reg yet. Stay close,' she said. If anything happened, Walker would be here in seconds with a pepper spray, baton, and cuffs—which he had hidden on his person—and she was confident she could take care of herself in the meantime, what with her training in self-defence and

CHAPTER TWELVE

restraining techniques. It wouldn't be the first time she'd been in a scuffle with a man, someone much stronger than her. 'Okay. I'm next to the vehicle now. Make and model is…'

An old man was walking up the car park from the opposite side, slowly. He looked frail, ill perhaps, off colour, using a walking stick.

'Excuse me miss,' he said, when he got close enough. 'Could you help me?'

'I'm sorry. Not right now. I'm just in the middle of something,' said DC Briggs, eyeing the man, keeping her suspicions of anyone now in case he might be the owner of the motorhome.

'It's just… I seem to be a bit lost, that's all. I have a map.' He got something out of his pocket, fumbled with it in the wind. 'Could you tell me which direction the windmill is?'

'Oh, it's on the south side, that way,' said DC Briggs, pointing.

'Thank you,' said the man, nodding, starting to amble away.

'Get someone on that guy now, just in case,' said DC Briggs. 'Just getting the make, model, and reg of the vehicle to you now.'

She went around to the windscreen side of the motorhome and saw a Blue Badge on display—now realising the vehicle was parked in a disabled spot—which contained a grainy photo of the owner. She squinted, trying to get it into focus, but before she could, the old man came back, tapped her on the shoulder with the bottom of a clenched fist.

'Oh, miss,' he said.

She felt a little prick in her shoulder, then some wooziness, and fell to the floor. But she wasn't unconscious—she could still see the old man, looking down at her, smiling, but she couldn't move a muscle. It was him: their killer. It had to be. But she was paralysed, couldn't even speak to tell Walker what had just happened. It had all happened so quickly. She was terrified, fear folding in, suffocating her thoughts, but she knew her colleague would be watching, or listening, or both. He'd have to be. He'd be coming, right now, wouldn't he? After all, he was her only hope.

CHAPTER THIRTEEN

Walker woke up with sand stuck to the side of his face. He pulled himself to a sitting position, felt his head. There was blood, his hair matted together with the stuff.

'*Briggs...*' he said, but his voice came out weak, not like himself.

He'd been tailing her, watching her every move. He'd been within only fifty yards of her when she'd entered the car park to their right, had her in his sights. He'd felt someone move, behind him, and then a sharp pain in his head; and then... *lights out.*

He pulled himself to his feet, urgency spurring him on, and got moving, tentatively at first, but then a little quicker. He was dizzy, but he was making some ground and got to the car park. He looked around. There was no motorhome there.

'Hogarth, Ainscough, you getting this?' asked Walker.

'Sir. You're back,' said DI Hogarth. 'We lost contact with both yourself and DC Briggs for a few minutes there. There was another voice. She was talking to someone, just before... We've mobilised some squad cars, and DC Ainscough is on his way to provide further backup, over.'

'I've lost Briggs,' said Walker. '*Shit.* She went to investigate a motorhome, the owner of which apparently upset or attacked another woman. It's not here.'

'We know,' said DI Hogarth. 'We heard all that.'

Right on cue, DC Ainscough pulled up in a pool car, abruptly, looking like a civilian, passenger window down.

'Come on. Get in,' he said.

Walker did so and slammed the door, and DC Ainscough got moving while he started to pull the seat belt over himself, as habit.

'North or South?' asked DC Ainscough, just before he came to the exit of the car park.

Walker thought about it. If their guy had knocked him out, he probably realised they were on to him and was about to get the hell out of dodge. He'd most likely be leaving Lytham St Annes. The question was, *which way?*

'North,' he said. 'But make sure there are some squad cars heading south too. She didn't inform you of the make and model of the motorhome while I was unconscious? The registration?'

'No,' said DC Ainscough. 'She was going to, but…'

'Damn it!' said Walker. 'Just tell them to look out for a sodding motorhome then.'

'Will do,' said DC Ainscough, as he reached for the short-wave police radio. 'But I have to tell you, since we got here, those motorhomes have been bloody everywhere.'

'Oh, great,' said Walker. 'Well tell them to check all of them then. One of them likely contains our colleague, and time is bloody well running out.'

CHAPTER FOURTEEN

Shelly Briggs must have passed out at some point, because she was now on the bed of what she presumed to be the motorhome, engine running, still paralysed, unable to move a muscle. The old man she'd talked to was now in the driving seat as they sped along—at least, she thought it was him; she could only see the back of his head, and not much of that from her horizontal position, what with not being able to move or sit up. He must have injected her with some medication, a paralysing agent. Fear crept in again, but she knew she must stay calm, have her wits about her, if she was to have any chance to survive. The one consolation, if it could be called that, was that it was her he'd taken, rather than some other poor unsuspecting woman, as at least she had Walker and the team looking out for her, probably trying to find her right now, doing all that they could. They'd have mobilised a force by now, looking out for such a motorhome. *Where was Walker? Why hadn't he come?* She suddenly worried he'd been hurt, that he was lying somewhere, needing help. He wouldn't have let her be taken if he could do anything, she knew that. But she couldn't do anything about that now, if he had been hurt somehow. She needed to get herself to safety first.

The motorhome pulled up. It was quiet, somewhere remote, she sensed. She could see a little, out the windscreen, but she saw only green and blue—trees, bushes, and sky. If he'd taken her somewhere rural, down some dirt track somewhere, they'd be difficult to find. The police could only do so much in such a short timeframe. She knew that from experience.

The old man from earlier turned the engine off, got up back with her. She could see him properly now: it was the same aged guy.

'Change of plan,' he said. 'Sorry about this, my dear. I usually try to make it quick—less suffering that way, you see. It's not my intention to cause pain.'

He started to tape her hands and feet with some black gaffer tape, and then her mouth too, but not before stuffing a used rag in there. It tasted of mould, but she couldn't even retch, the muscles in her throat also paralysed, it seemed. But she could smell and taste, unfortunately.

'Just in case the medicine starts to wear off,' he said. 'Succinylcholine, in case you're wondering. It's a skeletal muscle relaxant, a neuromuscular blocking agent that used to be used as an anaesthetic. Pretty easy to get a hold of, as it happens. At least, it was back in the day. I got a good stock.'

So, he had drugged her. That's how he got his victims, made them so pliant, easy to deal with. Those poor girls. They must have been terrified, just as she was right now. Only they would have had no hope at all, but at least she had that with her colleagues trying to find her right now—she hoped.

'You a cop?' he asked. 'Why were you and your friend following me? I know you can't answer me right now—just making small talk.'

He was talking about Walker; he knew about him. Maybe

CHAPTER FOURTEEN

he'd hurt him somehow, or injected him with the same stuff, paralysed him so he couldn't come after them.

The man finished tying her up and gagging her, made sure everything was secure and to his satisfaction. Then, he went to the door of the motorhome, opened it.

'Gaz, in here,' he said. *There was somebody else.* 'Where have you been? I told you I'd be starting early. At least you made it for the main event, though, got rid of that guy following her for me.'

Gaz? He had an accomplice, wasn't acting alone. This was quite the revelation for the case, if there was more than one person involved. They hadn't suspected that from all the evidence they compiled.

'I tried. Traffic. You got her?' said another voice, a bit younger sounding, not quite as frail and shaky.

'I did,' said the old man. 'Told you I still had it, told you I'm not completely washed up, not quite yet anyhow.' He seemed proud of himself, somehow, was showing off. 'You see how simple it is now? You just lure them in with some stupid story, and then inject them. Even an ill old man like me can do it. You can do whatever you want with them.'

The person called 'Gaz' entered the motorhome, stood over her, taking a good look. He was much younger than the other man, perhaps in his mid-twenties. He was rough-looking, hadn't shaven in at least a week or more, looked like he hadn't washed either. He was wearing a black leather jacket and some blue skinny jeans.

'Nice,' he said. 'Can I have a go?'

'No. You cannot *have a go*,' said the old man. 'I merely agreed to teach you how to do this, so you can do it for yourself when I'm gone. This one's mine. Hands off.'

'Fair enough', said the younger man. 'Since you're dying, and all. Last wishes, and all that.'

Dying? It seemed the old man was more than ill, didn't have much time. So, this would be his last victim, and their last chance to catch him. Hell, they couldn't even punish him in prison if he was going to die. He was going to get away with it—all those murders, spanning decades and countless broken lives. He was going to pass soon enough, and he'd done everything he wanted and got away with it for most of his life. Even if they did catch him now, it wouldn't be sufficient punishment for what he'd done, putting him away for the last few weeks or months of his life, if that's what he had. And he wouldn't even go to prison if he was terminally ill. He'd be put in a secure medical facility, and they'd just wait for him to die, probably before any trial even took place. His final days wouldn't be much different whether they caught him or not. But that didn't mean DC Briggs didn't want to escape, and arrest him, more than anything. She still wanted him to be held accountable, to make sure everybody knew what this man had done, what kind of a man he was.

But this younger man, that was another matter. If he was being taught to kill in the same way and do whatever nefarious things the old man had been doing to these women, it could go on for decades more, leading to God knows how many more dead women and grieving family members and friends. She had to get out of there, somehow, or get a message to Walker. She had to stop them, before anybody else got hurt; even if she got hurt, or worse, in the process. She'd rather save five more women's lives and die herself, than live with more women dying, knowing that she could and should have done something about it. She should have been more careful, at the motorhome, have had her wits about her better. The old man had seemed so frail, so harmless, she never imagined he could inject her with something like that, paralyse her. He'd been clever, and now she had to match that intelligence, stay calm, wait for her moment, her chance—if she had one—and take it. The medicine would wear off eventually, and if they hadn't killed her by then, which she was now pretty sure they were planning to do, she would have the opportunity to do something. She just wasn't sure what that *something* was, yet.

CHAPTER FIFTEEN

'We've got nothing? *Nothing?* What do you mean, we've got sodding nothing? This is DC Briggs, our colleague, my... friend. We must find her, before she gets hurt,' said Walker. He was in a panic, and that didn't happen to him often. Decades on the job had given him a certain calmness and objectivity, even in the face of danger. But this was different. He had feelings for Shelly Briggs, even if he wasn't entirely sure what those feelings were. He cared for her, he knew that—she was his policing partner and friend— couldn't think about her being hurt, or worse. He had to do something, anything, and fast, before it was too late. He'd let her down, was supposed to protect her. She'd trusted him. He'd messed up, and it was up to him to put it right.

'We're well aware of who it is,' said DI Hogarth.

They were back in their makeshift incident room at the hotel they'd checked in at, something they would never have done if the situation they had wasn't so urgent. It was radical, for sure, not the norm by any means, but there was no time to go back to Blackpool Police HQ as the CID normally would with a criminal investigation of this nature. The clock was ticking, fast, and if they didn't find DC Briggs soon, Walker knew they might never find her; and then she'd be a cold case

CHAPTER FIFTEEN

too, like those other poor women, and his sister too who was killed when he was just a kid. They knew exactly what this bastard was intending to do—they'd seen him do it to at least three women already. And it seemed DC Briggs was next, unless they intervened.

'I know it's hard,' DI Hogarth went on, 'but if we have any chance of saving her, we need to remain calm, think clearly, and work the case. I'm waiting for a call back from some of the hotels near that car park, see if they have any CCTV footage. If they do, we can most likely pull the registration plate of the motorhome, hopefully.'

'Well, if we can get that, we'll be able to get the registered owner as well, and then we'll have his identity,' said Walker. 'So that's something to cling on to. But it won't bring us any closer to finding him, will it? Not unless one of the patrolling officers can spot the vehicle—which he has most likely ditched by now if he has any sense. Hey, what about those infrared cameras I asked you to set up at the burial site? We get anything from those?'

'Negative, Chief,' said DI Hogarth. 'Just a stray dog and some other curious local wildlife almost breaking the camera.'

'Well, we could get some leads if we can find this other woman too, the one who DC Briggs said was running away from the motorhome,' said DC Ainscough.

'We should have had more sodding people on the ground,' said Walker, 'should have had someone to get after that woman in the first place, intercept her. We shouldn't be so bloody short staffed on an investigation of this nature. Things are going to shit recently.'

'Maybe she can be seen on CCTV, or we could ask around, see if she's said anything to anybody else in the nearby vicinity,' said DC Ainscough.

'Well, whatever we do, it needs to be quick,' said Walker, feeling unusually unfocussed. He was panicking alright. And his blood was positively boiling; he was just about ready to kill this bloody bastard himself if he ever got hold of him, got the chance. He needed to reel it in, get himself together, get focussed—just like DI Hogarth suggested—for *her*.

* * *

'There,' said DI Hogarth. He had the CCTV footage now, and they were going through it, still in the hotel room, Walker itching to get out of there, to look for DC Briggs, but needing some kind of a lead first to give him some direction. 'A motorhome, heading south near that car park, just minutes after we lost touch with yourself and DC Briggs.' *Damn. They'd gone the wrong way.*

'It has to be it,' said Walker. 'Can you zoom in and get the license plate?'

DI Hogarth did as asked. 'There. We have it. DC Ainscough, do the necessary and call the DVLA, tell them it's urgent.'

'Will do,' said DC Ainscough, moving to the other side of the room, getting his phone out.

'We have it again on the South Promenade, still moving, heading south,' said DI Hogarth, bringing up some more footage. 'And then again, exiting Lytham St Annes... And then we lose it.'

'Shit. They could be anywhere by now,' said Walker.

'They could,' said DI Hogarth. 'But my money's on him

CHAPTER FIFTEEN

coming back. If he's been doing this every thirteen years, on the same date—early July—for whatever reason, then it's a compulsion. He won't want to miss his window. He'll be bringing her back, dead or alive.'

'Alive,' said Walker. 'He'll be bring her back *alive*. She's going to be okay.'

DI Hogarth looked at him, forced something like a smile. 'Okay then, alive,' he said. 'He'll be coming to that burial ground at some point, or, if he realises we found the bodies, since he knows we're on to him, then he'll find an alternative burial ground, probably something similar if it's significant to him.'

'What about her phone? Nothing?' asked Walker.

'Dead,' said DI Hogarth. 'Most likely found and destroyed somehow.'

'I'm heading south, out of Lytham, see what I can find,' said Walker, knowing his odds were slim, but not knowing what else to do.

DC Ainscough hung up his mobile phone, looking at them. 'I've got his name,' he said. 'One Kevin Lawson, DOB April 4th, 1946. This guy is 78 years old. Clean record, not even a parking ticket, so no prints in our database. But we can track him digitally if he uses any credit cards, anything like that.'

He was older than Walker expected. He'd thought perhaps mid-sixties, at the most. He did the maths.

'So, for the previous murders, he would have been 65, 52, and 39. Why every thirteen years?' said Walker, but he was more talking to himself than the others, trying to spark an idea. 'DI Hogarth, run a background check on him, see what you can uncover? We need a profile on this guy. We need to know what makes him tick, and why, at his age, he's still doing this? It's unusual. Murder is typically a younger man's game.'

'Already on it,' said DI Hogarth, tapping away on his keyboard. 'No criminal record as DC Ainscough said. The rest is going to take time, I'm afraid.'

'Well, get it done as soon as you can,' said Walker. 'And in the meantime, DC Ainscough and I will get out in the field, see if we can spot anything. And get every cop in the area on this as well as a matter of urgency. We need all hands on deck for this one. She's one of us.'

'Will do,' said DI Hogarth.

'Wait,' said DC Ainscough. 'The scorpions buried with the bodies. That's been bothering me, why he'd do that. Perhaps there's a lead there we can explore now we have his name.'

'Yeah. It's been bothering me too,' said Walker. 'I guess this freak likes his scorpions.'

'Or maybe its broader, and he has an interest in bugs and insects in general,' said DC Ainscough. 'Creepy crawlies?'

'Maybe,' said Walker. 'We should see if he's a member of any such societies, or if it was related to his career in some way. What are people who study that sort of thing called?'

'*Entomologists*,' said DI Hogarth. 'I'll see if his name comes up anywhere in that field. If it does, maybe someone knows him, or knew him, remembers something that might point us in the right direction, give us an insight.'

'Okay. You do that. And we'll get looking,' said Walker. 'If you turn anything up, anything at all, let me know immediately.'

'Got it,' said DI Hogarth, getting his nose back in his computer. 'She'll be okay, sir,' he said, without looking up. 'She's tough as nails that one.'

'I hope so,' said Walker. And she was damned well going to

have to be if she had any chance of getting through this, he thought.

CHAPTER SIXTEEN

The medication was wearing off now, she could wriggle her toes again, and her fingers, but she wasn't going to let them know that. Better to have the element of surprise, should she have a chance to do anything. But at present, she was bound and gagged with gaffer tape, captive, so DC Briggs simply lay there, on the bed of the motorhome, impotent, waiting and listening, trying to get an idea of what was going on; trying, despite everything, to remain objective.

The two men were sat at a small dining table in the motorhome, arguing about something.

'How'd you find me to begin with, anyhow? I never told your mother my name,' said the old man. 'Not that I remember, anyway.'

'Look, Kevin. It doesn't matter how I found you, does it? The only thing that matters is we're now together. Reunited. Isn't that a good thing?' said the man called Gaz.

Kevin and Gaz. At least she had their first names. That was something.

'I remember your mother, you know. She looked just like her,' said Kevin.

'You mean just like me?' said Gaz, confused.

CHAPTER SIXTEEN

'No, just like her,' said the old man.

'Who the hell is *her*?' asked Gaz.

'Never mind,' said Kevin. 'There've been a couple who've got away over the years. I didn't always hit a bullseye with the first shot. Sometimes, things can get away from you. That's the first lesson you need to learn: to be flexible, and to let those fish go that resist, wriggle free. Don't waste your energy chasing them upstream. They won't have anything on you anyway. It will be your word against them. They don't usually take it any further anyway—never have with me, anyhow—just want to forget it, probably. I'm not sure the police would even take such things seriously. I mean, the one that got away before, I only touched her arm a little firmly. It's hardly a crime now, is it.'

Well, he was wrong there—the police would take such an accusation seriously. But he was teaching the younger man something. He'd got himself a student.

'Okay, *dad*,' said Gaz. 'Whatever you say.'

Dad? Jesus. Gaz was his son. He was teaching his own boy to kill women.

'We need to talk about it,' said Gaz.

'Talk about what?' said Kevin, sounding annoyed. 'In case you haven't noticed, we've got a woman tied to the bed here, with police probably crawling all over the place. We should get moving. She's probably a cop herself. I told you something was off. That guy was tailing her. They're on to us, somehow. They're ruining everything.'

'We're going nowhere until we've talked about it,' said Gaz, stubbornly. 'You want me to take her in my car, then we're going to have to have a conversation first.' He took some car keys from his pocket and dangled them in front of Kevin.

'Fine then,' said Kevin. 'What do you want to know?'

DC Briggs could move her whole foot now, but she made sure they weren't looking at her when she tested it, ever so slightly.

'I want to know why you... why you raped my mother, but didn't kill her, like the others,' said Gaz. 'Why'd you let her go? I wouldn't be alive if you'd done her in.'

'The truth is, I don't know,' said Kevin. 'She got to me, somehow. She was so much like my own mother, that one. It was uncanny. I remember her well. I couldn't hurt her. I cut her loose, found someone else. How'd you find me, kid? How'd you figure out what I've been doing all these years, something even the police had no idea about?'

'I guess it was just more important to me than it was to them,' said Gaz.

'What was?' asked Kevin.

'To know the truth,' said Gaz.

There was a pause in proceedings so DC Briggs just kept as still as she could, waiting for any opportunity, learning what she could.

'I've always had these dark fantasies,' said Gaz. 'To kill someone. Now it finally all makes sense.'

'Ah, *we are all fractured creatures trying to become whole,*' said Kevin. 'Profound, isn't it?'

'What?' said Gaz.

'Just something an ancient Greek philosopher once said: Plato', said Kevin. 'You heard of him?'

'Maybe,' said Gaz. 'I just think... this is my fate, what I was always meant to become.'

'No,' said Kevin, firmly. 'Fate is what happens to us when we do nothing. You did something. You found me. *This...* is

CHAPTER SIXTEEN

your destiny.'

'My destiny?' said Gaz. 'It's more like a compulsion. I just... *need* to do what you do. How do you wait so long, between kills? How do you have the patience?'

Kevin started to cough, couldn't catch his breath for a minute or so, before it settled down again.

'Are you okay?' asked Gaz. Kevin just held out a hand, communicating for him to wait.

'We must control the dark shadow, Gaz, or it will take over everything, destroy us. But we can't shackle it completely. We must feed it, keep it sated,' said Kevin. 'That's what I've been doing. That's how I survived for this long. It's a matter of self-preservation.'

Self-preservation. The guy was a lunatic.

'The dark shadow?' said Gaz. 'What's that?'

'It's something a psychologist called Carl Jung talked about. It's what makes people like you and me kill, even if we don't want to,' said Kevin. 'It's the beast inside, wanting to get out.'

'The *dark shadow*,' said Gaz. 'I like that. I can feel it, in me, moving around, trying to get out like you say, right as we speak.'

'Well, hold it a little longer, Gaz. We have work to do. How'd you find me?' said Kevin, again, more insistent this time.

'When I was thirteen, my mum brought me here, to Lytham St Annes, said she had some demons to face. I had no idea what she meant at the time, but I do now. She was weirdly superstitious about the number thirteen, had been acting funny ever since I turned that age. One day, on the beach—by pure chance, or perhaps not—we saw you, followed you to this very motorhome. She said you were my father, that you were a bad man, and that we should never come back to this place. I memorised the registration plate,' said Gaz. 'Later, when I grew up, I decided to track you down, find out who you are, where you live, everything.'

'And that's why you knocked on my door last week,' said Kevin. 'The timing of it... actually it does seem like fate a bit. And you were thirteen then too when you first saw me—the same age as me when my mother died. How very strange. The universe is a mysterious place, is it not?'

'I killed someone myself, this year. Some guy. Wrapped him in bin bags and dropped him in some water at an old, abandoned quarry. He was rude to me,' said Gaz. 'Very rude. It made me furious. I couldn't hold it. I wanted to do it. It was the excuse I'd been looking for.'

'And how old are you now, Gaz?' asked Kevin.

'I'm twenty-six.'

Kevin smiled, rubbed his face, seeming amazed by something, looking up at the ceiling, or the universe, perhaps.

'It's important you do exactly what I teach you, Gary, to carry on the ritual,' said Kevin. 'Do you think you can do that?'

'Don't call me Gary. Only my mum called me that. I told you, call me "Gaz",' said Gaz.

'You like insects, Gaz?' asked Kevin.

'I guess,' said Gaz. 'I mean, I don't—'

'Have you heard of the periodical cicada?' asked Kevin. 'They spend most of their lives underground, but one species emerges every thirteen years to transform and mate. I haven't been caught because I only do this every thirteen years. People forget, police staff change, investigations get lost under a pile of new investigations. If you hide the bodies well, no one important will remember a missing person after a few years. And if you hide all the bodies in the same location, the chances of discovery are minimised further. It doesn't matter if you get caught for one, or ten murders, you see. The sentence will be much the same. Do you see?'

'How long do you have now?' asked Gaz. 'To live.'

'Days, weeks, who knows,' said Kevin. 'I'm not feeling too great, to be honest.'

'Where is it, the cancer?' asked Gaz.

'Bloody pancreas. Giving me belly ache,' said Kevin. 'It'll be painful when the time comes, so I want to finish it early. And I want you to bury me with her. You think you can do that?'

DC Briggs already knew she was in a world of trouble, but now she'd had it confirmed: they were going to kill her. Panic started to well up from deep down in the pit of her stomach, but she pushed it back down, knowing she needed to remain calm if she were to have a chance of getting out of this.

'I do,' said Gaz, without hesitating.

'But first, I need to have my time with her, alone, do what I need to do. But not here. The police could come, spoil it. It must be perfect—the perfect end. I want some time with her, and then I'll kill her, before topping myself as well. We'll do it in your car, park somewhere remote. You go for a long walk, and when you come back, we'll both be ready for burying. You can put us with the rest, that place where you forced me to dig up the graves of the other women, to prove who I am, and what I've done. I'd like to be with them—all of them. It might be a kind of poetic end, don't you think?'

'And what do I get out of this?' said Gaz.

Kevin smiled. 'You know what,' he said. 'You came here to kill me, didn't you? That's why you really came.'

Gaz smiled back, started to nod. 'I suppose I did, initially. But you are my father, after all. I just couldn't do it—not without learning more about you first. And when you told me you were dying anyway, I thought there was no longer any point—you'll be dead soon anyway. I thought it better to watch you suffer, for what you did to my mum, maybe even add to that suffering. But then you started to tell me these things, and my life started to make so much more sense.'

'So, you'll do it? You'll bury us?' asked Kevin, seeming to want some confirmation.

'I will,' said Gaz. 'But I want something from you first?'

'Oh. What's that?' asked Kevin.

'I want you to call my mum, tell her that you're sorry,' said Gaz.

'Call your *mum*?'

'She's in a mental health facility. She won't even remember a few hours later, they pump so much medication into her. And nobody will believe anything she says anyway—she hallucinates all the time, gets confused. But I want you to tell her anyway,' said Gaz.

Kevin thought about it. 'Sure, Gaz. I can do that. But let's ditch the motorhome first in case the police come sniffing around. We'll be better off in your car for now.'

Gaz sniffed and nodded. 'Put her in the boot?' he asked.

'Yeah, in the boot,' said Kevin. 'And if she's a good girl, we might even give her some water. We wouldn't want her passing out at the vital moment now, would we.'

CHAPTER SEVENTEEN

'Is it hers?' asked PC Matlock, the Constable who'd found the pink mobile phone on Clifton Drive North, half dug into the lower lying sand dunes there.

DI Hogarth took it, had a good look. He entered the security number, which he'd set up himself for the operation, opened it up. 'It is,' he said, looking at Walker.

They'd met nearby Lytham Windmill, on a bench there, a popular tourist spot and a scenic one at that, which Walker might have noticed and appreciated at any other time. But not now.

'Did you see anything else? Talk to anyone who saw something?' asked Walker.

PC Matlock shook his head. 'Sorry. I just found the phone, that's all. Nobody I spoke to saw anything.'

'Well, that will be all then,' said Walker. 'You may resume your duties.'

PC Matlock walked away in a hurry, heading eastwards into town, leaving Walker with DI Hogarth and DC Ainscough.

'What are you hoping to find here, Chief?' asked DI Hogarth, who was out of his element somewhat, beyond the confines of his usual four walls and a computer. 'Surely I could do more back at base.'

'Somone must have seen Kevin Lawson out and about—before he took DC Briggs, that is,' said Walker. 'He would have been stalking, trying to find a victim. He's been here. And if he had any conversations with anyone, we might get a clue as to where he's gone next,' said Walker. 'It's a longshot, I know, but it's all we have unless that motorhome turns up.'

'But we already have a small army of PCs out canvassing the area, talking to people,' said DI Hogarth. 'We're wasting our time here.'

'No, we're not. Look,' said Walker. 'Police in uniforms often scare people off, make them tight-lipped, make them not want to get involved. Me and DC Ainscough will look around, see if we can find anything. You pretend you're this bastard's son, say he's not well or something, say he has dementia maybe, and that you need to find him. Someone might know something?'

'Why me?' asked DI Hogarth. 'Why don't you do that?'

'Well, because you look... You just look less like a cop, that's all,' said Walker.

'Because I'm fat?' asked DI Hogarth. His BMI was off the charts. Technically, he was obese. 'And no one would imagine a person like me could be a police officer?'

'No. I mean... Never mind. You just look more like a civilian, that's all,' said Walker. 'And you're more approachable than I am, more amiable. People like you, don't they.'

'Well, I suppose it doesn't matter, as long as we find her,' said DI Hogarth.

'No, it doesn't. We've got a mugshot each of this guy, from DVLA records. Show them that, say you'll be very grateful if they can point you in the right direction, some shite like that,' said Walker.

'I'll do my best,' said DI Hogarth. 'And where are you going?'

CHAPTER SEVENTEEN

Walker's phone rang.

'Hello? Yes, yes. That's *great!* I'll meet her at the Beach Café in ten minutes then. Thank you,' said Walker.

'What's that?' said DI Hogarth. 'You two going for some grub while I'm out here, sweating my arse off?'

'It's the woman who was attacked, the one DC Briggs mentioned running away from the motorhome,' said Walker. 'She's reported the incident. And get this, she works at the damned café we had lunch at: the Beach Café. Her name is Shannon McNaughton. I'm going to talk to her now, find out exactly what he did to her, or tried to do, why she was running away like that. Then we might have a better idea of what we're dealing with here, what his approach might be, what weapons he could have and all that.'

'Fine,' said DI Hogarth. 'Just get me a bacon butty to take out and give it me when we meet up again, hopefully soon. This is gonna be hungry work.'

'I'll do that,' said the ever-happy-to-help DC Ainscough. 'If we have time, that is. No problem.'

'We won't have time. Look, I shouldn't have to tell you that we're running out of time here, guys,' said Walker, raising his voice as his emotions started to get the better of him. 'And if we don't find something soon, and she doesn't find a way out of this herself somehow, it could be too late. So, sod the bacon butty, and let's focus here. Not eating for a few hours won't kill you. We'll eat when DC Briggs is back with us, safe and sound, end of. Got that?'

'I didn't mean anything...' said DI Hogarth. 'We all want to help DC Briggs. I just work and think better when I'm fully fuelled, that's all. I'm useless on an empty tummy. I said it so I can help DC Briggs better, that's all.'

Walker huffed. 'Fine,' he said. 'We'll get the damned butty. We'll get us all a bite to eat, keep ourselves fuelled and fresh. It will only take a minute or two if we tell them we're on urgent police business. Happy now?'

DI Hogarth nodded his appreciation. 'I'll be happy when DC Briggs is safe and sound, the same as all of us.'

'I'll take care of it,' said DC Ainscough.

'We're going to get her,' said Walker, trying to make it come true by believing it himself, visualising her safe and sound. 'Come on, DC Ainscough. Let's get to that café.'

* * *

'Shannon McNaughton?' asked Walker. A woman wearing an apron, a member of staff at the Beach Café, nodded, and they all sat down at one of the tables. 'Oh, and three bacon sandwiches and three bottles of water to go, while we're talking, please. And tell them we're in a hurry, on urgent police business.'

'Liz, these gentlemen need three bacon sandwiches and three bottles of water to go,' shouted Shannon, getting the attention of one of the other members of staff. The woman called Liz got out a pen and notepad, scribbled something down. 'And they need it quick. Really quick.' Liz nodded her understanding, probably already having been told that Shannon was meeting with some police detectives.

'Right, let's get down to business,' said Walker. 'We understand you made a call, reporting an incident you had.'

'Yes, that's right,' said Shannon. 'I wasn't sure if I ought to report it, but decided I should, in case he tried anything like that with anyone else, in case he was dangerous.'

'You did the right thing,' said Walker. 'In fact, we have reason to believe that the old man who attacked you may be a very dangerous individual, who has currently taken a person hostage. So, we need to know everything that happened, starting from the beginning. Now, what happened?'

Although Walker was in a hurry, could feel every second of the clock ticking, he knew he couldn't rush things too much, or he might miss a vital piece of information—information he'd learned, during his long career, could make or break an investigation, and could be a case of life or death.

'I was just walking on the beach, alone,' said Shannon. 'I needed to take a breath. I've had some stress at home...'

'Go on,' said Walker.

'It's my husband. He's—'

'Not *that*,' said Walker. 'I'm sorry. We need to focus as a person's life is at stake. You were walking on the beach. And then?'

'Well, this old guy approached me, said he needed some help,' said Shannon.

'What did he look like?' asked Walker. 'And what was he wearing? Is there anything you remember that stood out about his appearance?'

'Er, I don't know really. He was quite old, in his seventies or eighties, grey hair, thinning, but not bald. Don't really remember what he was wearing. He just looked like a frail, ill, old man,' she said. 'Weak looking.'

Walker showed her the mugshot of their suspect, the one they'd got from the DVLA, from his driving license. 'Is this him?' he asked. 'Is this the man you saw?'

'Yes, I think so. Yes, that's him. I helped him back to his motorhome,' she said.

'Can you describe it?' asked Walker. 'I don't suppose you saw and remember any of the vehicle registration plate, do you?' He figured her having noticed the license plate was a long shot, but he hoped she could at least give a matching description of the vehicle to corroborate what they had.

'I don't know. It was just a motorhome, like any other. White, or more like cream, maybe. Not one of those massive ones, but not tiny either. Medium sized,' said Shannon, staring into space, evidently trying her best to remember all the details. 'I'm sorry. That's all I remember.'

'That's great, Shannon. Anything else? Anything at all? Any distinguishing features, stickers on the vehicle, accessories, that kind of thing?' asked Walker, trying to jog her memory, spark something.

'Er... Oh! I remember now. It had a disabled sticker on the door, was parked in one of the disabled spots on the car park, near the toilets,' she said.

Walker made a mental note, and DC Ainscough did the same, only in his leather-bound notebook. 'So, you helped him back to the motorhome. Did you talk with him, on the way?'

'Not really. He was out of breath. Just kept saying sorry, that he needed help,' said Shannon. 'And thanking me.'

'And then?' said Walker, wanting to move things on.

'I went inside—the *motorhome*—with him. He looked harmless. I didn't see any problem. I offered him some water. Said he needed some help with taking his medication. He took out a syringe. I thought he was going to ask me to inject him. I couldn't have done that. I'm not good with needles, you see. But it turned out he just wanted help preparing it. Said his hands were shaking, so I loaded the syringe for him after he told me how to do it, then gave it to him.'

'Did you see what the medicine was, the one you loaded into the syringe?' asked Walker.

'Not really. I had a look, but it was nothing familiar,' said Shannon.

'Can you remember any of it?' asked Walker.

'S-U-C-C. It was a long word. That's all I remember,' said Shannon.

'Thank you,' said Walker, looking at DC Ainscough, making sure he'd got this.

'So, you gave him the loaded syringe...' said Walker, urging her on.

'And then he grabbed my arm, tight, tried to inject me with it, but I got away, ran. I saw this woman on the beach when I was running, told her not to go that way, warned her that some mad man was down there in a motorhome. She shouted something after me, but I couldn't hear, and just legged it. Is that who it is? Is that who's in danger?' said Shannon, looking mortified that someone could be hurt who she might have warned better.

Normally, Walker would dig deeper, go through all the details again, ask more questions, but they didn't have time. They needed to act.

'I'm sorry you had to experience this,' said Walker. 'Do you have anything else to add? Anything at all?'

The woman thought about it and then slowly shook her head.

'Then that will be all,' said Walker. 'Thank you for the information.'

Three bacon sandwiches and three small bottles of water

were put on the table in front of them, wrapped in a clear plastic bag. It was Liz from earlier. Their order was ready.

'On the house. We know who you are,' she said.

'Much appreciated,' said Walker, grabbing the bag and handing it to DC Ainscough.

Shannon got up, slowly, seeming to think about something. 'That motorhome, it smelled of something—smelled of death. Find this guy, detective, before someone gets hurt.'

'We'll do our best,' said Walker, and Shannon got back to work going behind the counter with Liz.

'S-U-C-C,' said Walker. 'What's that? Google it or something, will you, find out?'

DC Ainscough got out his mobile phone, started tapping on it.

'Oh, no,' he said.

'What is it, detective?' asked Walker. 'What is a medicine beginning with S-U-C-C?'

DC Ainscough took a deep breath. 'It's *Succinylcholine*,' he said. 'There's nothing similar. *Succinylcholine is a depolarizing skeletal muscle relaxant used adjunctly to anaesthesia and for skeletal muscle relaxation during intubation, mechanical ventilation, and surgical procedures.*'

'Shit,' said Walker. 'And in plain English?'

DC Ainscough studied some more. 'It basically paralyses a person for a short time while allowing them to remain conscious. It goes on to say: *Succinylcholine has no effect on consciousness or pain threshold and must therefore be used in conjunction with adequate anaesthesia.*'

'So, without anaesthesia, the person injected would remain conscious, would feel pain, but would not be able to move a sodding muscle,' said Walker. 'That about the size of it?'

CHAPTER SEVENTEEN

DC Ainscough gulped. 'That seems to be correct, sir.'

Walker slammed his fist down on the table several times, and almost everyone in the café—which was a considerable amount of people—looked at him, probably wondering what the hell was wrong with him. Only Shannon and Liz from earlier seemed sympathetic, or worried, or both.

'Damn it,' he said.

'Poor DC Briggs,' said DC Ainscough. 'What's he going to do to her?'

'That's how the old git bloody got her,' said Walker. 'He's drugged her, dragged her in the motorhome, somehow, or she went in there willingly first. Get word out that we're looking for a motorhome with a disabled sticker on the side. I want every bobby in the area looking for that vehicle, day and night, until we find her.'

'Will do,' said DC Ainscough.

'And find out what his bloody disability is with his local council. We've got his address from the DVLA: says he lives in Southport. That's Sefton Council, right? If he's got a Blue Badge, then he'll have to have applied for it through them, told them what his disability is. Knowing what's wrong with him might come in useful, when it comes to stopping him,' said Walker. 'And get a crew down to his house once the search warrant comes through. It should be quick since we've got Chief Constable Sarah Harriet on our side. I'm surprised it hasn't come through already. See what can be found there, any clues as to what makes this guy tick, what his modus operandi is. We'll need all of this if we have a chance of stopping him.'

'I'm on it,' said DC Ainscough.

'Good. I'll talk to DI Hogarth, see if he's got anything,' said Walker, getting up and going outside, taking a breath. His heart was racing, adrenaline pumped. It would be like that until he found DC Briggs, got her safe. He made the call. 'DI Hogarth. Anything?'

'Not really, Chief. The place is swarming with elderly guys like him. People just keep squinting at the photograph and saying they might have seen him, but they're not sure,' said DI Hogarth. 'You?'

'Keep a look out for any motorhomes with a disabled sticker on the door,' said Walker. 'It seems our guy might have a Blue Badge. We're looking into it, trying to find out what that disability might be.'

'Roger that,' said DI Hogarth. 'I'll keep my eyes peeled.'

'Let's meet up at our Incident Room in thirty then,' said Walker. 'See what we have.'

'Will do,' said DI Hogarth, sounding tired and out of breath.

'Oh, and Detective,' said Walker.

'Yes?'

'We got those supplies you wanted. We'll refuel in thirty, formulate a plan while doing so.'

There was a pause on the line. 'Oh, that's great,' said DI Hogarth, sounding slightly rejuvenated, but with a touch of guilt. 'I'm sure we'll be more productive if we do that. Good thinking, sir. Over and out.'

CHAPTER EIGHTEEN

Back in the makeshift Incident Room at the nearby hotel, Walker, DI Hogarth, and DC Ainscough were, as promised, refuelling themselves with a bacon sandwich and a bottle of water each—their takeouts from the Beach Café—while discussing their next plan of attack for finding the killer and bringing their colleague home. Tensions were high, with what was at stake, but Walker agreed for the need for them to stay sharp and in as good condition as possible, so he was forcing his food down, despite not having any appetite. He looked at DI Hogarth, who, conversely, seemed to be enjoying his, or at least having no trouble getting it down.

'I don't know how you can eat so comfortably at a time like this,' said Walker.

'I guess it's my drug,' he said. 'I need it to function. Don't judge me.'

DC Ainscough was not much interested in his food either. He was checking his messages, reading through them, having not had a bite of the unopened sandwich yet.

'Got our perps disability,' he said, leaning forward. 'He's... Oh, this is unexpected. He's got cancer.'

'Cancer?' said Walker. 'Can you get a Blue Badge if you have cancer?'

'Apparently so,' said DC Ainscough, pushing his round framed glasses further up his nose. 'If it renders you partially immobile. It's his pancreas, it says, and its terminal.'

'He's *dying?*' said Walker. This was good news and bad news, all rolled into one. On the good side, he would be in a weakened state, and he was old already, so he shouldn't give them too much trouble if they accosted him, if they were able to avoid his needles, that was. On the downside, the fact that he was dying made him an even more dangerous animal than he already was—he had absolutely nothing to lose.

'That's what they say,' said DC Ainscough.

'What are the symptoms of pancreatic cancer?' asked Walker.

DI Hogarth did a quick Google search for them. 'Belly pain, loss of weight, possible jaundice,' he said. 'Amongst other things.'

'Jaundice? That's yellowing of skin, right?' said Walker, wanting it confirmed, as anything related to his appearance could be of use.

'Er, skin and whites of the eyes, it says,' said DI Hogarth.

'Well, hopefully, all of this is slowing him down, giving us more time to find them,' said Walker. 'Add this to his description—possible yellowness of skin and eyes. It might help us locate him,' said Walker as his mobile phone rang. He picked it up, answered. 'Hello? He put the phone on speaker so the others could hear. I'm sorry, could you say that again?'

'*I said, this is Kevin Lawson. Do you know who I am?*' said the voice, weak and gravelly, old sounding.

Walker motioned to DI Hogarth, clicking his fingers, telling him to record what was about to be said. Hogarth seemed to get it, got his mobile nearby, recording.

'We do,' said Walker. 'Is DC Briggs with you?'

'Is that her name? Yes, she's with me.'

'We're going to need to speak to her, Kevin,' said Walker. 'Right now.'

'You're in no position to make demands right now,' said Kevin. *'Besides, she's unable to speak at the moment.'*

'Kevin... look, we understand you're not well. We can get you help, get you in a secure medical facility. You can see out your days peacefully. You just need to tell us where you are,' said Walker, more in hope than anticipation, just trying to keep the conversation going. He knew the longer it went on for, the more clues they might unearth.

'I just need to know one thing,' said Kevin. *'Why were you following me? How did you know? Was it that woman, the one who ran away?'*

'Kevin, I'm sure you've got a very good reason for doing this. But DC Briggs has done nothing wrong. She's innocent. Let her go,' said Walker. There was a pause, more than a few seconds, but Kevin was still on the line—they could hear his laboured breathing. 'Kevin?'

'You know, don't you?' he said. *'About the other women. You found them, somehow. You wouldn't dedicate this much police time to some batty old guy who grabbed some lady's arm.'*

Walker thought about it. There didn't seem to be much to lose by revealing what they knew at this point, but perhaps there was something to gain if they'd missed something, and he wanted credit for it. Perhaps there were many more victims than they currently had. Anything was possible.

'You mean Sally Fielding, Tracy White, Jackie Wakefield? Have I missed anyone?' said Walker.

'So, you never found the first, Cynthia... something. I forget now. She was the one that started all of this. So beautiful. So much like her,' said Kevin.

'Like who?' said Walker. 'She was so much like *who?*'

'Never mind,' said Kevin, sounding like he might be winding up the conversation, ready to hang up.

'Summer dress, blonde hair tied back, glasses?' said Walker. 'That's your type, right? That's the kind of women you've been looking for. Do they look like someone you knew? An old girlfriend, perhaps?'

'Goodbye, Detective Walker,' said Kevin, and then the line went dead.

'Shit. How'd he even get my number if DC Briggs can't talk?' asked Walker, exasperated that they just talked to their killer and not got any obvious useful lead from it.'

'Perhaps he took it from her phone before discarding it,' said DI Hogarth, his answer seeming obvious once he'd said it. Walker wasn't thinking straight. He was getting too twisted up with thinking that Shelly—DC Briggs—might get hurt; or that she had already.

'Well, at least we got the first name of his first victim,' said DC Ainscough. 'And since he's doing this in early July every thirteen years, we have pretty reasonable grounds for believing this may have been in 1972, thirteen years before he killed Jackie Wakefield in July 1985.'

'I'll run this through our database, see if we can get a match on a missing person in Lytham St Annes in early July 1972, with a first name of Cynthia,' said DI Hogarth.

Walker gave it some thought. They knew who he was, what he'd been doing, and how. But they didn't know why. Often, such homicide investigations were about finding out who the

CHAPTER EIGHTEEN

killer was, but this time they knew exactly who he was. There was no mystery there. What they didn't know, was *where* he was, and the clock had been ticking on that ever since they'd found out his kill dates; and it had been ticking even quicker since he'd taken DC Briggs. It was that sense of urgency that had forced their hand in the first place, got them to put her at risk—a risk they'd deemed just about acceptable if it offset the risk of someone else being hurt. That decision, right now, was not looking like such a good one, though. They'd underestimated him, something Walker wouldn't be doing again.

'You do that, try find out who she is. Maybe we'll get a clue to his location. Her body wasn't discovered with the others, so perhaps his MO wasn't yet cemented. He might have been sloppier, might have killed someone he knew before settling on his MO of targeting strangers. Try to find out who she is, where she's from, whether she knew him or not. If we're lucky we might uncover something we couldn't from the other cases. DI Hogarth are you able to do anything to track the location of his phone call?' asked Walker.

'It's possible to track it, but it will take time, by which time he'll probably have moved on to somewhere else,' said DI Hogarth. 'Maybe even discarded that phone too.'

'Then analyse the recording you just took, clean the audio up, see if there's anything in the background that we missed during the live call,' said Walker. 'Maybe there's something there.'

'Will do,' said DI Hogarth. 'Course. I'm on it, right now.'

'Before you do that, did we find anything about this guy being involved in any entomology clubs? Or writing any academic papers in this field, anything like that?' asked

Walker.

'Not really,' said DI Hogarth. 'He's a member of the Royal Entomological Society and the British Entomological and Natural History Society, but nobody knows much about him. He has some online presence, but it seems he keeps it at that.'

'Okay. Clean up that audio then, and let's see what we have,' said Walker, more in hope than expectation.

* * *

DC Briggs could hardly breathe. She was in at the boot of a car now, still bound, could feel it moving, going over bumps and dips in the road. They were going to kill her, and there wasn't a whole lot she could do about it unless she got free, got full control of her body again. She could feel her hands and legs again now, could wiggle her fingers and toes no problem, could even blink her eyes. She prayed that Walker and the team weren't far behind. But that was about all she could do right now: *pray*.

* * *

'You hear that?' asked DI Hogarth. He was showing Walker his findings of the audio clean-up, and there was something in the background they'd missed during the live conversation, just as Walker had hoped. It was what sounded like a cow *mooing*.

CHAPTER EIGHTEEN

'A cow?' asked Walker. 'So, he's near a farmer's field somewhere?'

'Well... yes. But there are loads of farmers' fields containing livestock around here. So, I sent it to an expert in livestock farming, and... get this... they said that cows, much like humans, have their own regional accents,' said DI Hogarth, looking pleased with himself. 'And get this: this cow, they are fairly certain, is a *highland cow*.'

'What, so they've gone to Scotland?' said Walker, not quite sure what DI Hogarth was getting at, knowing that would be a few hours' drive, thinking their chances of finding Briggs was slipping away, feeling himself being sucked into a well of despair.

'Possibly, but since this guy has a history of killing in Lytham St Annes on this date, for some reason, I think there's a good chance he'll want to stay close by,' said DI Hogarth. 'So... bear with me... I checked the area for any highland cows, and lo and behold, there's this one farm who stocks them—imported them from Fife in Scotland a year ago, say they've become something of a tourist attraction, so they let folks in to see for a small fee, feed them and the like. I have the address.'

'Great. I'm on it,' said Walker, relieved they might still be close by, that there was still some hope. 'Text me the address now and I'll go take a good look.'

'I'll come with you,' said DC Ainscough. 'In case you need backup?'

'Course. We have something, then. Let's go see if the bastard is still there, or if anyone has seen which direction he's heading in,' said Walker, picking up his phone, and already heading towards the door. 'This is our chance, fingers crossed.'

CHAPTER NINETEEN

'Haven't been out in the fields yet today,' said John Baines, the owner of Mossbank Farm, a farm, they'd learned, that specialised in livestock, and which crucially had a field full of Highland Cows—the only such cows of their type in the area. 'Been too busy with catering to tourists. We're making more from visitors than from our actual sodding farming business at the minute. It's a good job we had this idea, or we'd be in danger of going under. Our mortgage payments are—'

'So, you haven't seen any motorhomes around here in the past few days then?' asked Walker, who was stood in front of the Baines farmhouse and family home with DC Ainscough.

'Can't say I have,' said John. 'Except perhaps some visitors to the farm that parked up here one day—a family of four if I remember right, two young boys. They loved the cows, they did.'

'Is it okay if we take a look around?' asked Walker, waiting a couple of seconds, before adding, 'We're going to anyway.'

'Course,' said John. 'Knock yerselves out. There's a dirt track around the back if you wanna use that. It's big enough for your car. It'll take you all around the periphery of the farm, past the Highland Cows you were interested in, and out near

CHAPTER NINETEEN

the main road. Hey, why were you interested in the cows, if you don't mind me askin'?'

'That's police business,' said Walker, gazing off, looking around, while sensing that John needed some reassurance, so he added, 'but rest assured you have nothing to worry about. We're just looking for someone, that's all, and we believe they may have been here.'

Walker started to walk back to the car, which they'd left in the car park of the Baines' estate. On his way, he heard DC Ainscough say 'We'll be in touch if we need anything more. Thanks for your time, Mr Baines,' before catching up to him.

'Get in,' said Walker. 'Let's take a damned good look around here, see what we can find. Keep your eyes peeled, Detective. It's all in the details.'

* * *

'There!' said DC Ainscough. 'Up ahead, just around that corner.'

Walker's colleague had seen the edge of the motorhome slightly before him as the lane wound around a corner to the right, meaning DC Ainscough, sat in the passenger seat, could see a bit more around that corner before him. He drove right up to the vehicle and came to a stop, waiting for a few seconds, seeing if it was going to speed off. It didn't. He opened his car door, just a touch, waiting another few seconds, and then DC Ainscough followed suit.

'Be careful,' said Walker. 'Expect the unexpected.'

DC Ainscough nodded, took out his baton, steeling himself,

seemingly getting ready to use it if necessary. Walker trusted him. They got out of the car, engine still running just in case, and approached the motorhome. Walker motioned for DC Ainscough to stand in front of the side door, while Walker walked around it, peeking through some of the windows—but most of them had the curtains fully drawn, so he couldn't see much. What he could see was that there was nobody in the driver's or passenger's seat. When he got to the front of the vehicle, he could fully see through the windscreen, but still couldn't see the back side of the vehicle as there was also a curtain behind the front seats, pulled across on a string.

'Shel? You in there?' shouted Walker. There was no response. Walker returned to the side door that DC Ainscough was guarding, and he tentatively tried the handle. It turned.

'Hello? This is DCI Walker of the Lancashire Constabulary. I'm coming in,' he said, habitually, voice still raised, perhaps even a touch more than before. 'We are armed.' He opened the door and the smell immediately hit, catching the back of Walker's throat, his gag reflex being activated for a second, turning his stomach. 'Jesus—'

'What is— Oh, *hell*,' said DC Ainscough, who was a little behind Walker. It was the smell of human faeces, mixed in with something else, like ethanol, not a good combination.

They got inside, both with batons out now, ready to strike any assailant if necessary. DC Ainscough dropped his as soon as he saw: *human remains*, what was left of them—but thankfully, it was not DC Briggs as this was clearly a male. It looked like a trainee butcher had been practicing on them. There was blood everywhere, and evidently the bowels had been cut because faecal matter had spilled out as well. There was an empty bottle of ethanol in the kitchen sink amongst

CHAPTER NINETEEN

some dirty dishes. Walker picked it up, took a look. There was also an empty box of matches on the sideboard with two dud matches next to it, which had obviously been struck several times with no success.

'Someone tried to burn the place,' said Walker, getting closer to the body, covering his nose and mouth. 'Open a window or two, will you?' he said, so they could breathe a little easier, think better. DC Ainscough did as asked, being careful not to step in any of the biological slop.

Upon further inspection, the deceased was an elderly male. Walker could see that much, but he had to turn the head to get a good look at the face; and remarkably, his face seemed to be one of the few parts of him that hadn't been mutilated. There seemed to be various stab wounds all over the body.

'Shit,' said Walker. 'Is this our guy?'

DC Ainscough took a good look, up close, then compared it to the mugshot they had of Kevin Lawson. 'Looks like it,' he said, with some confusion in his voice, not quite being able to figure what had gone down, with Walker having the same bewilderment.

'What the hell has—? Has DC Briggs done this?' asked DC Ainscough.

'*Of course not!*' he said, shouting at the much younger Detective. 'Of course she sodding didn't...' He was shouting because he was scared. If she had got loose somehow, gone nuts on the guy, slaughtered him with a kitchen knife or something, and then ran, knowing she'd gone too far, she'd be in a whole world of trouble.

It quickly flashed in his mind that he should doctor the crime scene to protect her, put a weapon in Lawson's hand, perhaps. But he couldn't do that. Besides, he knew she'd never go to these lengths, whatever he'd done to her. This wasn't self-defence. Lawson was a frail old man, and he'd obviously been continued to be stabbed long after he'd been immobilised, probably long after he was dead. There were no two ways about it: he'd been executed, brutalised. It was carnage.

If she'd not done it though—then there must be a second killer, an accomplice, perhaps the person who'd knocked Walker unconscious. And that meant she was still in mortal danger. Either way, it wasn't good.

'What do we do now then?' asked DC Ainscough.

'What we do, is we find DC Briggs,' said Walker. 'She could be nearby. She could be hurt. Come on.'

CHAPTER TWENTY

'Hogarth, we have a situation here,' said Walker, now back in the pool car, doors open, talking on speakerphone next to DC Ainscough, who seemed to be struggling with this even more than he was. 'We've got our killer. He's dead. But DC Briggs is still missing. We've scoured the immediate area, but there's no sign of her.'

'What?' said DI Hogarth. 'Still missing? Do you think there's more than one killer then? There was no evidence of this.'

'I'm not sure yet,' said Walker. 'Kevin Lawson wasn't just dead: he'd been mutilated, slaughtered like an animal, most likely dead well before the final wounds were made. Someone went loco on him, alright. It was a real mess. Can't say he didn't deserve it, though.'

'But if there isn't more than one killer, then that means…' DI Hogarth paused, obviously having just realised what one other possibility was—the unthinkable: that DC Briggs killed him and ran away, however unlikely that might be given her character and professionalism.

'Whether it was DC Briggs or someone else that did it, it's hard to say. But we aren't going to jump to any wild conclusions,' said Walker. 'The most likely scenario at this point, in my book, is Lawson had an accomplice who turned against him for some reason. I don't think DC Briggs could have done this. By all accounts, Lawson wasn't just old but frail too—and our inspection of the body backs that up—so I'm not sure he would've had the physicality to knock me out near that car park and then get after DC Briggs so quickly. And that points to someone else being involved. Regardless, our main aim hasn't changed: we must find DC Briggs, get her to safety, as soon as possible.'

'But *if* it was her, that killed him, I mean, is there any possibility of an argument for reasonable force?' asked DI Hogarth. 'And absconding from the scene and not calling it in isn't going to look good too.'

All of this had already flashed through Walker's mind too, of course. 'Let's just find her first,' he said. 'Worry about that later.'

There was an uncomfortable silence while DC Ainscough rubbed his forehead, sweating.

'Call it in. Get forensics over here, pronto, to process the scene,' said Walker.

Another pause. 'You sure about that, Chief?' said DI Hogarth.

'Just do it,' said Walker, as assertively as he could, before hanging up.

'Right, now that's called in, we're taking another look,' said Walker to DC Ainscough. 'Maybe we missed something.'

'I'm sorry, sir. I feel a little woozy,' said DC Ainscough, looking like he might throw up at any minute. He took a deep breath, looking at Walker. 'Alright. I think I'm okay now.'

'Well, you don't look okay. Stay here, Detective. That's an order. Take a breath, regroup. I'll be out in a minute,' said Walker, exiting the car with no resistance from DC Ainscough,

CHAPTER TWENTY

and going back inside the motorhome through the same side door, closing it behind him.

He put some nitrile gloves on, which he always did when inspecting a crime scene, so as not to contaminate it.

He went through some drawers, found a pouch with some needles in, and a small bottle of Succinylcholine—the drug that Kevin Lawson had likely been using on his victims, the same drug they'd come up with from Shannon McNaughton's statement, the one beginning with S-U-C-C, that he'd tried to inject her with. As DC Ainscough noted, it was a powerful muscle relaxant used during certain surgical procedures, one that could render a person completely paralysed, whilst allowing them to remain conscious. Lawson had probably been using it so his victims would be aware of whatever terrible things he did to them. It was beyond evil, but he couldn't think about that now, especially when it involved DC Briggs.

Walker finished what he was doing, took one last look around the room, to see if he'd missed anything. He got that sense that someone might have been looking for something—there were a couple of drawers left open, and some bits and bobs spilled out of a cupboard onto the floor, though he guessed this could have occurred during the attack, or if Lawson had been in a rush for some reason, been messy.

He didn't think there was much more he could do here. He'd leave the rest to the CSIs and Forensic Team, including a more detailed inspection of the body. He didn't want to touch that any further in case he compromised any evidence. He'd already touched the head once to ID the face. He returned to the car, opened the door. DC Ainscough looked at him.

'You find anything?' he asked.

'Yeah, the drug that he'd been paralysing his victims with—it *was* Succinylcholine, just like we thought. Should have spotted that the first time. Must have been the smell, making us not think straight. It seems our DC Briggs may have been immobilised.'

'Then it can't have been her then—I didn't really think she could have done that. There must be someone else involved after all,' said DC Ainscough. 'But that means she's still out there, trapped, tied up or something.'

Walker took a closer look at the external surroundings now that forensics were on their way, and they'd ruled out DC Briggs being anywhere nearby. He saw something, on the floor.

'Hey, there's some tire tracks out here that may be from another vehicle,' he said. 'They look smaller than the motorhome's.' They hadn't seen them until now because first they'd been focussed on the motorhome, and then on scouring the wider area to see if Briggs might be there. The tracks looked like they'd been freshly made, clean. He got out, took a few steps over to the tracks, bent down, inspecting them. DC Ainscough also got out, joined him by his side.

'What is it?' he said, looking down, also now seeing the tire tracks for himself.

'Well, it's confirmed now. Someone else has been here, recently,' said Walker. He looked around, being careful where he was placing his feet. 'Wait. Don't move.'

Walker identified what looked like two pairs of footprints, both which seemed to stand still in a certain spot, but then one pair disappeared.

'Look,' said Walker. 'Here are the tire tracks, so the car was facing either this way', he said, pointing down the road, or

CHAPTER TWENTY

that way,' he said, pointing the other way. 'But the two pairs of footprints are here, and then one disappears. Someone is either getting into or being put into a car boot. It's Briggs and Lawson's accomplice-cum-killer. It must be. So, the car must have been facing this way, in the direction our car has come from. And then the other pair walks back to the motorhome, goes inside.'

'Oh, hell. He put her in the car boot and then went back inside to kill Lawson,' said DC Ainscough.

On the balance of things, Walker now wished DC Briggs *had* killed Kevin Lawson, was safe somewhere, and they only had to worry about getting her exonerated for any possible wrongdoings. But now they had a much different problem, even worse than before, in fact, as they knew nothing at all about this mystery person who it seemed had taken her. They were back to square one. It was obviously all a lot more complicated than they'd first thought.

'What do we do, Chief?' asked DC Ainscough, who was evidently way out of his depth now and in danger of going under, still struggling to come to terms with the fact that one of their colleagues had been taken.

'Get forensics to cast these shoe prints, and the tire treads, see if we can get a match on anything. At the very least, we should be able to match one of the shoe treads to those worn by DC Briggs, if what we're thinking is correct,' said Walker. 'Get it confirmed.'

'Got it. I'm on it,' said DC Ainscough.

'And chin up, Detective. There is one ray of light at the end of this dark tunnel,' said Walker.

'Oh, and what's that?' asked DC Ainscough.

'If she was stood here, making those footprints, then she

was still alive just before she was put into this car,' said Walker. 'Let's follow the tracks, see how far they go.'

DC Ainscough got on his phone, ready to instruct the forensic team, while Walker took out some police tape and barrier posts from his boot, which he kept there for emergencies just like this, when a scene needed to be protected in a hurry. He cordoned off the area, and then called the farmer from earlier, John Baines.

'Hi, John. It's DCI Walker again. We have an active crime scene on your property. I've cordoned it off with police tape, but I need you to close the road, somehow, make sure no more vehicles come down here until we get backup. Yes... Yes, a tractor at either end of the lane should suffice. Give me a minute or two to drive out first. We're coming out the way we came in. Okay. Thanks.' Walker hung up the phone and they both got in the car, Walker in the driver's seat again. He turned the car around, going back from where they'd come—the direction that DC Brigg's kidnapper had driven in, towards John Baines' farmhouse and the car park from earlier. They lost the car tracks as soon as they got to the car park, though, as the dirt track turned into a concrete gravel drive.

'Okay. There's nothing more with can do here for now. Let's get back to DI Hogarth, look at what we have, try to get some intel,' said Walker. 'But we must be quick. I have a feeling that time is well and truly running out on this one. We have to find her, and fast.'

CHAPTER TWENTY-ONE

'We just got data from forensics come through,' said DI Hogarth, staring at his Apple MacBook screen. 'Expedited, for one of our own.' He looked up at Walker, maybe hoping he was pleased, or approved, or something. But Walker was devoid of any such sentiments now—he was too worried about DC Briggs, too much in a hurry for giving compliments. 'I already got a photo of the soles of the shoes DC Briggs was wearing. Checked her receipt from when she went shopping for the operation—the ones we kept to get reimbursed later—called the store, got them to send me an image. They were Birkenstock 'Arizona Soft Footbed' sandals, size seven. Let's see then...' He clicked at his keyboard's trackpad a few times, lined up the two images. 'We have a match.'

'So, she was stood there, near that motorhome, and then her footprints disappeared, most likely because she was forced into the boot—possibly bound, gagged too. The question is, where is this mystery person taking her? And why did they kill Lawson?' said Walker. 'What about the tire treads?'

'Just looking at that too,' said DI Hogarth. 'Just a sec. It's a long shot, though, as you well know. We can't identify the make and model of a vehicle based on tyre prints alone—but we could narrow it down a little, maybe.'

Walker waited as patiently as he could, sat next to DC Ainscough, pinching at the skin on his leg without realising it, until it hurt, and then he did realise and stopped. 'So?' he asked, when he could wait no longer.

DI Hogarth took a deep breath. 'Interesting. Four different brands of tire, by the look of it seemingly coming from the same car—maybe a used car that was sold on? That's unusual, but it would still be very difficult to identify the car based upon this. However...'

'I like *however*. I can work with *however*,' said Walker. 'What is it?'

'It appears something else was dragging from the bottom of the car, making a hard line in the dirt,' said DI Hogarth. 'I'd say it's most likely an exhaust pipe, fallen down a bit.'

'So, we find a car with a drooping exhaust pipe, with different tyres, and we have our guy?' asked Walker. 'That it?'

'It seems so,' said DI Hogarth.

'Right. Let's get out there,' said Walker. 'Scour the area looking for a vehicle of that description. Get as many officers on this as possible, as a matter of urgency. We need to find that car. And let's hope to God they haven't left the sodding area, or we'll never find them.'

'I'll get on security camera footage,' said DI Hogarth.

Walker looked at him, questioning whether there was time for all that, whether Hogarth might be better used out in the field, looking with them.

'What? Look at me? I'm not going to be much help running around out there, am I? I'm hardly the dynamic type,' he said.

'Well, just make sure you find something here then, Detective,' said Walker.

CHAPTER TWENTY-ONE

'I'll check anything near or coming from that farm during the time in question, see if we can identify a car with a broken exhaust pipe,' said DI Hogarth.

'Fine. Come on then, Detective Ainscough,' said Walker. 'We have to find her, find out what the sodding hell is going on here, and bring her in.'

CHAPTER TWENTY-TWO

DC Shelly Briggs sat slumped in a wheelchair, the one that belonged to Kevin Lawson. She'd seen it folded in the bathroom of his motorhome. Perhaps he used it on his bad days, she thought, when his cancer got the better of him. Right now, she was being wheeled across the sandy beach of Lytham St Annes, heading South, unable to move because she'd been given another injection of succinylcholine, rendering her paralysed—not even able to speak. Nobody was looking at her, probably assuming she was severely disabled, the drug also making her drool. She was being abducted in plain sight. She wanted to scream, to tell anybody who would listen that she was being taken against her will, that they should call the police. But all she could do was sit, unmoving, impotent, and be wheeled slowly forwards.

The sun was slowly coming down now, maybe 8pm, she guessed, but the tide was still pretty low—although it wouldn't be soon. *Where the hell was he taking her?* 'Gaz' was his name, Kevin Lawson's son, apparently. But Kevin wasn't here. When Gaz had put her in the boot of that car, she'd heard a commotion, some shouting, but it was hard to hear much from the confines of the boot. And then, shortly after that, the car started to move.

CHAPTER TWENTY-TWO

'Almost there,' said Gaz, bending down, wiping her drooling mouth with a tissue, appearing to be caring for her—not that there were many people around at this time, just a few strollers and dog walkers.

Almost there? What was he going to do to her? she thought, panic rising once more. She was glad Kevin wasn't there too, at least, as they knew he was a serial killer, had all the evidence they needed. She didn't know that Gaz was—not yet—although he had claimed to have killed someone. So, he was either dangerous, or a liar, or perhaps both. But, on balance, perhaps the lesser of two evils, at least for now.

'We'll just wait a little while longer,' said Gaz. 'Take in the view, perhaps?' He looked at her, smiled—but it was a malevolent smile, one that made her stomach turn. 'Has anyone ever told you that you're a really *great* listener? Maybe I should hold on to you for a few months, or years, even.'

She couldn't allow that; she had to do something, and soon, but at the moment she was completely paralysed.

'Only joking. The police will be out looking for you. It's too risky. Gotta get rid,' he said, standing in front of her now, having stopped pushing.

She could now see he was wearing what looked like a fishing tackle bag—a long storage bag, army green colour.

He smiled again, making her skin crawl this time. He got close to her face, really close, and whispered, 'Do you want to know what I've got in my bag?'

An elderly couple walked by, not too far away, and Gaz stood up again, looked at them.

'Evening,' he said. 'Nice weather today.'

'It is that,' said the man, attempting a smile. 'Your wife?' he asked.

'Sister,' said Gaz. 'She has multiple sclerosis. Had it ever since she was a child, but it's progressed recently, isn't that right, Susan?'

DC Briggs attempted to signal something, anything, with her eyes, but the old couple just looked at her with nothing but sympathy.

'Oh, that's a real shame,' said the man, looking at Gaz's bag. 'You been fishing?'

'Yeah. Tried in the sea. Not got anything, though. Susan likes to watch,' said Gaz.

The old man nodded and walked on with his partner.

Gaz looked at DC Briggs again, got even closer to her face this time, almost touching—she could smell his breath: stank of beer and chips. 'I'll tell you a secret: it's not a fishing rod in my bag. Want to know what it is?'

He unzipped the bag and started to pull something out, looked like the handle of a spade. He dropped that back down in the bag and then pulled something else out—some bamboo rods. Then, he put those back inside the bag too and zipped it back up.

'I am going fishing though,' said Gaz. 'Want to know what my bait is?' He started to laugh, an insane chortle, a sound only someone deranged could make, before, in an instant, changing his expression to one of deadly seriousness, of something like bottled-up anger. 'It's you. My bait is *you*. When everybody is gone, I'm going to dig a hole for you, just before the sea, give you one of these bamboo rods for you to breathe through, and then bury you alive. It won't take long for the tide to come in, maybe a few minutes, and then it will slowly cover that bamboo rod, and you'll drown. And I'm going to be sat on those rocks back there, watching, drinking whiskey, maybe even give myself a little tug, if the mood takes.' He touched her on the face. 'It's going to be fun, eh? A nice little buzz for the both of us.'

If she could, she'd spit in his face, in defiance. But she still couldn't move a muscle, no matter how hard she tried. She hoped to God Walker wasn't too far behind. She trusted him, she'd seen him work, many times. She'd seen him save people before. He'd be here. He had to be. He was her only hope.

CHAPTER TWENTY-THREE

'We've got it,' said DC Ainscough. 'Car parked up near the South Promenade, four different tyre brands, exhaust pipe touching the road!'

Walker almost felt like he might cry, the relief was so intense. 'That's great! Then let's get—'

'The officer who found it says it's empty,' said DC Ainscough.

'Then they must be nearby, maybe on the beach?' suggested Walker. 'What are you waiting for? Go, go!'

It didn't take long for Walker to speed down to the South Promenade in their pool car, get to the location they'd been told the deserted car was. Just as described, it matched what they were looking for: it was a white Skoda Octavia, 2011 model with odd tyres and a broken exhaust pipe drooping down, touching the road. Walker got out, approached the car, and smashed one of the windows with his baton without hesitation. He opened the door, took a quick look inside: there were some bamboo rods in the back seat. He grabbed one, showed it to DC Ainscough. Then, he rooted in the cup holder, took out some receipts, quickly scanned through them.

'Here—bamboo from a DIY store. Also, one telescopic spade, some gaffer tape, and another receipt is for a fishing tackle backpack. To the beach!' he said, his mind racing, frantic now.

CHAPTER TWENTY-THREE

'And get some uniforms down here ASAP. I think he's going to try to sodding bury her alive!'

They got running, toward the beach, DC Ainscough getting ahead of Walker, with him currently being the fitter of the two. Even the wind was against them, in their faces, slowing them down, reducing visibility.

'Look out for any bamboo sticking out of the sand or water,' he shouted. 'And look carefully. Use your torch. She's running out of time.' It was pretty dark now, so their chances of finding such a bamboo rod sticking up wasn't great, and Walker knew it. But unfortunately, that was about the only hope they had.

* * *

Having almost given up, in the depths of despair—it now being too dark to see much of anything from any kind of distance, with their torches only illuminating a few metres or so out—Walker spotted something sticking out of the sea. It was only a few centimetres or so, and he wouldn't have seen it at all if the clouds hadn't parted, let some moonlight through. But it was there, like a beacon of hope. He scrambled out, into the black waves, dropped to his knees, inspected the thing—carefully, in case she was breathing through it, but as quickly as he could. It *was* one of the rods of bamboo, just like the ones they'd found in the car.

'It's her!' shouted Walker, over to DC Ainscough, who was further along the beach—along with several other officers who'd arrived to provide support—having evidently missed what Walker had spotted. 'Get over here, now!'

DC Ainscough soon joined him, but Walker was already digging with his hands, pulling up mounds of sand and throwing it to one side, like an animal digging for its very survival. Something below was moving, in the sand. It had to be her. She was alive. Once DC Ainscough started to dig as well, frantically pulling the sand back, beneath the water, a hand emerged, grabbing at them, pulling, fervently. Walker got a good grip, but the wet sand was sucking her in good and proper, like quicksand. He could feel it was her now—was sure of it. But the arm suddenly went limp and stopped pulling. She'd lost consciousness. They had to be quick. The waves were sloshing above the bamboo rod now—she could no longer breathe properly. They dug some more, as fast as they could, pulled more sand out, throwing it to one side, only for water to replace it. Eventually, working together, they heaved her by the arm, pulled her part way out, DC Ainscough losing his grip at the vital moment, falling on his arse in the sea. Walker pulled her the rest of the way out all by himself, finding strength he didn't know he had, and with several sharp tugs he dragged her to drier sand, then put her on her back, wiping more of the wet sand away from her eyes and face, scooping it out with his finger. DC Ainscough rejoined him.

'She okay?' he asked.

'She's not breathing,' said Walker, turning her head to one side, tapping her on the cheek, making sure there was no water in her mouth. He checked her pulse: it was weak. He was going to have to resuscitate her, give her mouth to mouth. He'd had some training but had thankfully never had to use it in a life and death situation—until now.

He put her head forwards again, tilted it back, the way he'd been trained, using one hand to hold her chin, lift it up, keeping her mouth open using his thumb and index finger. Then he placed his other hand on her forehead, pinched her nose with this index finger and thumb, and took a breath, placing his mouth on hers, forming a seal. He blew into her mouth for one second, watching her chest rise and sink again when he moved away. It was working. He gave her four more breaths, then checked her pulse again: he couldn't find it this time, panic welling up. She was in cardiac arrest. He'd have to give her CPR. He did one more breath and then started the first of thirty chest compressions. *One, two, three...*

'Get back to dispatch, chase that ambulance,' said Walker. 'Find out what's bloody taking so long.'

DC Ainscough was obviously in shock, paralysed with fear. 'Shit. Sorry. Yes.' He got to work on his phone and Walker repeated the process. She still wasn't breathing. He did it again: *two breaths, thirty compressions.*

DC Ainscough had his hands on his head now. 'Come on,' he said. 'Please... please.'

Walker repeated the process again. Nothing.

'*Come on!*' said Walker himself now, working even more frantically, doing harder chest compressions, more powerful breath work. 'Breathe, damn it.' He hit her on the chest now, twice, in anger and frustration, hoping to somehow jump start her, looking for a miracle.

DC Ainscough got down next to Walker, put his arm around him, trying to console him. 'Sir, she's gone,' he said. But Walker wasn't done yet. He wasn't giving up on her. Not now.

He gave it one more round: *two breaths, thirty compressions.* The sea was coming in even more now, the tide getting higher, almost covering them again.

'Sir, she's really gone,' said DC Ainscough, almost crying

now. 'It's not your fault. We did our best.'

'Shut the hell up and get ready to take over if need be. We're doing this until paramedics arrive,' said Walker. 'And we're going to have to pull her further in if this water gets any higher. I need you to get yourself together, for Shel. She's *not* dead yet I tell you!' said Walker defiantly, banging on her chest once more, giving her one more breath, the seal on her lips even tighter than before, probably enough to hurt her had she been conscious. Then banging on her chest again, with both hands.

And then *it* happened. He had his miracle, a real life one: suddenly, she came to life, coughing and spluttering, spitting sea water out. He gave her a few seconds, silently thanking a God he never believed in. 'Detective, you okay?' he asked.

She slowly sat up, with some effort, looked around, got her bearings. He could barely believe what had just happened. Then she looked at Walker, dead in the eyes. 'If you wanted a kiss, you only needed to ask,' she said.

Walker hugged her, tight. 'Thank God,' he said. DC Ainscough put his arm around her too, squatting down in the water to do so, which had now risen and left them in a pool of water.

'I knew you'd come,' she said. 'I knew you'd find me, somehow.'

Walker shook his head. 'We got lucky, that's all. We got *very* lucky.'

'You always do,' she said. 'Thank you, so much, Jon. You saved my life. Thank you.'

CHAPTER TWENTY-FOUR

DC Briggs was now being checked over in a hospital bed at the Accident & Emergency Department at Blackpool Victoria Hospital, Walker and DC Ainscough by her side. The doctor inspecting her was a Dr Adam, a guy of South Asian origin who still had a slight accent mixed in with some northern English, creating a curious mixture.

'There doesn't appear to be any serious physical effects,' said Dr Adam. 'A little bruising here and there, which might be sore for a while. We'll do a few more tests, as a precaution, but right now there's no reason to suspect there will be any further issues.'

'But she wasn't breathing for at least several minutes,' said Walker. 'It felt like forever.'

'I understand that. And we'll do some scans to check this out,' said Dr Adam. 'But I'm sure Detective Briggs will be fine. People underestimate just how long CPR can keep a patient going—up to thirty minutes in some cases. As long as there's air going into the lungs, and the blood is kept circulating, they're essentially on life support. You did the right thing, carrying on the way you did. Don't worry too much. She seems perfectly lucid, has answered all of my questions.'

'See. I'm fine,' said DC Briggs.

DC Ainscough gave Walker a guilty-looking glance. He'd been ready to give up on the CPR, had thought she was already dead. It wasn't his fault though. Walker wasn't aware of what Dr Adam had just said either—he'd just carried on the CPR out of sheer stubbornness and a belief that she'd be okay. They'd have to schedule a refresher course on CPR procedures soon, get up to date.

'Psychologically, of course, from what you've told me, she may need some on-going support,' said Dr Adam. 'These kinds of traumatic events often don't hit us right away, take time to process, and can lead to a whole host of issues, such as anxiety, panic attacks, or even depression. So, I'd recommend some counselling, once she's recovered, physically, that is. Please consult your local GP for that.'

'Thank you, Doctor,' said DC Briggs. 'But that won't be necessary. I feel fine.'

'We'll get her in with Police Care UK, get her an appointment as soon as possible,' said Walker, his thoughts already turning to getting information about her attacker, ASAP, but being aware that she needed a little time to catch her breath first.

DC Briggs shook her head but left it at that for now. 'Could I get some more water?' she said. 'I'm still thirsty.'

'I'll do that,' said DC Ainscough, heading towards the water cooler.

'Then I'll leave you to it for now then,' said Dr Adam. 'Someone will be with you soon and we'll get those scans done. Then I'll be back for a review in due course.' He nodded and hurriedly left the room. The emergency room was busy; there were lots of patients to see.

DC Ainscough gave DC Briggs the water and she took a

CHAPTER TWENTY-FOUR

big gulp, spilling some of it on her hospital gown. Walker intervened, taking the cup from her.

'Slowly,' he said. 'Detective Ainscough, how about you go get some snacks from the vending machine too? We need to refuel a bit here.'

'Will do,' he said, before leaving.

Walker grabbed a plastic chair and pulled it next to the bed DC Briggs was lying on.

'Well... that was a close one, eh?' he said. He took her hand, held it, just grateful she was still alive, being less guarded than usual, actually showing some of his feelings.

'Is this appropriate behaviour for a DCI and his inferior, Jon?' she asked with a little mischievous smile.

'Well, let's just say we're officially off the clock right now,' he said. 'When you're ready, you know the score: we're gonna need to know what happened, and fairly soon. But for now, for a few minutes at least, we're just two civilians who've just been through something traumatic, recovering.'

'I'm fine,' said DC Briggs.

'How can you be *fine*? You were buried, alive, and were about to suffocate to death,' said Walker. 'Nobody is fine after something like that.'

'I *know*,' said DC Briggs, a bit sharpish, 'but I'm okay.' She broke down, started to cry. 'I... I'd almost given up. I'd stopped breathing, had accepted it: my fate. I'd made peace with it, was ready to go. And then I felt your hand on mine.' That was good. She'd only just stopped breathing then when Walker found her. She squeezed his hand, tighter and tighter, before loosening it again, too loose. She went limp, just like she had in the sand, closed her eyes.

'Oh, no. Detective,' said Walker. '*Shelly!* Stay with me...'

She'd lost consciousness again, her breathing getting shallow. 'Nurse!' He pressed an emergency button, then popped his head out into the corridor. 'We need help in here!' he shouted, and a couple of medical staff came running their way.

He grabbed DC Brigg's hand again. 'Stay with me, Shel. It's gonna be alright.'

'Sir. You need to get out of here, give us room to work,' said one of the nurses, so Walker backed off.

'If you could just wait in the waiting room?' said the same nurse, but Walker couldn't leave her. He'd only just got her back. 'Sir!'

Walker nodded, exited the room, headed towards the A&E waiting room. He couldn't lose her like this, not after everything.

DC Ainscough stood in front of him.

'Chief? Is there a problem?' he said.

Walker just shook his head, put it in his hands for a few seconds, before looking up at DC Ainscough. 'She's… There's a problem. She lost consciousness again,' he said. 'She just passed out while talking to me.'

DC Ainscough put his arm around Walker once more, but this time Walker swatted him away.

'She'll be okay,' said DC Ainscough. 'It's probably just been too much for her, that's all. She was taking it all far too well. She was bound to crash at some point.'

'But she was barely breathing…' said Walker. 'You don't understand. She was barely sodding breathing.'

CHAPTER TWENTY-FIVE

Gary Cooper got up off the rocks. It was getting cold now, time to go. Darkness had descended quickly, and he could no longer see the bamboo rod he'd left for the woman to breathe through. He realised he didn't even know her name, and then smiled, laughed a little. It didn't matter. He'd got his kicks, didn't care about anything else, was calling it a night. He'd never been much good at anything, had never found any special skill or talent, not even a mediocre one. He failed at most things he tried, had been bullied at school, called all sorts, ridiculed. Even his mother had said he'd never amount to anything. But she'd been wrong. He'd finally found something he was good at.

He was a goddamned serial killer. That's what they called them—people who killed multiple times. He'd be a wanted man. He knew he'd have to be more careful in future, if he didn't want to get caught. But that really didn't concern him much. He didn't really understand his father, why he'd hidden himself away all those years like some dirty bug. He wanted people to know what he'd done one day, once he'd left an impressive enough body count in his wake. He wanted people to talk about him, analyse what he'd done. And for that he knew he'd probably need to be caught at some point, tell his story. Maybe some people might even look up to him, admire him, for what he'd done, his boldness.

He hopped over some sand dunes, got back to the main road, heading toward his car. Killing had been cathartic. He felt like a new man, felt like he could do anything now. All his life, he'd felt bound, restricted somehow, held back. But not anymore. He was reborn, like a butterfly emerging from a chrysalis. He was ready to fly. He'd taken his old man's prize, what would have been his very last: the woman. Had taken her for himself, used her, like the world had used him, chewed him up, spat him out. It had been fun, but now it was time to get some sleep. He was exhausted.

'Damn,' said Gaz. His car—the window was broken and there were a couple of cops stood nearby, guarding it. They must have got on to him somehow, tracked his car down. They'd know who he was now, or they would soon. But they didn't have him yet. He shrugged, now feeling somehow invincible, untouchable, even. He'd never felt this powerful before, this strong. Well, if they wanted him, they'd just have to find him. He didn't care anymore. Didn't care much about anything—except killing, experiencing that feeling again, that rush like no other. But even if they did catch up to him, he could still do that in prison—*kill*—slash some convict, bleed him out, get the respect of the other prisoners. He'd be a leader in there, a God. So, it didn't matter whether he was free or banged up. He'd still get what he wanted. It's not like he'd get the death penalty in Britain, no matter what he did. They'd take care of him, feed him, clothe him, look after his medical needs, provide entertainment; *and* he'd have a never-ending supply of possible victims. It was win-win. That's why he wasn't afraid of being caught.

CHAPTER TWENTY-FIVE

He ambled away, without a care in the world, intending to find a hotel, rest up for the night. He was meant for this. It was all a matter of faith. This was his destiny—he'd always known it; he just hadn't realised until now. It was his nature. He was born to kill.

After walking for some time, Gaz finally came across a hotel that had a room available. He'd been checking on a website called Agoda on his mobile phone as he went, trying to find a reservation. It was called the Inn On the Prom hotel. It was a bit expensive for his liking, but it was just for one night. It would have to do. There wasn't much else available.

He took a deep breath of the chilling night time air and walked up to the Reception Area, getting ready to check in.

CHAPTER TWENTY-SIX

'Sir, what are you doing?' asked DC Ainscough. He was following Walker at a pace, heading back to the pool car in the car park of Blackpool Victoria Hospital. Walker got to the car, fiddled with the key fob, nervously and a little jaded, unlocked it. '*Sir?*'

Walker turned and faced him. 'What else? I'm finding the bastard that did this to her, that's what,' he said. 'So he can't hurt anybody else.'

'But DC Briggs... She's not—'

'The Doc said its post-immersion syndrome or something, that her oxygen levels were likely too low during resuscitation, and that she has a good chance of a full recovery. There's nothing we can do for her here until she wakes up,' said Walker. 'She'll be alright. She's resilient. But until then, we're better off continuing with the investigation, tracking this guy down. There'll be nothing more that DC Briggs wants to hear when she wakes up than that we've got this guy.'

They got in the car, DC Ainscough offering no resistance whatsoever.

Walker was feeling as frustrated as hell. If only he'd asked her about her attacker before she'd lost consciousness, at least they'd have something to go on. If it had been any other victim,

CHAPTER TWENTY-SIX

he might have pressed on, asked what he needed ASAP. But it was *her*, and he thought she needed a few minutes to process it all.

He was still out there, that guy, whoever he was, and that was their first task—getting his name and identity. That would be easy enough though, *if* his car wasn't stolen. During the chaos, when paramedics had arrived at the scene, Walker had stepped back to let them take care of DC Briggs, told DC Ainscough to find out if their supporting officers had a name, address, and photo of the owner of the registered car yet from the DVLA database. They hadn't as all available officers had been out looking for DC Briggs at the time as a matter of urgency. But it would have been checked by now, and officers would be out looking for him, or whoever owned that car. The gears were in motion. DI Hogarth would also be checking any available CCTV footage, to try to get a visual on the guy at the car, and then checking security footage in the surrounding area to see if he could be picked up anywhere else, while his registered home address would also be searched for any clues as to his whereabouts. And since DC Briggs couldn't currently be interviewed to extract more information about him, it was time to see what else they had.

One thing was for sure: the guy would almost certainly know they had his car by now, would have returned to it at some point, most likely, saw the damage. It was an opportunity lost. If they'd left the car intact, they could have waited for him there, but Walker had to have a look inside. They'd been desperate for some clues, and out of time. If he hadn't done what he did, DC Briggs would never have had a chance. Without finding those bamboo rods, they wouldn't have known what to look for. So, there was nothing to regret there. They could still have left the car unattended after that, of course, and he still may have returned to it, even with the shattered window. But they'd have been leaving their only source of evidence unattended, and things had been so chaotic with DC Briggs that they hadn't had time to analyse the situation further. It had been all about saving her. But now she was back to relatively safety, in the care of medical professionals, they could focus on the case again, try to continue to track this guy down, focus on procedures that usually got them results.

'We're going back to our Incident Room at the hotel,' said Walker, already driving the car out of the hospital car park, probably a bit too fast. 'We'll see what we have on this guy, then formulate a plan of attack.'

'Seems like a plan,' said DC Ainscough. 'Do you think she'll be alright, Chief?'

Walker looked at him. 'How the sodding hell should I know? But if she's not, I'll tell you one thing: *this guy is gonna pay.*'

* * *

Walker entered the Inn On the Prom hotel, pressed the button of the lift to go up. They were on the second floor, and he didn't want to waste any time or energy going up the stairs. It took a few seconds, but the lift doors popped open, and Walker and DC Ainscough got in. But just as the lift doors were about to close again, a young chap with a shaved head and cool-looking sunglasses put his arm in the way, making the sensors reopen the lift doors.

CHAPTER TWENTY-SIX

'Alright?' said the man.

Walker nodded but didn't smile. He didn't appreciate being held up, even for a few seconds.

'Nice day, innit?' said the man, once he'd pressed the button for the first floor and the lift got moving. 'Done owt nice?'

Walker shook his head, not wanting to engage in conversation.

'Well, I had a lovely day at the beach with my girlfriend,' said the man. The lift stopped at the first floor, and the doors pinged open. 'Okay then, boys. Have a good one.'

He exited the lift and Walker and DC Ainscough got moving again and made it to the second floor. They got out and went to 'Room 22', which was where they'd set up their makeshift Incident Room.

Walker opened the door with the room's keycard and found DI Hogarth there, alone, as expected, with a serious expression on his face.

'How is she?' he asked, standing up from his desk in front of the computer, which he rarely did without good reason, which probably meant he'd been worried. They'd last been in contact with him during the ambulance ride, had instructed him to find everything he could about the attacker once he had a name, address, and photo of the registered vehicle.

'She's still at the hospital. She's in bad way,' said Walker. 'She lost consciousness again. Post-immersion syndrome, oxygen levels too low during resuscitation. But the Doc says she has a good chance, and we can't do anything about that right now. She's a fighter. She'll be okay. We have to put that to the back of our minds somehow, for now, stop this guy before he does something like that again.'

DI Hogarth sat back down, seeming to accept the situation,

no matter how bad it was.

'So, who is he?' asked Walker. 'We couldn't talk to DC Briggs before she lost consciousness again, so we got nothing there. Please tell me that the car *was* registered with the DVLA.'

'Yes. We have one Gary Duncan Cooper, aged twenty-six, Caucasian, as the registered keeper of the car, and as it hasn't been reported as stolen, we must presume this is our guy—at least for now. I have a mugshot of him. Here. Although it might not be of much use if he's been to a barber since.' He showed it to them. The guy in the photo had a full beard, long hair—not much to go on at all: brown eyes, medium sized nose, nothing identifiable, no spots or blemishes. 'No criminal record either. He's clean.'

'Twenty-six,' said Walker. 'Interesting.'

'What?' said DC Ainscough.

'Nothing. It's just... *twenty-six*—it's a multiple of thirteen, the periods between the kills of Kevin Lawson. Bit of a coincidence, that's all,' said Walker, wondering whether it might *not* be a coincidence, but simultaneously being aware that one can see patterns that aren't there if one looks hard enough.

'Lawson would have been fifty-two years old when Gary Cooper was born, in 1998, the same year that our Tracy White—the third known victim of Lawson—was killed,' said DC Ainscough.

'Well, we definitely know that Lawson was active that year, out and about, at least. Perhaps he raped some woman, decided not to kill her for some reason, got her pregnant?' suggested Walker. 'DI Hogarth, get a DNA sample of Kevin Lawson, and then if there's any DNA found in the Skoda Octavia, we can see if there's a familial connection.'

CHAPTER TWENTY-SIX

'Killed his father for raping his mother but carries on his work as he has the same evil coursing through his veins?' said DI Hogarth. 'It's a theory, that. I'll get on it. Let's see then.'

'Was there anything else found at the scene of the mo-motorhome?' asked Walker. 'I never inspected the body properly, except for a visual inspection of the face. Left it to forensics.'

'There was indeed,' said DI Hogarth. 'Under his clothing, around his neck, was a necklace of several teeth—five in total—presumably mementos from his victims, running DNA tests on them as we speak—along with one key. We couldn't find anything that the key fitted in the motorhome, so I got it to some officers to search his home, see if it fit anything there. They couldn't find anything.'

'Well, get it back here then. Let's have a look at it,' said Walker. He stood at the head of the room, updated his Evidence Board with everything he had so far.

'Okay. So, we've got one Kevin Lawson, recently deceased—murdered by someone thought to be driving a white Skoda Octavia, 2011 model with odd tyres and a broken exhaust pipe, registration PX11 4QT. The registered keeper is one Gary Duncan Cooper. Lawson is known to have killed at least three women over four decades or so—a Jackie Wakefield, Tracy White, Sally Fielding, while he also kidnapped and was thought to be going to kill Shelly Briggs.' He was just running through everything as much for himself than anyone else, recapping, getting it all set in his mind. 'But he never got a chance to kill her because someone else intervened, killed him—probably an accomplice, the driver of the Skoda Octavia—and took Shelly Briggs.' It seemed strange to be referring to her in this way, like a victim, rather than a colleague, but it was important to remain professional, try not to make things personal. That would only slow them down, interfere with the process. 'The first question is whether this accomplice was involved in any of the previous killings, and the second is what happened between them to cause this guy to do what he did to Kevin?'

'Maybe someone who was related to one of his victims, perhaps?' offered DC Ainscough. 'Found out it was him somehow, got revenge?'

'Oh, come on, *think*. If the killing was purely based upon revenge, then why take Shelly Briggs, inject her with succinylcholine, paralyse her, and bury her in the sand, not just to kill her, but to psychologically torture her first? This is one sick, twisted human being we have here—just as bad as Lawson. If this was just about revenge, they'd have simply killed Kevin Lawson and got out of there,' said Walker. 'Obviously, what we have is not one but two sick bastards working together for some reason, and it seems—and this is putting it mildly—they've had a bit of a "falling out". That has left our Gary Cooper free to try to murder DC Briggs with a completely different MO. So, that raises the question of what brought these two men together in the first place—two men of such different ages—and what got between them to cause such savage violence? Is this younger man just a loose cannon, who's gone off over nothing, did they argue over what they were going to do to Briggs, or is there something deeper, more personal? Were they lovers, perhaps, or related somehow? Were they friends, or colleagues? What do you have on Gary Cooper so far, DI Hogarth?'

'Bugger all,' said DI Hogarth. 'No CCTV footage to confirm his identity, seems to be unemployed, was brought up by a single mother with no siblings.'

CHAPTER TWENTY-SIX

'Well, that supports the familial connection theory, if he has no known father. What's his address?' asked Walker.

'17A, Marsh Way, Penwortham, Preston,' said DI Hogarth, tapping on his computer a few times. 'Little flat by the looks of it, not in the best condition.'

'You did get the warrant expedited, didn't you?' Walker asked to DI Hogarth.

'Course. Already got a Section 17,' said Hogarth. 'But only just, so haven't had any officer's over there yet.'

'We taking a road trip?' asked DC Ainscough.

Walker thought about it. There was nothing else to do here for the time being, no major leads to chase, nothing that uniformed officers couldn't handle. 'Damned well we are,' said Walker. 'I want to know what this guy does for a living, where he shops, what his hobbies are, if he has any friends, everything we can find out about him. Check his social media as well while we're away, all the usual stuff. And get forensics to thoroughly check that car for any DNA. Let's see if there is a familial connection to Kevin Lawson with any other samples or see if we have any previous unsolved crimes with that genetic sequence.' Walker thought some more, making sure he hadn't missed anything. 'Okay, people, I think we have our plan. Let's get to it then.'

CHAPTER TWENTY-SEVEN

Gary couldn't believe his sodding luck. Of all the hotels he could have checked in to, it had to be this: the *Inn On the Prom*—the very same hotel, apparently, that the Detective was staying at, the one he'd knocked unconscious back on the North Promenade, the one who'd been following Kevin. He couldn't bring himself to call Kevin his 'dad', even if he was his biological father. He didn't quite know how he felt about his father dying. He was glad and sad all at the same time. But at least his luck was in with this detective. He'd even managed to get a room right under theirs. He'd seen the number of the detective's room key when he'd met them in the lift, figured out which room was directly under theirs, asked reception if it was available and if he could change room because he wanted one with a better view. The receptionist had been reluctant at first—looked annoyed—but when he'd offered her twenty pounds for her trouble, she'd soon become more cooperative. Perhaps he'd make her regret that attitude one day, turn her into fish bait. But that could wait. This wasn't the right time. For now, he was just pleased to be directly under the detective's room. He could actually hear them talking. He was using the old ear to the cup trick, standing on the bed, placing the cup on the

CHAPTER TWENTY-SEVEN

ceiling. Surprisingly, he could hear pretty good with it. They were looking for him, and he was literally right under their noses! He'd laughed out loud when he found out, but he'd stopped laughing when he found out the woman was alive—the one he'd buried. They must have found the bamboo in his car, found her with the piece he'd left with her for her to breathe, until the ocean waves covered it. It left him with a feeling of incompleteness, and he didn't like it one bit. He'd have to remedy that, put things right: *find her*.

He had her name now though—one Detective Constable Shelly Briggs. And the nearest hospital was Blackpool Victoria Hospital, so she'd most likely been sent there. He'd ring them up from a public phone, inquire about her, say he wanted to visit and get the visiting times, and then finish her off somehow. A simple pillow over the face should do it, quick and effective. The staff might not even realise she's been murdered if she's in a bad way anyway. They'll probably just think she hasn't made it. He needed it though, to feel *complete*, to move on. Plus, she knew what he looked like.

Gary also had the name of the other Detective too, the one he'd knocked out, the one he'd seen in the lift at this very hotel: one Detective Chief Inspector Jonathan Walker. He wondered whether they had his name yet; probably, since they had his car. But he hadn't used his real name when checking into the hotel, had paid in cash too. He was smart, covering his tracks. It would be the last place they'd look. And they wouldn't recognise him if they got a mugshot. All his IDs—his driver's licence, passport, etc.—were all taken when he had long hair, a full beard, and glasses. But he had none of those things now: his head was shaved completely bald, his face was clean shaven, and he'd given up the glasses for contact lenses. He was like a different person. He really had metamorphosised. He was reborn.

He googled the address for Blackpool Victoria Hospital, wrote it down on a hotel notepad. 'There, my lovely,' he said. 'I'll see you again soon.'

He'd finish her off, and then get the hell out of here. But first, he'd nip down to the shop, buy something to eat—maybe some *ramyun*, that spicy instant Korean noodle he'd become a bit addicted to in recent years. He'd drop some hotdogs in there too, make a real meal of it. And then, he'd be on his way.

He looked in the mirror, licked his index finger, and smoothed down his eyebrows.

'Looking good, Gaz,' he said. 'We are looking damned good.'

CHAPTER TWENTY-EIGHT

'What are you doing back so soon?' asked DI Hogarth. 'Did he have a false address on file with the DVLA? Was it occupied by someone else?'

Walker slumped down in a chair next to the bed in the hotel room they had, while DC Ainscough looked similarly forlorn. 'Empty,' he said. 'Clean as a sodding whistle too. We tracked the landlord—the neighbours had his number. Said rent hasn't been paid for three months and he's pursuing eviction, has already served a Section 8 and is applying to the county court for a possession order. Cooper had cleared out of there, leaving the door locked and the curtains drawn. There's nothing there.'

'I've got the key back that was on the necklace of the deceased Kevin Lawson,' said DC Ainscough getting it out; it was inside of a clear evidence bag. 'As you requested. The one that couldn't be paired with a lock at his home. It has some letters and numbers on the back: MYMBL1409. I've done a cursory search but can't find anything obvious that it might be linked to.'

'Investigate it deeper then, find out what it might be. Get a locksmith to look at it, see if it's a part of a keying system, or a master key of some sort, or perhaps he has a storage locker somewhere and the 1409 is the locker number,' said Walker.

'I'm already on it,' said DC Ainscough. 'But it might take some time. This kind of thing... it could take weeks, and even then, we might come up with nothing. It's a needle in a haystack of millions of keys and locks.'

'Well, it's a good job that I do have something then,' said DI Hogarth. Walker looked at him, perking up, eyes wide. 'Forensics have now managed to recover some samples from the car. They've run the tests and got a match: Gary Cooper is a direct descendent of Kevin Lawson,' said DI Hogarth, before exhaling, sharply.

Walker did a mental fist pump, just glad they finally had something, but his nanosecond of elation was quickly eviscerated by thoughts of DC Briggs fighting for her life. 'Jesus. That *was* quick. Good work, Detective.'

'DC Briggs is one of her own, and Sally Fielding was the cousin of former Deputy Chief Constable Harry Potts. So, yeah, we got the super-expedited service on this one,' said DI Hogarth, before elaborating and saying, 'Chief Constable Harriet rubber stamped it.'

'Right. So, it's confirmed? Kevin Lawson is Gary Cooper's biological father?' asked Walker, wanting it crystal clear.

'99.9% sure,' said DI Hogarth. 'There's always a small chance of a false negative with such paternity tests, but it is beyond reasonable doubt.'

'So, he killed his father,' said Walker.

'It seems so,' said DI Hogarth.

DC Ainscough got a call, took it. 'Yes, thank you. We'll be right there.'

'What is it?' asked Walker.

DC Ainscough smiled, perhaps the first genuine smile any

CHAPTER TWENTY-EIGHT

of them had sported since DC Briggs had been taken.

'It's Briggs,' he said. 'She's awake! She's out of the coma.'

'Well, that's fantastic news!' said Walker. 'Is she okay? Let's get down there, talk to her.'

'Do you think she knows anything, about Cooper?' asked DC Ainscough.

'I never had much chance to talk to her last time, before she lost consciousness,' said Walker. 'If she is okay—and a mean *really* okay—we'll question her, see what she knows. But we must make sure she's well first. Let's get over there and see.'

* * *

'Oh, my God,' said Walker. 'It's so good to see you.' He was with DC Ainscough and DI Hogarth at the hospital, by DC Brigg's bed. She was still in a private room in the A&E Department, having not been moved to a ward yet, such was her condition.

DC Briggs was sat up, in bed, slowly sipping on some orange juice with a straw. She forced a smile. 'You didn't all have to come down here,' she said. 'Shouldn't you be working the case? Did you catch him?'

'Not yet,' said Walker. 'But we will.'

'He's called Gaz,' said DC Briggs. 'The man that did this to me. It wasn't Lawson. He's called Gaz.'

'We can talk about all that when you're feeling better,' said Walker, against his instincts, really wanting desperately to talk about it, but wanting to make sure his colleague was okay before they began.

A nurse popped his head in, a male nurse of African origin

with a big smile and bright eyes. 'How are we doing?' he asked. 'You've been very lucky, you know. We were worried about you.'

'I'm fine,' said DC Briggs. 'Just a bit thirsty, that's all.'

'That's great then,' said the nurse, before checking her IV drip and leaving again.

'Gaz is Kevin Lawson's son,' said DC Briggs. 'I heard them talking. Gaz tracked him down, was going to kill him but changed his mind because Lawson was dying anyway—cancer. Lawson raped Gaz's mother, you see, intended to kill her, but changed his mind for some—'

'Slow down there,' said Walker. 'We know exactly who he is: One Gary Cooper. And we know he's related to Lawson too. We had it confirmed via a DNA test.'

'They both still out there?' she asked.

'One of them is,' said Walker. 'Lawson is dead.'

DC Brigg's eyes went a little wider.

'If you really are feeling okay, whenever you're ready, we need you to work with a forensic imaging specialist, so we can get a picture of this guy's most recent appearance,' said Walker. 'All we have is his DVLA photograph—has a full beard and long hair, could be anyone.'

'I told you, I'm fine,' said DC Briggs, but she was pale, weak looking. 'Get someone down here. He was clean shaved when I saw him, short hair too.'

Walker looked at DI Hogarth, a little sheepishly. 'Bring him in,' he said.

DC Briggs shook her head and smiled. 'Of course, you already have someone here, don't you?' she said. 'Always well prepared. Silly me.'

DI Hogarth brought a small looking chap into the room—at

CHAPTER TWENTY-EIGHT

the top end of middle age, white, bald, glasses. He was holding an iPad.

'This is Derek Lewis, our forensic imaging specialist, here to help construct a facial composite of the man who took you from Kevin Lawson—presumably Gary Cooper,' said Walker. 'He'll take you through the process, ask you a few questions. Take your time.'

Walker, DI Hogarth, and DC Ainscough all sat there while DC Briggs worked with Derek on the iPad, using some facial composite software called EvoFIT. He asked her to select various faces that resembled the man who'd buried her rather than building the face piece by piece, and the system then generated a further series of faces, from which DC Briggs choose the one most resembling the offender, before making finer adjustments to the chin, hairstyle, and facial expressions. Once they were both happy with it, Derek said, 'Just give me a few minutes to finalise the image.'

Walker nodded. 'Is there anything else you can tell us, about what happened?' he asked.

'He wheeled me there in a wheelchair,' she said. 'I was paralysed. People were looking at me with pity in their eyes as we passed them.'

'Must have got the chair from Kevin Lawson,' said DC Ainscough. 'He had a Blue Badge. The medication too.'

'Kevin Lawson could walk, I saw him,' said DC Briggs. 'But he had cancer, so maybe he just used it sparingly.'

'Anything else?' asked Walker. 'You heard them talking?'

'Yes. Like I said, Gaz said Kevin raped his mother. Then he said he'd recently killed some guy, and... it seemed like he wanted to kill more. And they talked about Carl Jung, something about a dark passenger, or shadow,' said DC Briggs.

'It's all a bit fuzzy now.'

'That's good,' said Walker, touching her arm to reassure her.

'All done,' said Derek, turning the iPad around for them all to see. 'Is this the guy you saw?'

'Yes,' said DC Briggs. 'That's him.'

The facial composite depicted someone with a shaved head and no facial hair.

'Wait a minute,' said Walker. 'We've seen this guy.' It was taking him a few seconds to place him, and DC Ainscough got there a split second or so before him.

'In the lift, at the hotel,' he said, with some urgency.

'Oh, bloody hell,' said Walker. 'You're right. We've got to go. He's only staying at our bloomin' hotel!'

CHAPTER TWENTY-NINE

'This is the room?' said Walker.

'Yes,' said the hotel receptionist, who had a name badge on that said 'Jade McAvoy'. 'This is the one. He asked to change rooms, for this one specifically.' Not good. It seemed to be directly below their room. He must have been on to them, was probably trying to listen in on their investigation.

'And this man...' Walker held up the facial composite he had of their suspect, which he now had on his phone. 'You think he's in there now?'

'I think so,' said Jade. 'But he might not be. I'm not sure. I can't keep track of everyone who comes and goes, and not everyone leaves the hotel key with me when they go out, you know—even though they're supposed to.'

'Okay. Give me the spare key then. If he does come back, do not alert him to our presence. Just let him come up to his room or let me know immediately if he just goes out again. Do you understand?' said Walker. Jade nodded. 'Then that will be all,' he added, taking the keycard from her, and she left.

'Here we go then,' said Walker, swiping the keycard on the door's sensor, opening it up. He went in cautiously, holding his baton, followed by DC Ainscough and DI Hogarth, who did the same. The room was empty, the bathroom too. There was nowhere else to hide.

'Damn it. He's obviously not here,' said Walker. 'Close the door, in case he comes back, quick.'

DI Hogarth did as asked.

'No talking from now,' said Walker, putting his finger on his lips. 'In case he comes up and hears us. Take a quiet look around. See if you can find anything, in the bins, everywhere. Go.'

DC Ainscough and DI Hogarth did as ordered, quietly going through all of Gary Cooper's belonging, and carefully emptying the bins to see if there was anything there too. Walker scanned the room and found a small notepad on a coffee table. He opened it up. The top piece had been torn out, but on the next piece were some writing indentations. Walker held it up to the light, this way and that. He could just about make it out.

'*Shit!*' he said.

DC Ainscough looked at him, eyes wide. 'Sir, I though you said to be—'

'He's got the address of Blackpool Victoria Hospital. He's going back to DC Briggs!' said Walker. 'We need to get back over there. *Now!*'

* * *

'How far?' said Walker.

'About ten minutes sir, according to the Sat Nav,' said DC Ainscough. DI Hogarth was not with them as he'd not been able to keep up when they ran down the stairs of the hotel,

CHAPTER TWENTY-NINE

with them bypassing the lift this time as it had been occupied.

'I'll make it in five,' said Walker, standing on the accelerator even harder, driving dangerously fast, but alerting other road users of his passing via the mobile siren he'd put on the roof of the car. 'Keep trying, but we'll probably make it there before anyone else can now.'

He meant for DC Ainscough to keep calling for backup, and to alert hospital staff, who he'd not been able to get through to yet in the few minutes he'd had since getting in the car. They weren't answering, which could suggest that something had already gone down at the hospital, while their colleagues in the immediate vicinity might also be occupied with urgent situations of their own.

'Hold on, Shel. We're coming,' said Walker.

* * *

'But sir, it's not visiting time now,' said one of the hospital staff as Walker barged his way through.

He flashed them his ID card. 'DCI Jonathan Walker, on urgent police business. Coming through,' he said.

He made it to the room DC Briggs was located and opened up the door without knocking. There was a man stood over the bed, holding a pillow down. Walker grabbed him, threw him to the floor, knocking over an IV drip stand and some trays on a side table as well, rattling on the floor. The man was still gripping on to the pillow, sitting up on the floor now, using it to protect himself.

'Please, sir, calm down,' he said, his eyes pleading, not

understanding what was going on. The bed was empty. He'd just been making it up, in the process of putting a pillowcase on the pillow. Walker's imagination had done the rest, thought DC Briggs was being suffocated.

A toilet could be heard flushing and DC Briggs came out of the adjoining ensuite.

'Chief,' she said. 'What are you doing?'

Walker helped the man to his feet, who still looked a little scared. He was a nurse.

'Sorry,' said Walker. 'I'm DCI Walker. I thought we had a situation here, misread the situation. Your patient is in danger. We need to closely guard her from now on.'

'Gary Cooper?' said DC Briggs, looking perturbed. 'He knows where I am? He's coming after me?'

'You can leave us now,' Walker said to the male nurse, so he exited, closed the door.

'Found his hotel room, had the address of this hospital written on a notepad,' said Walker. 'Scared the hell out of us. Thought he might get here before us.'

'Well, I'm fine,' said DC Briggs. 'Help me back on to the bed, will you? I'm feeling a little dizzy.'

Walker and DC Ainscough both pitched in, got her comfortable.

'DC Ainscough, could I have a word with DCI Walker, in private, please?' asked DC Briggs.

DC Ainscough nodded and left the room, also closing the door behind him.

'What is it, Detective?' asked Walker.

DC Briggs put her hand to his cheek, gently caressing it.

A solitary tear rolled down the side of her face before her top lip curled up a touch and quivered in a little snarl. 'Go get the bastard,' she said. 'Will you do that for me?'

'I will,' he said, a bit taken aback with the power of the emotion behind those words. 'Once we've got you safe and secure here, that is. He's not going to get away with this. One way or another, he'll be punished for what he did to you, I promise you that.'

CHAPTER THIRTY

'You stay here with DI Hogarth,' said Walker to DC Ainscough, stood outside of DC Briggs's hospital room. 'Wait until back up arrives, and make sure they're well-armed and ready for a possible attack.

'Understood. Will do,' said DC Ainscough.

A call came in on Walker's mobile. It was the hotel receptionist from earlier, Jade McAvoy.

'He's just come back, gone to his room?' said Walker, looking at DC Ainscough, urgency in his eyes, clicking his fingers, telling him to get some coppers over there immediately. 'Call me again if there's any change. I'm coming right over.'

Walker hung up the phone and started to leave. DC Ainscough was already on his phone, but he stopped, mid-sentence, put his hand up to show Walker he wanted to say something.

'I should assist you, sir,' said DC Ainscough. 'He could be dangerous. He *is* dangerous.'

'I'll be fine, Constable. You must stay here and protect DC Briggs, in case he comes back, or in case the receptionist is mistaken, and it's not him,' said Walker. 'Join me when she's being adequately guarded. Just make sure a team is assembled and isn't far behind me.'

CHAPTER THIRTY

DC Ainscough visibly gave up. 'Okay. Go get him then, Chief. But be careful.'

Walker left, galvanised by Shelly, her touch, and her wish for him to go get this guy, punish him for what he did to her, burying her alive, torturing her, and whatever else he might have done. He deserved to die for what he did, but he was going to get the next best thing if Walker had anything to do with it: he was going to prison, and for a very long time.

* * *

The receptionist at the hotel, Jade, was sure Gary Cooper had gone back to his room, and Walker had been waiting for backup before entering, just to make sure he couldn't get away if he was in there. Walker now had a team of five coppers, excluding himself, so they should have more than enough to overpower any attempts at escape, he thought. He held the spare room key, took a deep breath, and entered.

Inside, was a *bloodbath*. The white sheets and blankets of the hotel bed contrasted sharply with the blood that was on them, surrounding a body that was face down.

Walker went in, took a look around. 'The area is clear,' he said, putting his baton away. Then, he got closer to the body, put some nitrile gloves on, did an initial inspection, tilting the head so he could see the face. It was a male, bald, matching the profile of the facial composite they had. It seemed, against all the odds, it was Gary Cooper.

Walker pointed at one of the officers who'd followed him inside. 'You, stay with me. The rest of you, scour the area, try to find anyone acting suspiciously, get everyone's name and ID who's staying at the hotel, all the staff too. I want to know everyone who has been coming and going in here today. You got that?' They nodded and got to it.

Gary Cooper had been stabbed several times, just like Kevin Lawson had. They'd got it wrong. They must have. Cooper hadn't killed Lawson—it was somebody else. DC Briggs said she'd heard Lawson and Cooper arguing at the motorhome when she was locked in the boot of that car nearby. But Walker now thought that Cooper had left Lawson there alive, that someone else was involved in his death.

'What's your name, officer?' asked Walker to the copper who'd stayed with him.

'I'm PC Mathew Leek,' said the Officer.

'Like the vegetable?' asked Walker, still looking at the body.

'Yes, sir, but slightly less pungent,' said PC Leek.

'Go get me some evidence bags from the car,' he said, passing PC Leek his key fob. 'And call forensics, get them here ASAP. We need to process the crime scene.'

'Will do,' said PC Leek, leaving the room.

Walker squatted down next to the bed, looking under it—nothing there except for a few drops of blood that had leaked through the mattress. The body was still bleeding, which could happen immediately after a person was killed. It meant he wasn't long gone. He looked at the man's face again; his eyes were still open. Whoever had done this to him had only just got away, and given what Cooper had done, Walker wasn't exactly cut up about it. DC Briggs had got her wish, and, to his surprise, Walker hadn't been made to work too hard to get him. But there was obviously much more at play here.

He was just about to stand up again, make a call to DC

CHAPTER THIRTY

Ainscough, when Gary Cooper, the man he thought deceased, coughed, spitting some blood in Walker's face.

'Oh, my...' said Walker, wiping at his eyes, hoping the guy didn't have any diseases to pass on.

He'd been stabbed several times, was unmoving until now, presumed dead, but somehow, he was alive.

Walker got his phone out, opened it up, but hesitated. This man was in a critical condition, he'd need immediate medical assistance if he had any chance of survival. He had to call it in. But this was also the man who'd killed at least one person, and had tortured his friend and colleague, leaving her to die a horrible death. So, he wasn't entirely sure if he wanted him to survive. If he did, he'd go to trial, would most likely get a long custodial sentence, but he'd survive, might even get out one day as he was only twenty-six. He was a dangerous animal that needed to be put down. Walker hesitated a few more seconds, toying with the idea.

'Help me,' whispered the man, more blood oozing out of the side of his mouth.

He couldn't do it. If Walker didn't call it in, he was as good as a killer himself. It was a line he didn't want to cross, and he knew DC Briggs wouldn't want it either—she just wanted the man stopped.

'DCI Walker here. We have a man in need of emergency medical assistance at the Inn On the Prom hotel in Lytham St Annes, Room 12. I repeat, we have a man in need of emergency medical assistance at the Inn On the Prom hotel in Lytham St Annes, Room 12. Yes, that's right. Stabbed, by the look of it, several times. Okay, I'll stay with him, put pressure on the worst looking wounds until the paramedics arrive,' said Walker, ending the call.

'It's you,' said the man, smiling.

'Shut up,' said Walker, grabbing some of the man's clothes from an open wardrobe, using them to put pressure on the wounds. 'I'm only doing this for myself, not for you, you understand?'

'She was so scared,' said the man, almost laughing now.

Walker pressed more firmly into one of the wounds, making the man yelp. 'You're going down for this,' he said. 'And if you ever get out, I'll come looking for you.'

'There's no need for that,' said the man. 'It wasn't anything personal.'

CHAPTER THIRTY-ONE

Several weeks had passed since Gary Cooper had been attacked, and Walker had now set up a team and an Incident Room at Blackpool Police HQ to investigate the crime further. Cooper had somehow survived the attack and continued to recover in a secure medical facility, awaiting trial—although his injuries had been extensive, so this caused some delays with proceedings. DC Briggs, who was currently on leave attending a course of counselling because of her ordeal, was dropping by today to say 'hello'; and now she was here, at the Blackpool station Incident Room.

'I want to come back,' she said to Walker. 'I *need* to come back. I'm going mad twiddling my thumbs at home.'

'Yeah, I know what you mean,' said Walker. 'Been there, done that, several times. But we must follow protocol, cross the I's and dot the T's, that kind of thing.'

'Well, the counsellor says she's ready to sign me off. Says I've responded well to the therapy, am ready to return to full duty,' said DC Briggs, a little proudly.

'And are you? Really?' said Walker. 'It hasn't been that long.'

'I'm a *fall off the horse and get right back on* kind of girl, me,' said DC Briggs. 'It's the best way. And my counsellor agrees. Sort of.'

'Well, I don't care what she says. It's too soon,' said Walker. 'What you went through...'

'Look. I've dealt with it. Women can do that, you know. We don't just bury things and let it fester like you men. We're a bit braver. I cried, I shouted, I let it out, several times, and now I'm ready to come back,' she said. 'I need this. I just need to carry on, do what I do.'

Walker shrugged his shoulders, knowing he wasn't going to convince her to take any more time off if she'd been given the okay. Why should she? He knew he wouldn't, so it would be hypocritical to expect her to. She had her own demons to face, as did he.

'Is that a yes then? I can come back? Work the case?' she asked, clearly wanting confirmation.

'Work the case? *This* one?' he asked. 'Seriously? Are you sure you can be objective after everything that's happened? I don't think—'

'Are you sure you can?' she asked.

It was a good question, and one he preferred not to answer, at least not directly. He'd wanted to do what had been done to Gary Cooper himself after what the bastard had done to her. He'd deserved it, and there was a part of him that wanted to slap the man's attacker on his back rather than put him in cuffs—if it was a *him*, but likely so, given the nature of the attack and how Gary Cooper had obviously been overpowered.

'Point taken,' he said. 'When do you want to come back then?'

'I thought I already had,' she said, taking a seat, getting comfortable. It seemed she had. He'd been played, good and proper. 'So, what do we have so far?'

CHAPTER THIRTY-ONE

'DC Ainscough, do you want to take this one?' asked Walker, wanting to give the young Detective some experience in leading a case, heading an Incident Room investigating a major crime.

'Certainly,' said DC Ainscough, appearing a little surprised, standing up, going to the front of the room. 'The Inn On the Prom hotel provided us with a list of guests who were staying at the hotel on the day that Gary Cooper was attacked. Our theory is that the attacker was a paying guest, or someone who worked at the hotel, as the receptionist—one Jade McAvoy—did not witness any visitors entering the hotel lobby during the time of the attack, and she stated she was there for several hours, never once leaving her desk. However, one of the guests in the list has been impossible to locate—a Derek Smith—so we're assuming that this alias was made up, for some reason, but this does not necessarily mean this person was the attacker. Does anybody have anything to add to this?' he said, seemingly running out of steam, or perhaps panicking a bit, not being used to leading a group of Detectives.

'DC Briggs, can you tell us again, exactly what you remember about the day Kevin Lawson was killed, when you were abducted by Gary Cooper,' said Walker. 'We can go in an interview room if you wish, just the two of us.'

Their investigative team now consisted of Walker, DC Briggs, DC Ainscough, DI Hogarth, and two other trainee detectives on placement—a Trainee Investigator Luke Stevenson and Trainee Investigator Emily Sharrock, both in their early twenties, and both highly intelligent, having graduated from university with first class degrees. All six members of the team were currently present in the Incident Room, ready for the briefing, hence Walker's question about whether DC

Briggs would like to go over the events of that day in private.

'I don't mind talking here. But we've been through this a couple of times already, haven't we? I'm not quite sure what else I can add.'

'I'm just asking because sometimes, our mind hides things from us, and they leak out when the time is right,' said Walker. 'So, if you'd just humour me, we'll compare the accounts. It's page six of the handout,' he said to everyone in the room. 'If you want to compare as we go.'

Papers shuffled as everyone found the correct page, and then DC Briggs started, looking uncomfortable, but going on anyway.

'Like I said, I was incapacitated as Lawson had injected me with what I later learned was the skeletal muscle relaxant succinylcholine. I was paralysed, but I could see a little as my head was angled slightly forwards on the bed against the edge of the pillow,' said DC Briggs.

'You can skip the part where you describe their conversation, for now. We went through that in some detail already. It's your transfer to the car's boot I'm most interested in right now,' said Walker. 'You said Gary Cooper put one of your arms around his neck to support you, and walked you to the car, before putting you in the boot and closing it. Did you have full control of your body at this time?'

'No. I was only just regaining control. I wouldn't have been able to walk without his help,' said DC Briggs.

'So, that's why you didn't try to escape?' asked Walker.

'Correct. I would have had to crawl out of there,' said DC Briggs. 'I was waiting for a better moment, but it never came. He injected me again when he opened the boot near the beach.'

'Okay. But back up for a second. When you were first locked

CHAPTER THIRTY-ONE

inside the car boot, next to the motorhome, you heard some commotion, right? Could you go over that bit again?'

DC Briggs closed her eyes, seemingly trying to concentrate, go back to the time.

'I was panicking, wondering what they were planning to do with me. All sorts was going through my head. I was terrified. I think I was in the car boot for a few minutes, maybe more, with nothing happening. I'm not sure. But then I heard some shouting. I heard Kevin's voice, frail, and then Gary's. They were arguing about something. Then Gary laughed and I heard a car door slam, and then the car started moving, quickly,' said DC Briggs. 'I think the tires screeched a bit. I could feel the sudden motion, and the sound of the engine. It also sounded like something was dragging and banging on the floor,' she said, her eyes suddenly becoming rooted in the present again, meeting Walker's gaze. 'It couldn't have been Gary who did that to Lawson. The last time I saw Lawson he was fine—and then I heard his voice right next to the car before it took off—and then Gary was with me the whole time, right up until just before you found me'

'That dragging and banging sound on the floor would have been the broken exhaust pipe. Is there anything else you can remember?'

'Not really. Just the smell of oil, or petrol, or both,' she said.

'I think we can theorise that Kevin Lawson and Gary Cooper were initially planning to take you somewhere together, but then they had an argument, perhaps Gary didn't agree with Lawson's plan, or he wanted you for himself. Whatever it was, he would have been stronger than Lawson and could have pushed him away with ease. Then, once Gary drives you away, leaving Lawson alone at the motorhome, our mystery person turns up, slaughters him.

'That seems to be about the size of it from the information we have,' said DI Hogarth, who'd been listening intently to it all until now.

'Motive?' asked Walker.

'Since these two are killers, and they've both had attempts on their lives—one successful and one not—the most likely motive is probably revenge, for someone they've hurt or killed,' said DC Ainscough. 'I'd say.'

'I second that,' said DI Hogarth. 'It'd be a hell of a coincidence for this to be a random attack on two known killers. Do you think this is one of the Blackpool lot?'

He was talking about the case they'd recently been involved in at Blackpool, when a movement had been started by a bunch of vigilante types, using violence to make people be kinder to each other.

'I'd say not,' said Walker. 'Different M.O. completely. The way they were cut, the viciousness of it—it seems personal. The killer would have had to have known that motorhome was here if they were after *him* specifically. And even if it was a civilian whose investigation was ahead of ours, they'd still be unlikely to have found that motorhome on this random farm road like that. So, that means they had some sort of intel; perhaps they got the location from a police scanner and got here before we did. But that would make the timeline tight. More likely they identified the farm before we did, and that means they knew about the cows, heard that recording.'

'Are you suggesting that we have a leak, that this is someone connected to the force?' asked DI Hogarth.

'I'm not suggesting anything,' said Walker. 'I'm just laying out the most likely scenario based upon the facts. Who might

CHAPTER THIRTY-ONE

have known about the lead on the farm?'

DI Hogarth thought about it. 'Well... I had to do a fair bit of research—talked to an expert in livestock farming and a few other people in that field, and then there's the farmer, John Baines, and anyone else he's talked to, and then we also had all available officers out looking for a motorhome near any farms containing cows. But that was before I found out they were highland cows. Once I had that information, I informed Chief Constable Harriet of where we were with the investigation, and made sure we had officers around the Baines farm, ready for backup if required.

'Well, that doesn't narrow it down much, does it?' said Walker. 'Perhaps the most plausible explanation is that our comms were being monitored, and that someone got to the location before we did.'

'I concur. We'll have to be more careful from now on. I'll start by sweeping this place for surveillance equipment, just in case, and we'll only communicate via encrypted software moving forwards,' said DI Hogarth. 'Are we thinking that revenge is the most likely motive for all this, given that we have one serial killer dead, and one aspiring serial killer with an attempt on his life as well—two men who had been working together?'

Everyone nodded, and some of them uttered 'yes' or 'mm'.

'It's hard to think that there could be any other possible motive now, but things can change quickly in this job, so we'll see what else turns up. Unfortunately, our "victim" in this, Gary Cooper, has not been very forthcoming with his witness account of the attack. He says he never saw them, that they got him from behind, and he lost consciousness,' said Walker.

'But the forensic evidence doesn't support this,' said DC

Ainscough. 'All of the knife wounds are on his front side, and there was no blunt force trauma to the head.'

'So, either he's lying, or he's just confused,' said Walker. 'There doesn't *seem* to be any motive for protecting the identity of this attacker, but if he's not confused, then that's what he's doing.'

'What about his mother?' asked DC Briggs. 'Lawson raped her, was going to kill her. And then her son started going down the same path. Might she be involved?'

'We've already looked at her,' said DC Ainscough. 'She's currently in a mental health facility, is on medication, and hasn't left the place in over a year.'

'Then the question is, who would want to see these two dead?' asked Walker, already knowing the answer himself, but wanting the trainees to get involved. 'TI Sharrock?'

'Anyone who knew any of the victims,' she said, clearly, without hesitation. 'Perhaps someone with experience in the investigative process, or in the field of criminology?'

'Why do you say that?' asked Walker.

'The crime scenes,' she said. 'They both seemed chaotic at first glance, but they were impeccable—no prints, hairs, footprints from the blood, DNA, nothing. It seemed methodical, textbook, as if they'd been designed to look messy, but were in fact the opposite.'

Walker thought about former Deputy Chief Constable Harry Potts, the cousin of Kevin Lawson's third victim, Sally Fielding. He would have known how to organise a crime scene like this, keep it clean—but then again, anyone in CID would. It was possible that someone on the force tipped Potts off as to Gary Cooper's location, but he'd have to have been quick to get there before Walker did. It felt off. He wondered if Chief

CHAPTER THIRTY-ONE

Constable Harriet had kept Potts in the loop, had updated him on what they'd found.

'I want to discuss this with Chief Constable Harriet before we go any further with it,' said Walker. 'Take a break and work on your other cases, for now. One of our killers is dead, and the other is in custody, so our primary aim has been completed. There's no reason to believe any further attacks will take place if these were indeed motivated by revenge.'

'But, sir,' said TI Sharrock, perhaps a bit too boldly, before visibly shrinking back. 'No matter what the reason, a killer is a killer, and we must get them off the streets, right?'

'We will resume the case soon,' said Walker. 'Don't you worry about that. Let's reassemble here in a couple of hours, sound good?'

Everyone dispersed and went their separate ways, leaving only Walker, DI Hogarth, and DC Briggs in the Incident Room.

'Chief?' said DC Briggs, raising an eyebrow. 'What are you doing?'

'Nothing,' said Walker. 'I just want to check something with Chief Constable Harriet, first, that's all.'

'You do want to catch this person, don't you?' she asked. 'I'm the one who was abducted, remember?'

'Both of them deserved it, as far as I'm concerned,' DI Hogarth chipped in. 'But the law is the law, and we have to get them.'

'Of course I want to catch them,' said Walker, not lying, but he had to admit he had a few reservations about it all and wouldn't be losing much sleep over it if they didn't get Kevin Lawson's and Gary Cooper's attacker for some reason.

'But you don't seem quite as motivated as usual,' she said. She was perceptive, tuned in, which was usually a good thing—

but not right now.

'This is a sensitive case,' said Walker. 'We were only assigned at all because—' He was saying too much, didn't want to stir up a hornet's nest.

'I'll leave you to it,' said DI Hogarth, probably not wanting to get involved, not wanting to hear what was about to be said. 'Toilet break.' He left the room.

'Former Deputy Chief Constable Harry Potts? The cousin of Sally Fielding, the third victim. Do you think he might be a suspect?' asked DC Briggs in a hushed tone.

'I'm... not saying anything yet,' said Walker. 'Chief Constable Harriet told Mr Potts to go home, and he most likely did, has been with his family this whole time for all we know. I just want to touch base with her, that's all, update her on the case, get her thoughts on how to move forward.'

'But this is, technically, a separate case, isn't it?' said DC Briggs. 'The murder of Sally Fielding, and the other victims, has been solved, their killer deceased, while my abductor has been captured. The person who attacked them is now filed as a separate case.'

She was right. It was a separate case, technically, despite the two cases being linked.

'Well, Chief Constable Harriet might not see it like that—so that's one of the things I want to discuss with her,' said Walker. He was lying. He didn't want to be involved in a case where a former high-ranking officer was in the firing line. If Harry Potts was involved, it could mean big trouble. These things tended to get very complicated, very quickly.

'I'll see you in a bit, Constable,' said Walker, leaving her to it, heading reluctantly to the Lancashire Constabulary Headquarters, and the office of one Chief Constable Harriet.

CHAPTER THIRTY-TWO

'Harry Potts?' said Chief Constable Harriet, laughing, and yet somehow deadly serious at the same time. 'No, no. I know him. He's by the book, as straight as they come. He wouldn't be involved in anything like this. And no, in answer to your question, I haven't been keeping him in the loop. I can understand his interest, but I'm not about to compromise an ongoing investigation'

Walker and Chief Constable Harriet were sat in her office at the Lancashire Constabulary Headquarters in Preston. It was a humble office, not what he'd expected at all—basic chipboard furniture, a couple of filing cabinets, a bookshelf, very little decoration.

'But we have to check out all possible persons of interest, right?' said Walker.

'Look, I understand why you felt the need to bring this to my attention,' said Chief Constable Harriet. 'I really do. But Harry's not worth police time investigating. He's one of us.'

'But retired,' added Walker.

'Retired, but still one of us,' said Chief Constable Harriet, with an edge to her voice telling Walker to back off. 'And we don't go after our own, not unless there's very good reason to. There are several other victims in this case to consider before this. I heard you yourself are quite close to DC Briggs. Doesn't that make you a suspect too, since she was abducted?'

Chief Constable Harriet held out her arm, stopping Walker before he could respond. 'I'm just making a point,' she said. 'Of course, I'm not saying you had anything to do with this. Do you see now, how dangerous your line of questioning is?'

Walker exhaled, a long, slow breath. She had a good point there. 'Fine. We'll leave Harry out of it for now, explore other avenues,' he said. 'But I expect we're going to need an alibi for him sooner or later, especially if the press get hold of this.'

'Then make sure they don't,' said Chief Constable Harriet, that initial good humour now evaporating completely. 'That would be a real shitstorm.' She was right. If the media got hold of this case, they'd be like a dog with a rag doll, tearing it apart.

'I'll tell my team to make sure everything is watertight, but they already know to keep this under wraps,' said Walker. 'I do think that revenge is the most likely motive for this, though. It's too coincidental that two connected killers have been attacked like this.'

'But you have no actual evidence of this yet,' said Chief Constable Harriet. 'So, why don't you follow the evidence trail instead, and see what emerges, rather than coming up with unsubstantiated and fanciful theories like this. Really. Whatever next, Detective Walker? Are you going to accuse me as well because I'm an old friend of Harry's?' She scoffed, dismissing the whole thing as something ridiculous, but Walker wasn't entirely convinced.

She was right in a way, of course, but coming up with unsubstantiated theories was partly how he worked. Every detective was different, had their own methods, but his had

CHAPTER THIRTY-TWO

achieved a high level of success over the years—hence his position and rank—so he wasn't going to change now just because a former police officer might be involved. Even if Harriet hadn't been keeping Potts in the loop, there might be other old friends and colleagues still on the force that could. There was no evidence of a second car leaving the motorhome and following Gaz, watching him bury Briggs, and following him to the hotel room to kill him there—which again pointed to someone having intel on their investigation. It was unlikely that Gaz was involved in Lawson's last murder, though, as he'd only have been thirteen at the time, so revenge didn't appear to be motive for killing him. Gaz might have spotted them when he was driving away from the motorhome, which would tie them to Lawson's murder. Walker felt that the motorhome had been searched though, so perhaps they thought Gaz had whatever they were looking for. That *would* provide motive. What that was, though, Walker had no idea. But he was concerned about the consequences of implicating someone on the force, or someone who used to be in a high position on it, so he had to back off for now, make sure he got there via the evidence trail, as Chief Constable Harriet put it, so there was no doubt about who did this.

'Will do,' said Walker, somewhat deferentially.

'Oh, and DCI Walker,' said Chief Constable Harriet.

'Yes?'

'Don't try too hard on this one,' said Chief Constable Harriet. 'The fact is, whoever did this got those two murderers off the street before we could. Who knows, they may have saved DC Briggs's life, and perhaps many others too. Police time and resources are limited. We must see the bigger picture. You start to see that, and you might just get my job one day.'

Oftentimes, Walker might feel Chief Constable Harriet was out of order, being dismissive of a case like this, but on this occasion, he felt the same deep down; he was almost grateful to be told to back off. It was true that the only thing driving him on with the case at the moment was habit, and decades following such procedures and evidence trails. It had become second nature.

Walker nodded, but it was a hesitant one, filled with complexity and ambivalence.

'You can see yourself out,' she said.

CHAPTER THIRTY-THREE

Walker now had his team assembled back at the Incident Room at Blackpool Police HQ—himself, DC Briggs, DI Hogarth, DC Ainscough, and the two young trainees, TIs Stevenson and Sharrock. He'd dug deep on the drive back, trying to figure out if he could live with himself if he let the case go, moved on to something else. But he decided, against his better judgement, that he probably could not. He'd never let a case go before, for political reasons or for anything else, and he wasn't going to start now.

'TI Stevenson, TI Sharrock, I'm reassigning you to another case,' said Walker.

'But, sir,' protested the young male, TI Stevenson, a handsome, strapping young lad with impeccable manners. 'Have we done something wrong?'

'Quite the opposite,' said Walker. 'Your work so far has been exemplary. Which is exactly why I want you off this case.'

'But that doesn't make sense,' added TI Sharrock. 'We don't want to be protected from anything, do we, TI Stevenson? We want real world experience.'

'Look,' said Walker. 'This case... it's complicated. Your careers could be over before they've started if it doesn't go smoothly.'

'We just want to uphold the law,' said TI Sharrock. 'So, if it's nothing dodgy, I'd like to be involved.'

'Me too,' added TI Stevenson, stubbornly, digging in.

'Very well,' said Walker, admiring their attitudes, hoping that it wouldn't come back to bite them. 'But before we start, I must underline that what we are about to do must stay very much under the radar, for the time being. The reasons for this will become clear if you all agree.'

Everyone nodded, muttered their complaisance.

'Okay then,' said Walker. 'It might be nothing. And then we can all move on with our lives. But we only have one real person of interest to explore with regard to the murder of Kevin Lawson and the attempted murder of Gary Cooper at the moment, and that is... *former Deputy Chief Constable Harry Potts.*' He let it settle for a few seconds, sink in. DI Hogarth whistled. 'If the killer wasn't stalking Lawson and Cooper, and we have no evidence of that, then the only people who knew where they might be found would be one of us. Police Constable Harriet told Potts to go home and says that she has not been providing him with updates. But someone else on the force might have, as he wanted to be kept in the loop. He's a relative of one of the victims, and he knows crime scenes.'

'Heads will fall,' said DI Hogarth, 'if this goes tits up. And even if it doesn't.'

'Chief Constable Harriet basically ordered us to let this one lie,' said Walker. 'In her words, she said to *not try too hard*, as the killer has taken two dangerous men off the streets, and she wants us focussing our energies elsewhere. She also warned against going after Harry Potts. He's an old friend of hers, you see, and a former colleague. She doesn't believe Harry has anything to do with this.'

CHAPTER THIRTY-THREE

'And yet, here we are,' said DI Hogarth.

'Yes, here we are,' said Walker. 'One murder has been committed, and we also have one attempted murder by presumably the same person, and it's up to us to ensure that justice is done.'

'I think whoever did this might have already done that for us,' said DI Hogarth. 'For those poor young girls, I mean, and for DC Briggs.'

'That's enough of that, Inspector,' said Walker. 'We must proceed with caution, to investigate covertly for the time being with anything regarding Harry, and above all we must make sure that none of this leaks to the goddamned press. That would be the last thing we need.'

'But... how are we going to investigate Harry, if we're not going to investigate him?' said DC Ainscough. 'I mean, we have to question him, don't we? Gather information. Establish an alibi, that kind of thing, follow procedure.'

'We need some hard evidence to bring this to the CPS,' said Walker. 'He's probably not involved, remember, hopefully, so let's gather all available evidence first, and keep in mind that he has a good motive for killing both of these men.'

'Both?' asked DC Ainscough. 'I mean, I get why he might want to kill Kevin Lawson, for murdering his cousin, but what about Gary Cooper?'

'Cooper might have seen Lawson's killer near the motorhome before the murder took place. So it's self-preservation,' said Walker. 'The killer needed Cooper dead as he could place him at the scene.'

'Makes sense,' said DI Hogarth,

'We must keep in mind at all times that any other family member or friend of any of Kevin Lawson's victims would also have the same motive to do this, so we must investigate other possibilities too. Also keep in mind that the motorhome appeared to have possibly been searched for something—although what that might have been, if it was, we're not sure; maybe that key we found around Lawson's neck and whatever it's linked to. Or perhaps that's nothing. But the reason we've got Harry Potts on our radar first is because he was right here, in Lytham St Annes, and he might have inside information about the case from someone on the force.'

'So, what do we do then, Chief?' asked DI Hogarth.

Walker thought about it. 'We need to know if Harry went home after we saw him at the mortuary. Sod it. I'm going to talk to his wife. I'll just tell Chief Constable Harriet, if she finds out, that we needed something to eliminate him from our enquiries, for his wife to say he'd been home all the time, something like that. She might buy that; be glad we've done something to neatly tie things off. Let's see how the wife reacts, see if there's anything there. I'll go to an interview room right now, make the call from there. Be back soon.'

* * *

'Mrs Potts? Yes, this is Chief Detective Inspector Jonathan Walker. I've been heading the case investigating the death of your husband Harry's cousin, Sally Fielding. That's right. Yes. I just needed to talk to you for a few minutes, ask a few questions, if you don't mind—pertaining to the case. We're trying to wrap things up now that the man who killed her is dead,' said Walker. 'I'd been informed you've already been

CHAPTER THIRTY-THREE

notified of this. Yes. Would you mind if I put you on speaker phone now, so I can be hands free, look through a few files while I'm talking. I can assure you there's nobody else here. It's just me.'

Walker was sat in Interview Room 3 at Blackpool Police HQ, alone, with a file he'd started to put together on Harry Potts, just to get a picture of who the man was. He wasn't going after him exactly, was just a person of interest in the investigation, for now.

'That's great, Mrs Potts. Putting you on speaker now,' said Walker, having gained her permission to do so. He pressed the icon on his phone to go on speaker mode, which he'd only recently discovered, thanks to DC Briggs, who'd laughed at him when he said he didn't know how to do it. But now he did.

'You can call me Alison,' said the woman, with the volume on the phone a little high, Walker adjusting it a tad with the volume controls.

'Okay, Alison... so, I last saw your husband at a mortuary called D Hollowell & Sons in Lytham St Annes on 1st July. He came to discuss the case with me after Sally Fielding's body had been exhumed,' said Walker. 'Do you recall this?'

There was a pause. 'Yes, I remember,' she said, a bit abruptly. There was something on it, though, her answer, an attitude Walker couldn't quite pin down, which made him hesitate.

'And your husband... he came home the same day, correct?' asked Walker.

She paused again, even longer this time. 'No. He didn't. I think he was with *her* again, that sodding woman.'

Chief Constable Sarah Harriet had ordered him to go home, but he evidently had not.

'I see... And when did you see him again then, Alison?' said Walker.

'Is Harry in trouble?' she asked. 'Why are you asking all these questions about him?'

'We just need to know where he's been, and who with, for the record, that's all,' said Walker. 'Kevin Lawson, the man who killed his cousin, Sally Fielding, has been murdered, so we need to eliminate your husband from our line of investigation, that's all, as a person of interest. We are simply following procedure, and I apologise for any distress this might cause. I'm sure there's no problem. So, if you wouldn't mind?'

Mrs Potts breathed a heavy sigh. 'I didn't see him for over a week,' she said. 'Told me he was assisting with the case, that you needed him up there. But I knew different, of course. I found out.'

'You found out what, Alison?' asked Walker.

'I found out that *she* was heading the case,' she said.

'You must be mistaken, Alison, whatever you're thinking. I've been heading this case myself. Who's this woman you're referring to?' asked Walker. 'Somebody on the force?'

'He's been seeing her for years, on and off,' said Alison. 'I found out shortly after we got married. He's been having a frigging affair. I've had to live with it all this time.'

'And this woman, do you know her name?' asked Walker.

'I told you, she's been in charge of your investigation—bloody *Sarah Harriet*,' she said, crying now. 'That's who.'

Well, that would explain why Chief Constable Harriet had been so adamant about him leaving Harry alone, for him to focus on other cases—if Alison was correct, that was. He knew that some people, some *women*, were the jealous type, got knotted up about things that weren't even there. One of his ex-girlfriends had been that way. He'd never understood it, but it ruined their relationship. So, he wasn't taking Alison's accusations as fact until it was proven, but he would certainly keep an open mind about it.

'If what you're saying is true, then I'm truly very sorry to hear that,' said Walker, trying to calm her down. 'But, just to be clear, you're saying that Harry did not come home at all from the 1st July until over a week later. I don't suppose you could you pin down the date exactly, by any chance, could you?'

'Wait,' she said. 'I'll just look at my calendar.'

Walker gave it a few seconds, taking it in, processing what she'd just told him, and the implications it might have. If Harry was to have an alibi, then it might need to come from Chief Constable Harriet herself, which would probably require an admission of adultery. The case wasn't getting any simpler, and if he was going to continue with it, against the wishes of Harriet, then there could be some serious repercussions.

'Here it is,' she said. 'He came back on July 10th with his tail between his legs. I remember, because it was the same day as a doctor's appointment I had—which I'd written on my calendar.'

'And you never saw or spoke to him during that time?' asked Walker.

'I never saw him, but we spoke on the phone a few times— just kept telling me he was assisting with the investigation, that he'd be home soon, was staying at some hotel,' she said.

'And the hotel he was staying at?' asked Walker. 'I don't suppose he mentioned the name of it?'

'No. He did not,' said Alison. 'I asked but he said he couldn't remember. He was lying. He was with her, I know it.'

'Is Harry there now?' asked Walker.

'No. He's taken the dog for a walk,' she said. 'At least, that's what he said. I don't know if I can believe anything he says anymore. He could be anywhere.'

'Alison, if you don't mind, would you not mention this conversation to Harry, for now, just while we tie off a few loose ends?' asked Walker. 'We just need to get his whereabouts nailed down, that's all, so we can—'

'Eliminate him from your enquiries?' said Alison. 'Yes, you already said that.'

'So?' asked Walker.

'I won't say anything,' said Alison. 'Why should I tell him everything when he lies to me. Is there anything else?'

'No. That will be all,' said Walker. 'Have a good... I mean, I'm sorry about this. I hope you feel better soon.'

'Goodbye, Detective,' said Alison.

'Goodbye, Alison.'

Walker hung up. He had work to do, and he needed to do it as much under the radar as possible, before Chief Constable Harriet got wind of any of this.

CHAPTER THIRTY-FOUR

Trainee Investigators Luke Stevenson and Emily Sharrock left the Incident Room with a stack of papers, after being ordered by Walker to make some copies. He didn't really need any copies. He just wanted them out of there. He didn't want them to be privy to what he was about to tell the rest of his team.

'Okay. So… Harry Potts's wife, Alison, says he didn't come home from July 1st, when we saw him at the mortuary, until July 10th, after Kevin Lawson had been killed, and also after Gary Cooper's attempted murder,' said Walker.

'Not good at all,' said DC Briggs. 'That would now make him our number one suspect. Chief Constable Harriet told him to go home, didn't she. I remember.'

'His wife believes the reason he didn't come home is because he's having an affair,' said Walker.

'Or… he was getting revenge for his cousin's murder?' said DI Hogarth.

'Or *that*,' said Walker, not quite sure how to tell them the next bit.

'What is it, Chief?' asked the ever-perceptive DC Briggs. 'There's more, isn't there.'

Walker nodded. 'The woman that Alison Potts believes her

husband is having an affair with is on the force.'

'Well, it certainly isn't me!' said DC Briggs. 'I was too busy being abducted.' It was good she had some humour about it. That would help in the long run.

'It's... the name she gave was... oh, my... *Chief Constable Sarah Harriet*,' said Walker, feeling like he'd just dropped something with a heavy weight in the room, the impact reverberating, changing everyone's expression.

'You're kidding,' said DC Ainscough, who'd been quietly listening to it all before now.

'Unfortunately, I am not,' said Walker.

'Is that why you just asked Luke and Emily to do all that photocopying?' asked DC Briggs. 'You didn't want them to hear this?'

'I thought it a bit strange that Chief Constable Harriet would place them with us. Perhaps she's asked them to keep tabs on us. Best to keep them busy from here on in,' said Walker, his paranoia levels now rising fast.

'If Potts and Harriet are having an affair,' said DI Hogarth, 'it would make complete sense for her to try to protect him, if he has done anything.'

'Which is perhaps why she asked us to back off with this case,' said Walker.

'But... we're not, are we?' asked DC Briggs.

Walker shook his head. 'We've got to get to the bottom of this,' he said. 'Our job is to uphold the law, whether that involves one of us as the perpetrator of a crime, or not.'

He let it settle for a minute or two, for everyone to get their thoughts together, him included.

'DC Ainscough, get out the autopsy report for Kevin Lawson again, read the section detailing the analysis of the knife

CHAPTER THIRTY-FOUR

wounds,' said Walker.

DC Ainscough shuffled through some papers on his desk, found the report.

'Here it is,' he said, flicking through it. 'The coroner states that regarding "Force and Depth of the Wounds", *the force used to stab and cut indicates a person of reasonable upper body strength.* Then, under "Target Areas", it says, *the strikes appear as a random or broad pattern, likely aiming for the chest or abdomen, with these types of attacks more predominant among male attackers.* Then for "Angle and Trajectory", it states, *the angle of the wounds provide clues about the assailant's height, which in this case suggests a person of average height, as the angle of the attack are neither upwards or downwards, with the exception of one wound, which demonstrated a downward thrusting motion, which could have been achieved by standing, by jumping, or by standing on an object.* Then for 'Hand Size and Grip,' it states, *the size of the weapon is indicative of average sized hands.* And the coroner's conclusion is that *no definitive conclusions about the attacker's gender can be achieved based upon this analysis, but the weight of evidence suggests that this is most likely a male of average height and build.*'

'And for the attack of Gary Cooper?' said Walker. 'Same, wasn't it?'

DC Ainscough flicked through more papers, nodded as he did so, evidently already knowing the answer, but just wanting to confirm it for himself. He found the relevant paper, scanned through it, and said, 'yes, almost identical.'

'Almost?' asked Walker.

'Yes. Pretty much word for word,' said DC Ainscough. 'Apart from that one downward thrusting wound, which is not present on this report.'

'Perhaps Kevin stepped out of the motorhome for a second,

down the step, whilst the attack was ongoing, and this caused the downward thrusting action,' said Walker.

'Sounds like a reasonable assumption,' said DC Ainscough. 'Although no blood spatter was reported on the step, but perhaps he was simultaneously dragged back inside, or the step had been cleaned.'

'I need to talk to Gary Cooper again,' said Walker. 'He's the only possible witness we have. He must have seen something, either with his own attack, or that of Kevin Lawson. Why's he not talking? Why's he letting the person that did this to him walk free?'

'Perhaps Harry got to him,' said DI Hogarth. 'Warned him to keep quiet, or else.'

'Or else what?' said Walker.

'You know... he'll arrange to have him offed, with his contacts at the prison, or whatever,' said DI Hogarth.

'I want to talk to this guy,' said Walker.

'And I want to come with you,' said DC Briggs.

'Detective,' said Walker, his tone softer than usual, concerned. 'I really don't think—'

'I want to come,' she said, stubbornly.

'May I have a word in private, DC Briggs?' said Walker. 'Outside, in the corridor, perhaps?'

DC Briggs nodded and joined him there, Walker closing the door so the others couldn't hear.

'After what that man did to you, I really don't think it's a good idea for you to see him. It'll bring it all back, hurt you,' said Walker. 'You need to try to let it go.'

'Chief, with the greatest of respect, you've agreed to let me work this case, so what's the problem?' she said.

'The problem is, I don't need you with me to interview him,'

CHAPTER THIRTY-FOUR

said Walker.

'Why not? I usually accompany you to such interviews.'

She had a point there. She did.

'Look, I just don't think it's necessary for you to see him, face to face,' said Walker. 'You were one of his victims too. It will cloud your judgement.'

'And what about yours?' said DC Briggs. 'Will it cloud yours?'

'You know what I mean,' said Walker.

They were at a standstill.

'It's very sweet, Jon, but you don't need to protect me like this. I'm okay. I've had therapy. I'm over it. And facing him might actually help me to get over it more,' she said. 'Come face-to-face to the man that buried me alive, see him in prison. It will be empowering, or something. You know.'

'If you're over it, then you don't need to *get over it more*, do you?' said Walker, feeling like he sounded a bit childish when he said it, and he probably did.

'You know what I mean,' said DC Briggs.

Walker felt his resistance crumbling. He felt protective of her, even more than before. He realised that it was probably him who wasn't being objective.

'Fine,' he said. 'You can come.'

'Thanks, Jon,' she said.

'*Chief*,' he reminded her.

'Thanks, *Chief Jon*,' she said, smiling, instantly disarming any negative feelings he had about it.

CHAPTER THIRTY-FIVE

Gary Cooper was handcuffed to a hospital bed in a secure medical facility at the Royal Preston Hospital, a unit specialising in serious injuries including stabbing incidents like the ones Cooper had been the victim of. When he saw Walker and DC Briggs walk in, his eyes went wide, his focus intent on Briggs. He looked excited.

'It's you,' he said. 'They told me you were alive. Fancy that.'

'Yeah, *fancy*,' she said, with an edge to her voice.

'We need to talk to you, about your attack,' said Walker.

'Again?' said Gary. 'I already told you everything I remember.'

Walker got up close to Gary, pressed on one of his bandaged healing wounds, just like he had when he'd found him, making him yelp. 'Well, tell us *again*,' he said, before easing off.

'I think I was… yeah, that's it. I was in the middle of putting a clean T-shirt on, so my vision was restricted, when someone came in. I felt a pain in my chest,' he said, touching himself where he'd been stabbed, 'and then again, and again. I guess I started to lose consciousness before I could see them,' said Gaz. 'That's all I remember. Honest.'

Walker got close again, started pressing on his wound even harder than the first time. 'Our reports show that the T-shirt you were wearing had the same pattern of stab wounds, so you must have had it on. You're lying!'

Gary laughed a hysterical laugh, one mixed with pain. 'Just checking, that you're real detectives, I mean.'

'Who was it?' said Walker, grabbing the man by his collar.

DC Briggs touched Walker on the arm, tugged him back. 'Easy, Chief,' she said.

'Yeah, *easy, Chief*,' mocked Gary. 'What are you, married or something?'

DC Briggs looked at Walker, just fleetingly, but Gary noticed. 'Oh, my God, are you two banging? Is that why you're so angry about this, *Chief*? Did I take your bit on the side?'

'Why are you protecting the person who did this to you?' asked Walker.

'I told you. I never saw anyone,' said Gary. 'And even if I did, I wouldn't tell you who she was.' Gary closed his eyes, either knowing he'd made a blunder, or bluffing.

She. He'd said the attacker was a *she*. But did he say it on purpose, to mess with them, or did he say it by accident?

'So, a woman did this to you?' asked Walker. 'Is that why you won't tell us—you're embarrassed that a woman messed you up real good? Almost killed you.'

'What are you, the grammar police?' said Gary. 'He, she, they... What's the difference. I saw nothing.'

'Did you see the person who killed your father, Kevin Lawson?' asked Walker. 'Was that a woman too?'

'What, he's *dead?*' said Gary. He knew damned well that he was dead. He'd been told when he'd regained consciousness.

'Did you see them?' asked Walker.

'No. I didn't see *them*, or *her*, or *him*,' said Gary. 'Are we done here?'

Walker sat down, leaned back, as he was finished with him, but wanted to give DC Briggs the opportunity to say anything she wanted to say, if she needed to find closure, or anything like that. She'd unlikely have a reason to see him again, so this might be her only chance, he thought.

'Why'd you do it?' asked DC Briggs.

'Do what?' said Gary. 'Are you trying to trip me up again, make me imply that I killed my own father.'

'No. Why'd you try to kill me?' she said. 'Why'd you bury me in the sand like that? Was it not enough just to kill me? Did you have to try to psychologically torture me and break me as well? Did you feel so utterly powerless that you needed to overcompensate by doing this shit?'

'I just... needed a buzz, that's all, luv,' he said, smiling. 'Nothing personal.'

Walker slammed his hand down on the bedside unit, making a plastic cup full of water spill everywhere. He grabbed Gary again, by the neck this time, shaking him.

'You bastard,' he said. 'I should kill you myself.'

Gary was smiling, seemingly enjoying the drama, even if it was him on the receiving end. DC Briggs started to whack Walker on the back now.

'*Get... off... him,*' she said, peeling his hands away from Gary's neck. 'Are you crazy?'

Walker stepped back, got himself together. 'I wasn't going to...'

'I just needed to look you in the eye, that's all... face my demons, you might say,' she said, her gaze penetrating Gary Cooper's, staring him out, making him look away for a moment. 'I've learned that if you don't face up to your demons, they'll haunt you forever. Have you faced yours, Mr Cooper?'

CHAPTER THIRTY-FIVE

With that, she got up, her head held high and exited the hospital room of her abductor and tormentor: one Gary Cooper.

CHAPTER THIRTY-SIX

'Do you really think the attacker was a "she", or do you just think he was messing with us?' asked DC Briggs. Walker and her were back in the pool car now, driving away from the Royal Preston Hospital, heading north, back to Blackpool Police HQ and their team—Walker in the driving seat.

'Anything is possible,' said Walker. 'It could have been a mistake, a slip of the tongue, or he could have been *pretending* to make a mistake and mess with our investigation, like you said. But none of that explains why he isn't identifying his attacker or attackers, unless he really didn't see them, for some reason.'

'I suppose sometimes things happen quickly, and it's hard to say why we did or didn't see something,' said DC Briggs. 'Memories are imperfect, even at the best of time. He could be telling the truth. It's not impossible.'

'Then we must keep our minds open, for now. But I doubt he and the truth are very well acquainted. Although the forensic evidence is skewed slightly in favour of a male attacker, it's hardly conclusive,' said Walker. 'At the moment, the best suspect we have is still Harry Potts, and we also need to look more deeply into his relationship with Chief Constable

CHAPTER THIRTY-SIX

Sarah Harriet, if indeed there is one beyond their working relationship, although I'm not quite sure how we're going to do that without them finding out.'

'And if they do find out?'

'If they do find out, then that could put the brakes on our investigation completely, and if we're wrong about it, we could find ourselves in a heap of trouble,' said Walker. 'With our jobs, I mean. She is our boss, after all. She wouldn't be very happy about being implicated in all this, and that's putting it mildly.'

'And if you weren't putting it mildly?' asked DC Briggs.

'Then I'd say she'd skin us alive and hang us out to dry for every misdemeanour I've ever been pulled up for,' said Walker. 'And there have been one or two over the years.'

'Like getting a little rough with Gary Cooper, for example,' said DC Briggs, although she said it almost like a reprimand. It was clear she didn't approve, despite what that bastard had done to her.

'Yeah. Like that,' said Walker.

'Do you think I'd be in trouble too?' asked DC Briggs.

'I don't think she'd be happy with any of us if we take this route in our investigation, and that includes you. She'd find something on you. We all have something,' said Walker. 'Even you.'

'What? Like I'm no longer fit for duty or something because of the trauma I experienced with Gary Cooper?' asked DC Briggs.

'Yeah, exactly like that,' said Walker.

'So?' asked DC Briggs.

'So, I'd understand if you don't want to be involved in this, and that goes for any of the others too. I can pursue it alone,' said Walker.

'But you're hell bent on pursuing it, one way or another,' said DC Briggs.

Walker nodded. He couldn't let this go; he couldn't let a potential murderer walk free just because of the position they held, or used to hold.

'Then I'm going along with you. We're a team,' she said, stubbornly. 'We're a team. And you saved my life. I owe you.'

Walker looked at her, in the eyes, making sure, before returning his attention to the road. It had started raining, and he flipped the windscreen wipers on.

'Well, okay then,' he said. 'But this is a sensitive operation, and we must be careful, or it'll be stopped before it even gets started.'

'*Careful* is my middle name, from now on,' said DC Briggs. 'I've got your back, Chief, always. You can rely on me, I promise.'

'Appreciated. And one more thing: if that motorhome was being searched after the killer did Lawson in—and it did look like it to me—then it stands to reason that they were looking for something of great value to them. But that's not necessarily of monetary value. It could be something else,' said Walker.

'Like what?' asked DC Briggs. 'Like something they could use to blackmail them?'

'That's what I'm thinking,' said Walker. 'Something that could wreck a person's life, perhaps. Something they did wrong, that no one else knows about, and they desperately want to keep it that way.'

'If that's the case, then wouldn't Lawson stand to make some money out of it if he threatened to out them, for whatever he had on them?' asked DC Briggs.

CHAPTER THIRTY-SIX

'That's exactly why I need you, Detective, to keep the wheels turning,' said Walker, smiling. 'We'll check his bank records then, see if he's been receiving any regular payments from anybody. It could be the lead we need, *if* we're lucky.'

CHAPTER THIRTY-SEVEN

Now back at Blackpool Police HQ, Walker was talking to his team—DCs Briggs and Ainscough, and DI Hogarth, with the two trainees in the copy room again, compiling some reports, Walker keeping them out of the way.

'Now, whenever those two youngsters come back in here,' he explained, 'you put the real case files away, work on something else, tell them the Cooper case is going nowhere, that we have no workable leads, just in case they are reporting back to Chief Constable Harriet. I know that might sound a little paranoid, but we must be if we're to get anywhere with this, fly under the radar. Now, are you sure you all want in on this? I wouldn't hold it against you one bit if you wanted out.'

'I'm in,' said DI Hogarth. 'We're doing nothing wrong. We're just following up on a lead in a criminal investigation, that's all.'

'Me too,' said DC Ainscough. 'Our careers will all end at some point. We just have to make sure we do the right thing, no matter what. And this is the right thing, I believe. I'd expect to be investigated if I'd been implicated in anything. It's just procedure. I want to end my career with a clear conscience, whether that's now, or in thirty years. I want to do what's

CHAPTER THIRTY-SEVEN

right.'

'Okay then,' said Walker. 'Let's get on it then. What do we have?'

'The bank records of Kevin Lawson have come back with nothing unusual. Not much going through his account, really. The only regular payments were disability living allowance payments from the DWP,' said DI Hogarth. 'Checked Gary Cooper's bank accounts too. Nothing of note.'

'Great. Another sodding dead end,' said Walker, feeling the frustration of the case, of being unable to unlock it.

DC Ainscough took out a metal evidence box, opened it up. Inside was the necklace that Kevin Lawson had been wearing, encased in a clear plastic evidence bag with some information written on it.

'The necklace of teeth that Kevin Lawson was wearing,' said DC Ainscough.

'I know what it is,' said Walker.

'We've not been able to identify one of the teeth yet, but three of them have been confirmed as belonging to the three bodies that were found in the sand dunes. And get this,' he said, hesitating.

'Get on with it, Detective', said Walker.

'One of them was quite old and was difficult to get any DNA from. But... forensics were able to get a degraded sample, and after several weeks of advanced amplification techniques, PCR and the like, they've been able to get a familial match—it's from Kevin Lawson's mother.'

Walker shook his head. 'Killed his mother too?'

'His first victim, perhaps,' said DC Ainscough.

'We don't know that,' said Walker. 'But it's more than possible. What about the key that was also on the necklace?

Did we get any further ideas about that—the numbers and letters that were on it. Any possible leads?'

'I've not been able to get that key out of my mind,' said DC Ainscough. 'I don't like unanswered questions, and it's been bugging me, keeping me awake at night.'

'Perhaps you're in the wrong job then. Sleep is important,' said Walker, knowing that he was also affected by the same affliction. 'Go on. Get to the punchline, would you, before those two spies come back.'

'Potential spies,' said DI Hogarth, smiling a pained smile.

'The numbers and letters on the key—MYMBL1409. Now, initially, I'd just Googled MYMBL and came up with nothing. But I had a hunch: if Kevin Lawson had something to hide, or keep safe, where might he keep it? You said it could be a locker somewhere, or storage facility, but that came back with nothing. I talked to several locksmiths as well. The numbers and letters were not from any keying system that they recognised. I considered a safety deposit box at a high-street bank, but those services are no longer offered. Then I thought maybe a secret safe, hidden somewhere at his home, but we couldn't find anything—tore the place apart. Thought it could be a locked box buried in his garden, got forensics to get a metal detector in his back yard when they were checking for any further victims buried there, then dug the place up in case it was a wooden box. Nothing. So, as I was running out of ideas, sat at my computer, I had another check for any safety deposit box services offered elsewhere, something more obscure.'

'I considered that too, but the banks shut them all down years ago, along with most of the high street branches. It's all gone sodding digital, hasn't it?' said Walker, his annoyance

CHAPTER THIRTY-SEVEN

with this change leaking out. 'I thought about getting one myself, for the deeds for the house, and a few other bits, but they'd already stopped the service at Barclays, where I bank, and I couldn't find one anywhere else either.'

'That's correct,' said DC Ainscough. 'However, with a deeper search, I discovered that there are still some independent companies and private firms out there that provide safety deposit box services in secure facilities across the UK.'

'And are there any around here?' asked Walker. 'We can't go travelling all around Britain, now, can we, trying every sodding safety deposit box with this key—even if we did get a warrant to use it.'

'No. Course not,' said DC Ainscough, smiling. 'But I've just got that warrant come through, and there is one such facility on Paradise Street Liverpool—a Metro Bank.'

'Sounds like a long shot,' said Walker, 'but worth a try. You thinking the "M" is for *Metro*, then?'

DC Ainscough smiled, even bigger. 'No. I'm thinking that MYMB is for Metro Bank, as that is their SWIFTBIC code—the code that identifies their bank—and the "L" is probably to mark it as their Liverpool branch. 'So, MYMBL1409 is Metro Bank Liverpool, safety deposit box 1409, I think.'

Walker sat up straight, coughed a little, getting excited that they actually had something. It wasn't a long shot any more.

'DC Briggs, looks like we're taking a little trip out to your backyard,' said Walker, referring to her occasionally scouse accent, which was mostly mild, but which tended to get stronger whenever she got overexcited, like now.

'Sounds good to me, Chief,' she said. 'What do you think we might find there, if DC Ainscough is correct.'

'Nothing good,' said Walker. 'But find it we must.'

CHAPTER THIRTY-EIGHT

'Harry, we need to talk,' said Chief Constable Harriet. She was off duty now though, so she was just plain old "Sarah" to him. They were on the phone, separated by many miles, with Harry at his home in Chester, Sarah sat in her car on a Tesco carpark in Chorley, the rain pelting down on it, making it hard to hear.

'What is it, Sarah? I thought we agreed not to contact each other anymore,' said Harry. 'We're done, aren't we?'

'We never should have done what we did, Harry,' said Sarah.

Harry sighed. 'Are we going over this again? Really? What's done is done. We have to move on now,' he said. 'My wife, she knows... *something*, you know. I didn't come home for days, Sarah. I'm properly in the doghouse for this. She won't even speak to me now.'

'Oh, there are bigger things to worry about than your sodding domestic life,' said Sarah, getting riled by his selfish attitude. 'They found a key, on a necklace around Kevin Lawson's sodding neck. I couldn't tamper with evidence. It's only a matter of time before they find out what it's for.'

'Then do tamper with the bloody evidence then!' spat Harry. 'It's not like you haven't done worse things.'

'It's not that easy. Things are tighter these days, more

regulated. And it would clearly implicate me,' said Sarah. 'There's no need to take me down with you, Harry.'

There was silence on the line, so much so that Sarah thought Harry had gone for a second. 'You need to get that key or we're both screwed,' said Harry. 'Just do what you have to.'

Now Sarah paused, knowing Harry wasn't going to like this next part. 'Walker has it. One of his detectives logged it out this morning. He has authority—he's on the case.'

'Oh, that's just sodding great,' said Harry. 'They'll find out what it's for eventually. That Walker is like a bloody dog with a bone. 'We should have put someone else on the case. Or just found Lawson ourselves.'

'I'm sorry, Harry. I thought he'd be easier to control, after everything that happened in Blackpool, and his suspension. Can't you just keep me out of this? Isn't it time to give me those damned tapes, so I can get rid of them, once and for all? Haven't you tortured me enough with all this?'

'Give you the tapes? That wasn't the deal, and you know it,' said Harry. 'Look, I appreciate what you've done, for me, and my family. I really do. But I just want to be left alone now, grow old in peace. We're done. It's finished. It's over.'

'I wish I'd never met you, Harry Potts,' said Sarah. 'You ruined my life.'

'I got you off the booze, is what I sodding did,' snapped Harry. 'You'd probably be dead now—overdosed in some alleyway or something—the way you were drinking, if you'd not met me.'

'There are times when I think I'd rather *be* dead,' said Sarah. She'd loved him, once, had been absolutely smitten with the man, before they'd broken up. She'd have done anything for him—*anything*. They say love is blind, and that it had been. She'd made excuses for him, tried to understand him, tried to support him. But in the end, he'd just gone back to his wife, just like he had now.

'Oh, don't be silly, Sarah,' said Harry. 'Think of all those people you've saved, all those criminals you've put away, making the streets safer. You've done good. We both have. People aren't perfect. We all make mistakes. The important thing is to find retribution, to make up for those things. If you aren't proud of yourself, then do something to tip the balance. Get more of these freaks locked away, like Gary Cooper. That's what I'd do, if I were still on the force. At least you have your job. What do I have? A pension and never-ending dog walks, and a wife who isn't speaking to me? It's hardly a happy ending for me either.'

'Goodbye, Harry,' she said. And she meant it. She never wanted to see the man again. But she'd been there before, and he'd always crept back into her life, somehow. He was the stain that couldn't be removed. He'd always be there. He was a part of her that couldn't be removed any more than her DNA could.

CHAPTER THIRTY-NINE

'Here it is then, sir, box 1409,' said the member of staff from Metro Bank who had taken them inside the vault. The safety deposit box had two identical keys, one which was held by the bank, and one that was evidently held on the necklace of the now deceased Kevin Lawson—the key that Walker now had, along with a warrant to inspect the contents of this box. 'Please turn the key simultaneously, with me,' he said.

Walker did as requested, and the hatch opened, revealing a metal container inside, which Walker took out and placed on an inspection plinth.

'That will be all, for now,' said Walker.

The member of staff nodded and left them to inspect the contents of the box.

Walker took a deep breath, having absolutely no idea what they might find. 'Here we go then', he said.

'Chief,' said DC Briggs. 'Whatever it is, I'm proud of you for pursuing this case.'

Walker nodded and opened the lid. Inside, was an envelope, marked 'To the police', alongside a tape player. He put on some nitrile gloves, lifted the envelope out. It had some weight. There was something inside, more than just a letter.

He carefully opened it up and let the contents slide out into the container. There was one note, neatly folded, and one dictation tape, about 5cm by 3cm.

'Oh, my. What do we have here then?' asked Walker, opening up the note first, looking together.

To Whom It May Concern: In the event of my capture, or death, please listen to the enclosed tape as evidence of the real perpetrator of the death of Sally Fielding.

That was all it said.

'Play it,' said DC Briggs, being unable to wait, the suspense obviously killing her.

Walker looked at her, 'I am,' he said, slowing things down a touch, knowing that hurrying these things never got anyone anywhere.

He carefully placed the tape in the tape player, and pressed play.

There was some muffled static, some odds noises, rattles and muffles and the like, but then a voice started to speak.

'If you want the evidence to go away then you must do exactly what I say'.

Walker stopped the tape. 'I know that voice,' he said, with some concern. 'That's Harry Potts.'

DC Briggs looked at him, quizzically. 'You know what, I think you're right. Go on... play the rest of it.'

Walker did as asked this time, without any further delay. He was just as keen to hear the rest of this as she was.

'How do I know you have CCTV footage of me with her?'

Walker stopped the tape again. 'Is that Lawson?' he asked.

DC Briggs nodded. 'It is. One hundred per cent. I'll never

CHAPTER THIRTY-NINE

forget that voice,' she said. 'Please, sir. Play it.'

He played it again, ready to listen to the rest of the unlikely conversation between Harry Potts and Kevin Lawson. They thought Harry had killed him, had never met him before doing so, but it seemed he had.

'Here, have a look for yourself,' said Harry.

There were a few seconds of silence.

'There,' said Harry. 'Satisfied. That's clearly you, with Tracy White, a missing person, injecting her with something, before she goes limp, and you stuff her in your car boot. We had no idea who you were until that allegation was made about you recently—that woman who said you grabbed her near the beach in Ainsdale, got a little rough, before she ran away. You weren't prosecuted because it was her word against yours, but we logged you in the system, got a match on this.'

'What, exactly, do you want me to do, Deputy Chief Constable Potts?' asked Kevin.

'I want you to make a problem go away for me,' said Harry. 'This one.'

There were a few more seconds of silence as Walker and DC Briggs listened on, getting even closer to the tape player.

'Who is she?' asked Kevin.

'It doesn't matter who she is,' said Harry. 'She's become a problem, and she needs to disappear.'

'Well... I suppose I'm due for another one anyway,' said Kevin. 'Can I dress her up how I want?'

'Do whatever you like. Just make her go away,' said Harry. 'For good. And make sure nobody ever finds her.'

'I'm going to need her name, at least,' said Kevin. 'What am I going to call her?'

'You can just call her "Sal",' said Harry. 'Meet me at this location,

just outside of Birmingham, at this time and day. We got a deal?'

'If you make the evidence against me go away, then we have a deal,' said Kevin.

'Just make sure you tie off any loose ends, and be careful,' said Harry. *'Or I'll be coming after you.'*

There was the sound of a car door slamming, and a few more seconds of silence, before the tape recording went dead.

'Holy, shit,' said Walker. 'He offed his own sodding cousin. Poor girl.'

'But why?' asked DC Briggs. 'And if he killed Kevin Lawson and tried to kill Gary Cooper as well, why did he do that too? Because Lawson was going to expose him with this tape if he got caught, and because he thought Gary might have the tape when he killed Lawson and couldn't find it?

'Well, that, now, is the million-dollar question, isn't it, Detective,' said Walker. 'And it's up to us to find out. But we have the bastard now. We bloody have him.'

CHAPTER FORTY

'This is unbelievable,' said DI Hogarth. 'Lock that door, would you?' he said, to DC Ainscough, who was also with Walker and DC Briggs in one of the interview rooms at Blackpool Police HQ, away from any prying eyes. 'Potts? I thought there was a slight possibility that he may have sought revenge for his cousin's murder, but this? Why would he want his own cousin dead?'

DC Briggs shook her head in evident disbelief. 'And he knew that Kevin Lawson was a killer, and he let him go free, buried the evidence? What kind of a copper does that?' asked DC Briggs, but they all knew the answer to that.

'A bad one,' said DC Ainscough, just in case there was any doubt. 'The worst.' He was disgusted. They all were.

'Perhaps his wife was right about the affair, but wrong about the person,' said Walker 'Maybe it wasn't Chief Constable Harriet at all, but Sally Fielding. Or, at least, it could have been over thirteen years ago. Maybe they had some kind of incestuous affair, and she threatened to tell everyone, shame him? Shame can do strange things to people. His wife may have thought it was Harriet, and that it was still going on when he didn't come home—but perhaps he was busy offing Lawson and trying to do the same with Cooper.'

'We have to take this to Harriet now, don't we? The evidence is unquestionable,' said DC Briggs. 'We have it all on tape.'

'And what if they frame it as some undercover work, an attempt to catch Lawson red handed, which never stuck for some reason, probably because due process was not followed,' said Walker. 'No. We need a little more. We need some hard evidence against Potts, DNA, fingerprints at the scene, that kind of thing. Something irrefutable. It could even be argued that this isn't Harry's voice on the tape, even though it sounds very much like him. People can be impersonated, after all. Did you ever watch that Phil Cool, back in the day?'

DCs Briggs and Ainscough shrugged their shoulders, while the older DI Hogarth smiled a knowing smile. 'Man, that guy could do anyone. And he had a face of bloody rubber, too, eh?' said DI Hogarth.

'I have an idea,' said Walker. 'What if Potts somehow got to Gary Cooper, had a word with him, somehow, warned him that he knew people, at the prison, who would make his life a living hell if he said anything, or end it altogether? He might have even gone the other way too, promised him some treats if he towed the line, make his stay in prison more comfortable. A man of Pott's former position would more than likely know people in high places, might have a few people owe him a few favours, if he had something on them too.'

'So, what are you suggesting, Chief?' asked DC Briggs.

'Let's start by checking the visitor logbook at the secure medical facility, see if he's had any visitors, beyond his lawyer and police security staff. Let's see if Harry Potts has been there.'

'Still wouldn't prove anything though, would it?' asked DI Hogarth. 'Harry visiting the son of his cousin's murderer is

CHAPTER FORTY

not exactly evidence of wrongdoing.'

'No,' said DI Walker. 'But at least it's a starting point. We can't show our hand just yet. We must wait for the right time, make sure Potts doesn't have anything we don't know about too. We need to know what his hand is, first.'

'You're talking about playing cards, aren't you?' said DC Ainscough. 'Poker or something. I've never really played much cards. I'm not a gambling man.'

'Well, you don't need to be, Detective,' said Walker. 'All you need to know is that we have the upper hand now, and we need to make sure it stays that way.'

* * *

'No Potts,' said Walker, looking at the visitor logbook at the Royal Preston Hospital, the medical facility that Gary Cooper was staying at, under the watchful eyes and security of Lancashire Constabulary staff members. 'But it seems that Chief Constable Harriet has been here.'

'No surprise there,' said DC Briggs, who was accompanying him, as per usual. 'Probably been following up on a few things, making sure we haven't missed anything. She was getting involved for a former colleague, after all, and probably wants to make sure everything is as it should be.'

Walker thought about it. 'Let's talk to Cooper again,' he said. He looked at the Ward Manager, who was showing them the logbook, a skinny middle-aged woman with round glasses who appeared overworked, with dark bags under her eyes. 'We need to see him.'

'That's fine,' she said. 'Right this way.'

She led them back to the room of Gary Cooper, where they'd been before, and let them go inside, closing the door after them on her way back out, with the security staff also moving outside the room with her. It was just Walker, DC Briggs, and Cooper left inside.

'Mr Cooper,' said Walker.

'You again?' he said, fidgeting, both hands cuffed to the table he was sat at. 'I've nowt else to say. Why don't you bugger off.'

Walker sat down, next to him. 'I see you've had some visitors.'

Gary shrugged his shoulders, gazed out of the second storey window.

'Chief Constable Sarah Harriet has been to see you,' said Walker. 'It's in the logbook.'

Gary looked at them. 'What? You can't just ask your colleague about it?' He started to laugh. 'You lot are a joke.'

'I will discuss the visit with her when I see her,' said Walker. 'But for now, I'm asking you.'

'Why?' asked Cooper.

'Because we want it from you,' said Walker. 'We have reason to believe you may have been blackmailed by someone, and we must do our due diligence to find out who that person is.'

'Blackmailed?' said Cooper. 'How'd you get to that?'

'Because you won't give up your attacker,' said Walker.

'Because I *didn't see them*,' said Cooper, in a sarcastic tone. 'How many times do I have to say it to you people.'

'Then if that is true, you won't mind telling us about the private conversation you had with Chief Constable Harriet.'

'It was nothing,' said Cooper, shrinking back. 'She just wanted me to go over what happened again, comparing it

CHAPTER FORTY

to the report she had. That's all.'

'Well, thank you for cooperating, Mr Cooper,' said Walker.

'Could one of you pass the jug of water before you leave?' asked Cooper.

Walker looked at DC Briggs, and Briggs looked at Cooper. 'No,' she said. 'We cannot.'

The man had tried to kill her in the most torturous way imaginable, and now he wanted her to pass him some sodding water. Walker wanted to punch him in the face, pour the bloody water on his head, and then hit him in the balls for good measure. But instead, they just stood up and exited the room.

CHAPTER FORTY-ONE

Walker and DC Briggs entered the Incident Room at Blackpool Police HQ, to be met by DI Hogarth and DC Ainscough, with Trainee Investigator Luke Stevenson and Trainee Investigator Emily Sharrock also present.

'Sir, something has come in while you've been away,' said DC Ainscough. 'About the Gary Cooper case.'

Walker looked at the two trainees that were with them. 'I don't suppose you two could run a little errand for me, could you? I have some files and some evidence that needs putting away.'

TI Sharrock frowned. 'Chief, why do you keep sending us away every time something comes up with the Gary Cooper case? Have we done something wrong?'

'No. Of course not,' said Walker. 'You've done nothing wrong. I just need these files putting away.'

'Okay, Chief,' said TI Sharrock, taking a pile of files and evidence bags from Walker, giving some to TI Stevenson to carry. 'Let's go,' she said, somewhat unhappily, and the two trainees left the room.

'What is it?' asked Walker. 'What do we have?'

'Interview Room 3,' said DC Ainscough. 'We have one Emma

CHAPTER FORTY-ONE

Shawcross, a Room Attendant at the Inn On the Prom hotel. When we interviewed her previously, she said she didn't see anything, but now she has something to add.'

'And has she given any indication as to what that is?' asked Walker.

'Not yet. I didn't push it. Wanted to get whatever she said officially recorded in a formal interview,' said DC Ainscough. 'And I thought you would want to do that.'

'You thought right,' said Walker. 'DC Briggs, Let's go to Interview Room 3, find out what this is all about.'

*

'Okay, Miss Emma Shawcross, we are now recording this conversation, for our records,' said Walker. 'I believe you came here today wanting to tell us something about the day that Gary Cooper was attacked and left for dead at the Inn on the Prom Hotel, where we believe you work as a cleaner?'

'*Room Attendant*,' she said. 'That's what they call us. But you're right. I am essentially a cleaner, although there are a few other tasks too.'

'So, what do you want to tell us?' asked Walker.

Emma ran her fingers through her hair, nervously. 'I didn't want to get in trouble, that's all. I need my job. I have a young girl, you see, Lily, three years old. It's just the two of us.'

'Go on,' said Walker.

'Well, I was having a smoke, near the fire exit of the hotel at the back. We're not supposed to, but I've been getting a bit stressed recently, and starting smoking again—not every day, just now and again, when I need it. Lily's dad had started calling again, you see, trying to see her. He hit me a couple of times, so I don't want him anywhere near her. But he's got a lawyer now, has started "proceedings", whatever that means,' she said.

'Okay. So, we understand why you were smoking, and why you don't want the hotel to know about this,' said Walker.

'They have a no-smoking policy for all staff and guests,' she said. 'I'd get in trouble.'

'And what happened, while you were smoking?' asked Walker.

'Some woman suddenly appeared, said she was conducting some checks on the building, PAT tests and something else. I don't even know what that means. So, I let her inside,' said Emma.

Walker looked at DC Briggs, and then back to Emma. 'Why didn't you just tell us this before, Emma? It could be important for our investigation,' said Walker.

'I... I guess I just panicked. I've never talked to the police before. I didn't want the hotel to find out about me smoking,' she said.

'So why didn't you just tell us and miss the part about the smoking?' asked Walker.

'Because we're also told not to open the fire doors under any circumstances except in the case of a fire, or if the fire alarms go off,' she said. 'It's policy.'

'So why are you telling us now?' asked Walker.

'Well, I just haven't been able to sleep at night since, in case this woman had anything to do with the attack,' she said. 'It's just... the right thing to do. I'll just have to find another job if I get in trouble.'

Walker smiled, as warmly as he could. 'There's no need for us to mention to the hotel that you opened this fire door,

CHAPTER FORTY-ONE

Emma,' said Walker. 'You might have to testify, but unless your boss likes attending trials... well, it's not police business to tell him about a little smoke you had. Now, this woman, can you describe her for me? Age, ethnicity, hair colour, height and weight.'

'Er... I guess middle aged, white, dark hair—brown or black—average height, average weight. Sorry, that's not very helpful, is it?' said Emma.

She'd just described what millions of women in Britain look like, but it could still come in useful by ruling out anyone not of those characteristics. 'We're going to need a little more. Can you talk to one of our forensic imaging specialists? They'll ask you a few more specific questions about her appearance, try to draw up an image. That okay?'

Emma though about it. 'I think so,' she said. 'I mean, I'll try my best.'

'Well, that's all we're asking for, Emma,' said Walker. 'And what time, approximately, did you see this woman? Can you remember?'

'I remember it was an hour or so before you and all the other police turned up. I guess it was about 12-ish then,' said Emma, 'because I was just opening up my sandwich when you arrived, and we have lunch at one o'clock.'

Walker's report logged the time of his arrival at 1:07pm. It seemed her account was accurate. 'That's great,' he said. 'Before we get the image done, can you just go over everything that was said in the exchange with this woman? That would be very helpful.'

'Well. I was startled that she was there, to begin with, as I shouldn't have been smoking, as I said, and I didn't expect to see anyone back there. There's nothing out back, you see.

Nothing at all. She said hello. Asked if she could enter through the back way since I'd opened it, said she was doing some checks on the building—PAT tests and one other that I can't remember, with an abbreviation. I didn't know what it was, and don't remember. I think it began with an "E". Anyway, I was a bit taken aback, didn't want to cause any trouble, didn't want her mentioning that I'd been smoking to the hotel manager, so I just let her inside, and that was that. We didn't say any more than that to each other,' said Emma.

'That's great,' said Walker. 'Is there anything else, anything at all? What she was wearing, any accessories, bags, accent, etc.?'

Emma gave it some thought. 'Just, a Lancashire type accent, I suppose, nothing specific. Her clothes were normal too, nothing memorable. I do remember that she had a bag though—maybe a leather handbag, black and white. That's it. That's all I remember.'

Walker nodded. 'Please stay here, and I'll send a forensic imaging specialist to join you ASAP. That will be all from me for now. Thank you for coming in. That's much appreciated.'

*

'There you go,' said Arnold Peters, the bald, ageing forensic imaging specialist with unsociable body odour that Walker had worked with several times before during his long career—a guy who'd previously been a traditional police sketch artist, before getting trained in electronic facial identification techniques. Derek Lewis, the forensic imaging specialist who'd recently worked with DC Briggs to get a current image of Gary Cooper, was now away on leave, so he'd got Arnold

CHAPTER FORTY-ONE

this time. Walker still often requested a more traditional sketch, which Arnold could provide, if he felt it needed a more human approach, but he was coming around to the speed and efficiency of digital systems, especially in time-sensitive cases like this. So, on this occasion, once again, he'd requested the digital facial composite.

They were now stood outside of Interview Room 3, and Arnold passed Walker a piece of A4 paper inside of an envelope of the same size; and he took it with both hands, like it was some precious artefact. There were moments during a case that felt big, that felt like they could make or break the case, and this was one of those moments.

'Used the Bluetooth printer in the corner for you, in case you wanted a hard copy. She did well,' said Arnold. 'Got some good detail from her. She just needed a little guidance, some sequential recall, that kind of thing. We got there in the end.'

'That's great. Thank you,' said Walker. 'That will be all.'

Arnold Peters left, leaving Walker alone in the corridor. He opened the envelope. Early impressions were often crucial with such things. What the forensic imaging specialist often did was to point the investigator in the right direction, rather than provide a definitive answer, but they had to be focussed and clear thinking on this first viewing, or it could be wasted— hence waiting until Arnold Peters had left.

He took a breath and slid out the image. What looked back at him was the unmistakable face of Chief Constable Sarah Harriet.

'Holy, bloody, shit,' he said, turning the paper back over, just for a couple of seconds, and then back again. 'Shit.' He turned the paper back over one more time, and then back again.

It seemed Chief Constable Harriet had been to the Inn on

the Prom Hotel in the timeframe of the attack on Gary Cooper, and she'd entered the back way, lying her way in, telling some nonsense about doing some checks on the building. She'd entered without invitation, and she'd likely left the same way, as nobody else had reported seeing her. It didn't look good. But why would she attack Gary Cooper, if it had indeed been her? There was clearly more at play here than met the eye. Perhaps Alison Potts, the wife of Harry Potts, had been right— maybe Harry and Chief Constable Harriet *had* been having an affair, and maybe Harriet had been doing it for him, to stop him going to prison, if Harry had been the one who killed Kevin Lawson, and Gary Cooper had seen him at the scene. But that wouldn't explain why Harry hadn't been the one to try to off Cooper himself. It just wasn't adding up.

Walker popped his head inside of the interview room, where Emma Shawcross was still sat.

'Did I do okay?' she asked, eyes wide, vulnerable.

'You did,' said Walker. 'You're free to go, Miss Shawcross. We appreciate your cooperation on this. But before you do go, could I ask you to look at a photo, and tell me whether this is the woman you saw?'

She looked at him, nodded.

Walker needed to be very careful. The facial composite didn't prove it was Chief Constable Harriet who'd been there, even if the image was a good likeness. He needed to be sure it wasn't just his mind playing tricks on him. So, he'd need Emma Shawcross to ID her actual face.

'Wait a minute,' he said.

He got on the Lancashire Constabulary website on his iPhone, trying to find a photograph of Chief Constable Harriet. He found one easily enough, took a snapshot of it—something

CHAPTER FORTY-ONE

DC Briggs had taught him to do by simultaneously pressing and releasing the side button and volume up button on his phone. Then, he found the snapshot in his photos folder and zoomed in on the face, so her police uniform couldn't be seen. He didn't want Emma knowing she was a cop, freaking out, clamming up. He needed the ID of the woman she saw verified.

He showed her his phone. 'Is this the woman you saw at the Inn at the Prom Hotel around the time that Gary Cooper was attacked?' he asked.

Emma squinted, took a good look, but just as she was about to say something, Walker must have touched the screen of the photo, because the zoomed in photo snapped back, showing Chief Constable Harriet in her full uniform, with her title above the photo.

'Chief Constable?' said Emma. She looked scared. 'I'm sorry, but I've done all I can.'

She got up, put her jacket on.

'Emma, we really need to—'

'You said I was free to go, and I'm going,' said Emma. 'I have things to do.'

She walked out of the interview room, leaving Walker kicking himself for his mistake. She was just about to confirm, or not, if Chief Constable Harriet was the woman she'd seen.

He rubbed his head, got up, got after her, knowing he needed to give it another shot.

'Miss Shawcross!' he shouted, but she was already gone.

He got outside, found her hailing a taxi and one pulled up nearby and a man popped his head out of the window.

'I'm sorry, I have to go,' said Emma, moving toward the taxi.

'Emma, wait,' said Walker. 'Off the record then. I need to

know. Is this the woman you saw?'

'I have to go,' said Emma, and she got in the taxi, and it sped away.

CHAPTER FORTY-TWO

If it hadn't been her—the woman that Emma Shawcross had seen—if it hadn't been Chief Constable Sarah Harriet, then Emma would have said so when she looked at her photograph. She'd been predicably scared when Walker had messed up the zoom function on his phone, exactly what he'd been trying to avoid. When you go up against the establishment, you'd better be damned sure you're squeaky clean, and almost nobody is. She didn't want to testify against the most powerful police officer in Lancashire, and Walker had to admit that she was probably sensible to walk away. But that didn't help his case, or his conundrum about how to move forward with this thing. He was pretty sure the woman she saw was Chief Constable Harriet, based on her reaction, but if she wasn't going to testify against her, then it meant nothing as a piece of evidence.

Walker had been home, had slept on it, somewhat uncomfortably, and was sitting outside of DC Briggs's home, waiting for her to come out, start work. While he was waiting though, he got a call—it was DI Hogarth.

'Up bright and early as usual, Detective,' said Walker.

'I'm at the station,' said DI Hogarth. 'Some new evidence has come in, regarding the Kevin Lawson murder. It's Potts.'

'What?' said Walker.

'They only found some of Harry Potts's DNA at the motorhome Lawson was killed in. On the matchbox, apparently, of all things. Perhaps he was struggling to get a light, took a glove off, maybe. Whatever happened, we've got him,' said DI Hogarth.

'You sure?' asked Walker.

'He had a sample taken years ago, to eliminate his DNA from a crime scene,' said DI Hogarth. 'So, he was in the database.'

'So, he killed Lawson to cover up his own crime,' said Walker. 'In case he squealed.'

'Apparently so,' said DI Hogarth. 'We have everything we need for a prosecution now. Are you going to pick him up?'

Walker hesitated. 'I am,' he said. 'It looks like DC Briggs and I are taking a trip to Chester. I'll see you in a few.'

* * *

'Mrs Potts?' said Walker. He was stood outside of Harry Potts's home address in Chester with DC Briggs. Should he give them any trouble, they were armed with batons, PAVA sprays, and Tasers. But Walker hoped he would come quietly, and there wouldn't even be any need for handcuffs. He hoped that the guy would come with a little dignity, if he had any left after what he'd done, that is.

'Yes?' she said.

'It's Detective Chief Inspector Jonathan Walker, and my colleague DC Briggs. We spoke on the telephone recently. Is your husband home?' said Walker.

CHAPTER FORTY-TWO

'I told you, it's *Alison*,' she said, looking perturbed, perhaps stalling for a few seconds, trying to gather her thoughts.

'Sorry. Alison. Is he home? We need to speak to him, urgently,' said Walker.

'Harry!' she shouted. 'Someone for you.'

'He was just in the kitchen,' she said, waiting, but Harry didn't appear.

'May we come inside?' said Walker.

Alison opened the door fully and let them through.

'Er, your shoes?' said Alison, ushering them to remove their footwear.

'Sorry, luv,' said Walker, thinking that if Harry ran, they'd not want to be running in their socks. 'We're in a bit of a hurry.'

Harry was stood in the kitchen, behind a block kitchen island, his hands low, out of sight.

'Harry, didn't you hear me? There's someone here to see you,' said Alison. 'A Detective—'

'I know who they are,' said Harry. 'We've met. It's a little impolite to come unannounced, isn't it?'

'Harry Potts, we are arresting you for the murders of Kevin Lawson and Sally Fielding. You do not have to say anything, but it may harm your defence if you do not mention, when questioned, something which you later rely on in court. Anything you do say may be given in evidence,' said Walker. 'Would you come with us?'

'That bastard deserved it. He was a goddamned serial killer,' he said. He brought his right hand up, onto the kitchen island, revealing that he'd been holding a knife all along. 'And so do I. I'm sorry, Sally, I'm sorry, Alison.'

And then he slit his own throat, right in front of them, blood pouring down the white shirt he had on. He got himself good, no holding back—this wasn't a cry for help—and slipped down, onto the floor.

DC Briggs immediately called it in, thinking on her toes.

'This is Detective Inspector Shelly Briggs. We have a male, mid-sixties, cut his own throat. Requesting immediate medical assistance at 31, Donville Road, Chester,' she said. 'Yes, we'll wait.'

She joined Walker, who had gone to Harry, his hand now putting pressure on the wound, trying to stem the tide of the bleeding, but not really making much impact. She did a few checks while still on the phone, testing his nostrils for any breath, opening his eyes.

'Harry? You there? The individual is unresponsive. Yes, we'll be waiting until you arrive. Thank you,' she said.

'Harry, why?' said Alison. 'What the hell did you do?' She got on the floor, near him, sobbing, holding his hand. 'You are the worst thing that ever happened to me,' she said, anger rising, before going back to the sobbing.

'It's going to be alright, Alison,' said Walker. 'Shel, take her to another room would you, help her calm down? I've got this. She doesn't need to see this.'

'Sir?' said DC Briggs.

Walker looked at Alison, who had her eyes closed now, still crying. He shook his head, to indicate that Harry Potts was not going to make it. He'd seen injuries like this before, which tended to be fifty-fifty, survival-wise. But Harry had gone deep. He'd made sure he wouldn't be coming back with that cut. No-one would survive that.

DC Briggs took Alison's hand, and slowly guided her out of the kitchen, while Walker kept his hand on Harry's wound,

CHAPTER FORTY-TWO

and he would do until the ambulance arrived. But he had little hope that he might survive.

CHAPTER FORTY-THREE

Harry Potts was pronounced dead at the scene by paramedics. He'd bled out from the interior jugular vein, and it seemed like he'd known exactly what he was doing. He didn't want to face the music, probably, whatever that music was, so he'd ended it there and then. His wife was beside herself. The poor woman had thought he was just an adulterer, but now he was a murderer too—or, at least, he would be, when it all came out. Walker had Kevin Lawson for the murder of at least three women, he had Gary Cooper for the attempted murder of DC Briggs, and possibly one other murder, to be confirmed, and he had Harry Potts for the murders of Kevin Lawson and his cousin, Sally Fielding, the latter of whom he arranged to be killed by the former. The only thing he didn't have, was someone responsible for the attempted murder of Gary Cooper—and regarding that, the only tangible evidence he had, at present, was a witness who'd provided an image with a likeness to their very own Chief Constable Sarah Harriet, of someone who had entered the Inn at the Prom Hotel via the back entrance, just prior to the time of the attack. Unfortunately, it seemed she was unwilling to testify and identify her in a court of law. It was a real mess. He considered that while the audio tape only explicitly implicated

CHAPTER FORTY-THREE

Potts, the promise of making the charges go away for Lawson might have also been made based on Lawson knowing about Potts' affair with Harriet. Perhaps that's how Harriet had got dragged into it, somehow.

Walker had just dropped by his home with DC Briggs, to get cleaned up, get a clean pair of clothes on after being stained with the blood of Harry Potts. He'd showered and changed, and DC Briggs was waiting for him in the living room.

'Come on,' said Walker.

'Don't you wanna take a little break after all that, grab a cup of tea or something, take stock?' asked DC Briggs.

'We're still on active duty, Detective,' said Walker. 'Besides, I want to go see Chief Constable Harriet, tell her the bad news—about Harry, I mean.'

DC Briggs looked at him, quizzically. 'I think she'll probably already know, sir. The whole station will, probably most of the constabulary by now. I think the top person in that organisation is likely well informed, especially since they were friends as well.'

'Well, I still want to go see her, make sure,' said Walker.

DC Briggs leaned forward in her seat, seeming ready to get up, getting a bit closer to Walker, who was stood nearby, car keys in hand.

'You're not going just to tell her about Harry's suicide, are you sir?' she said.

Walker shook his head. He wasn't getting anything past her, so there was no point even trying.

'Come on,' he said. 'I think it's time we had a good talk with our Chief Constable, tell her what's what.'

'But Chief,' said DC Briggs. 'She warned us not to pursue this, and we did, and now Harry is dead. Don't you think she'll be, you know, a little bit furious?'

'We're not going to tell her any of that,' said Walker. 'I just want to tell her that we'll be handing over this case to the Merseyside Police, to ensure impartiality and fairness. I can no longer head this investigation, as the Chief Constable herself has become a person of interest, as a result of Harry Pott's wife believing they had an affair, and the hotel cleaner providing an image that looks very much like her, of a person entering the hotel illegally just minutes before Gary Cooper's attempted murder.'

'Oh, Chief,' said DC Briggs. 'Are you sure about this?'

'I've not been sure about much with this case for quite some time,' said Walker. 'But we solved Sally Fielding's murder, which is what we were brought here to do, and her killer is now dead, along with the person who instructed it. Our work here is done where that is concerned. The attack on Gary Cooper can be treated as a separate case, for now, unless the Merseyside Police deem it to be connected to the Lawson and Potts cases—which it might well be due to Cooper being Lawson's son and all, and being involved with his crimes. But I want to tell Harriet, face-to-face, as a... courtesy.'

'A *courtesy*?' said DC Briggs, with some suspicion. 'You mean you're going to try to rattle her cage, see if she implicates herself further before we hand this over to the Mersey lot?'

'I mean... I'd just like to see what she has to say for myself,' said Walker. 'Before we move on to the next case.'

'Okay then. You know I'm always with you, no matter what,' said DC Briggs.

'Yes, yes you are, Detective Briggs. Let's go.'

CHAPTER FORTY-THREE

* * *

Walker and DC Briggs were travelling to the home of Chief Constable Harriet. They'd called her office to set up a meeting, but staff at the Lancashire Constabulary HQ in Preston had told them she'd gone home, having learned of Harry Pott's suicide, said she needed a little time to process it, make arrangements. Walker told them he had something for her, that he wanted to post it through her letterbox, so they'd given him her address, not having anything to be suspicious of with a fellow officer, and another high ranking one at that. He wanted to catch her off-guard, see how she really was. Although the case would be handed over to the Merseyside Police in the long run, he still wanted to know exactly what kind of involvement Harriet had in all this, how deeply she was involved.

'Here we are,' he said. 'This is the address we were given.'

'Nice place,' said DC Briggs, and she was right. It was a modern, detached house, likely at least four bedrooms, with a double garage and two expensive-looking cars parked out front.

They got out, approached the house.

'Is that smoke?' said DC Briggs. 'Smells like it.'

Walker looked through one of the windows of the house. All looked normal.

'Probably just one of the neighbours, burning some garden waste, or having a barbeque or something,' said Walker.

'In this weather?' said DC Briggs. She was right of course, but not all British BBQ enthusiasts were put off by the weather.

Walker knocked on the door—his customary three raps.

Then he waited. No answer. One more time: nothing. He walked over to a side gate, tried it. It opened and he motioned for DC Briggs to follow.

They found Chief Constable Harriet stood at the bottom end of a long garden, her back to them, stood over a rusty-looking steel drum, smoke billowing out from it. She'd obviously not heard them approaching, so Walker got a little closer, curious as to what she was doing. He was close enough now to see that she was holding something in her hand, a VHS video tape, and there was a box half full of them on the floor next to her, right by a black and white leather handbag; just like Emma Shawcross —the cleaner at the Inn at the Prom Hotel—had described. She started pulling the magnetic tape strip out of the VHS tape, cutting it with some scissors, and then dropping it into the fire, letting it burn, before dropping the rest of the cassette shell and its various components. She slightly turned, picked up another tape, when she caught sight of Walker and DC Briggs, a little startled. She'd obviously been crying.

'Chief Constable Harriet,' said Walker. 'I'm sorry. There was no answer at the door and we smelled smoke, thought we should check everything was okay.'

She wiped her face, dried the tears, and her face turned to stone—probably the mask she wore at work being mentally put on.

'DCI Walker,' she said, angrily. 'What are you doing here, *at my home*? You can't come here unannounced like this. It's just not how things are done.'

'I was told you'd been informed about Harry,' said Walker. 'Sad news.'

She just stood there, tape in hand, frozen, glaring at him.

'What do you have there?' asked Walker.

CHAPTER FORTY-THREE

'Just clearing out some rubbish,' said Chief Constable Harriet, dropping the VHS tape she was holding into the fire, this time not removing the magnetic tape strip first, and then picking another one up. 'I like to do this when my mind's a mess. It helps me calm, not that it's any of your business what I do in my own home. Now, if you wouldn't mind—'

'No labels,' said Walker.

'What?' said Chief Constable Harriet.

'On the tapes—there are no labels,' repeated Walker. 'People used to write on the side of the boxes, or on the sticker on the side of the tape, to remind them what they'd recorded. You only have numbers.'

'Do you value your job, Detective?' asked Chief Constable Harriet. 'You're not welcome here. I did not give you permission to enter my premises. Now, kindly see yourself out.'

Walker took a few steps toward her.

'*Sir*,' whispered DC Briggs, but it sounded more like a warning, a caution to tread carefully.

'Could I see one of those tapes,' asked Walker.

'*Detective Walker!*' said Chief Constable Harriet. 'You're overstepping here. Whatever it is will have to wait. I'm not currently on duty.'

'I'm afraid I'm not here as your subordinate,' said Walker. 'I'm here as a Detective Chief Inspector for the Lancashire Constabulary, investigating a person of interest in an attempted murder.'

He let it settle for a second.

'And that person of interest is *me?*' she said. 'Is that what you're saying. Is that why you're here?'

'I'm going to need to see the tapes,' said Walker.

'Look,' said Chief Constable Harriet, appearing flustered, more scared than angry now. 'Even if that's the case, then there are impartiality issues to consider. The case must be passed to the Independent Office for Police Conduct, and the IOPC will then likely delegate the investigation to another police force to avoid any possible internal bias. You should know that.'

'I do know that,' said Walker. 'Merseyside Police will be taking things from here. I just came here to inform you, face-to-face, as a courtesy. But now I also have a duty to seize any evidence for the Merseyside Police, if presented.'

'Why am I a person of interest, Detective?' asked Chief Constable Harriet.

'There was a cleaner at the Inn at the Prom Hotel,' said Walker. 'She saw someone come in the rear fire exit in the timeframe of the Gary Cooper attempted murder. She's since provided a description of that person to a forensic imaging specialist—it looks just like you.'

'And has she identified me?' she asked. Walker didn't respond. He didn't want to tell her about his blunder with the zoomed in photo of her face, that the witness had clammed up. 'Oh, come on, Detective Walker. You know as well as I that a sketch or a facial composite like that could be anyone. The mind sees what it wants to see.'

'Harry's wife, Alison Potts, also thinks you were having an affair with Harry,' said Walker. 'We have hard evidence that Harry put a hit on his own cousin, used a suspected serial killer to do his dirty work, let him get away to kill again. If you were involved with him, romantically, and sexually, then we need to investigate that, to rule out any involvement in these crimes.'

CHAPTER FORTY-THREE

'You have nothing on me, Detective,' she said. 'You shouldn't have come here. You'll regret this. All that will take time, and the Merseyside Police will need to get a warrant if they want to search my premises.'

'Well, they're not here, and I am, and I'm going to need to see those videotapes,' said Walker, his tone firmer now, demanding.

'You don't have my permission to enter my home,' said Chief Constable Harriet. 'Or to look through my things. Now, if you have no warrant, I must ask you to leave.'

'Open fields at the back,' said Walker, 'No fence. Just a few low-lying bushes.'

'If you don't bloody leave right now, Detective, I swear, I will destroy you!' said Chief Constable Harriet, now full of rage, eyes bulging, veins just about ready to pop.

'I wouldn't say it's exactly enclosed,' said DC Briggs.

'Which means we don't need a warrant to search the garden,' said Walker. 'Especially since we haven't had to break any locks to gain entry, and we were just investigating a possible fire—which by the way, is illegal in itself: the *Environmental Protection Act 1990* outlaws the burning of plastics in one's home or garden. You should know that.'

'I will finish you...' said Chief Constable Harriet, but this time her words were less rageful, and more fearful. She picked up the box half full of tapes, was about to throw the lot in the fire, but Walker grabbed it, prevented her from doing so—them both having two hands on the box now.

'Let go!' said Harriet.

'What are we going to find on these, Chief Constable?' asked Walker.

Chief Constable Harriet let go of the box, her shoulders

slumping forward, the weight of the world seeming to be on them.

'He's a bloody coward,' she said.

'I'm sorry?' asked Walker.

'Harry. He's a coward, killing himself like that, leaving it all to me,' she said, before looking at DC Briggs. 'I want to talk to Detective Walker alone, if you wouldn't mind, dear.'

DC Briggs looked at Walker. 'Chief?'

'It's okay,' said Walker. 'You go and wait in the car. I've got this.'

'You sure?' asked DC Briggs.

'Go,' said Walker, so she did, cautiously exiting the garden the way they'd come, looking back several times as she went.

'So?' said Walker.

'I have a daughter, Detective,' she said. 'I need to think of her now, how all of this is going to affect her. Her dad left, has another family now. We're not on bad terms. She can probably go and stay with them, if need be. But she needs to know that her mum is not a monster. It will affect her. I'm not a monster, Detective. I just went through a difficult time and made some bad decisions.'

'Well, that's not for me to decide,' said Walker. 'What did you do?'

Chief Constable Harriet thought about it. 'It's more what I didn't do,' she said. 'It's all here on these goddamned tapes.'

'What is?' asked Walker, feeling that familiar sense of dark foreboding that he sometimes got whenever something grotesque was about to be revealed—call it instinct, or a premonition, or whatever; he knew he wasn't going to like it, not one bit.

'I only just got them back off Harry—the tapes. He'd been

CHAPTER FORTY-THREE

blackmailing me with them, for years, but he finally gave them up,' she said. 'I didn't know he was going to kill himself though. I really didn't. I'd have tried to stop him if I knew, even after everything he did.'

'And what did *you* do?' asked Walker.

She shook her head. 'I worked so very hard to try to put this right,' she said. 'In my job, I mean. I thought if I can keep stopping people from getting hurt, then it might just make up for what I did.'

'And what did you do?' asked Walker. Chief Constable Harriet took a deep breath. 'Start at the beginning?'

'It was... twenty odd years ago. The first time it happened, it was late. We'd been watching England play Argentina in the World Cup finals, and they lost on penalties. Harry was beside himself,' she said. 'Bloody Beckham and his petulance. Red card.'

'1998,' said Walker. She looked at him. 'That game was in 1998. Michael Owen scored a wonder goal. They're still replaying it on the telly.'

'Yeah. That sounds right. 1998. I was with Harry at Sally Fielding's parents' house. He watched her every Tuesday, while they went out on a "Date Night". They were having marital issues apparently,' she said.

'And were you and Harry married, at the time?' asked Walker. 'To other people, I mean.'

'I wasn't. But Harry was already married to Alison. Two years. He told me it wasn't going well, and I liked him, so we started having an affair,' she said. 'The only time and place we could really meet, comfortably, was at Sally's house every Tuesday. I'd come in when he told me she'd fallen asleep. We thought if she woke up and saw me, and said anything, we'd

249

just say Harry left something at work, and I was dropping it off for him on my way home. It seemed like we had a watertight alibi.'

'Go on,' said Walker.

'There were two sofas, and on the night of the football, Sally fell asleep on one of them,' she said. 'She was sleeping like a log, so we just fooled around next to her. Harry said the risk excited him, and we were drinking and taking drugs to take the edge off work stuff, so I just went with it because I really liked him. He'd been working in vice, dealing with all sorts of dark shit—you know how it is. He'd confiscated some ecstasy off some kid in a club, just a small amount, hadn't taken him in. So, we were a bit loved up, just trying to let off some steam. Also, I suppose I found it all kind of exciting too—a bit kinky—and the truth was, I wanted his wife to find out, because I wanted to be with him. So, I didn't mind if Sally woke up and saw us. That was how it started, anyhow.'

'How what started?' asked Walker. He literally had her over a barrel, and it seemed she was ready to tell him everything. It seemed like she needed to get it all off her chest, after decades of keeping it to herself, locked inside, festering. It was surprising it hadn't made her ill.

'The... *abuse*,' she said, almost whispering it. 'I still don't completely understand how it happened, really. Things just spiral, perspective gets lost, especially when you're wasted like that.'

'Have a try,' urged Walker. 'Explain.'

'Well, the fooling around turned into full sex, actually, next to Sally—both of us properly wasted. I think I must have forgotten she was there. But then she woke up. Harry freaked, started bargaining with her, said he'd let her try a pill and have a drink if she kept quiet. So, she did. Things started getting a bit touchy-feely soon after that, as Harry and I were already horny from the sex we hadn't finished. Then Sally started canoodling with us, and it went from there. Before I realised what was happening, she'd somehow joined us, and we were all naked. Harry said it was too late anyway, whatever we did, encouraged me to go with it, said she was old enough, that they weren't even blood cousins, that she was adopted. Like I said, I'd been drinking and taking drugs, and I was ready to believe just about anything to be with Harry. I was completely smitten with him. I never asked how old she was—she looked like she *could* be sixteen. When I found out she was just thirteen, later, I was mortified.'

'And this happened just the once?' asked Walker.

'No,' said Chief Constable Harriet, looking down, unable to make eye contact with Walker. 'I told Harry it could never happen again. We had a big serious discussion about it the following week over some drinks—I was stressed out about it you see. Sally had gone to bed in her room this time, and Harry and I both agreed it was just a stupid mistake. Once it was all settled, we had a few more drinks, and eventually took some E again to lighten the mood. Harry told me everything would go back to how it was before, and I believed him. I wanted to keep seeing him. But then Sally woke up, came out of her room, naked, saying she didn't want to be left out, that she was lonely. I was wasted and went with it again. It just felt too loving and good to be wrong. It somehow became a weekly thing. The comedown was awful, though, and it made me drink more and take even more drugs—and so the cycle continued. I think it all really excited Harry. He said there was no harm in it, that she was enjoying it too, that it was just a bit of consensual fun. When I said I wasn't sure, he said that *maybe we shouldn't see each other this week*, and I needed to see him, like a drug—I was addicted—so I just said "Yes". He said I was so exciting, and he felt I'd do anything for him. I guess he was right. The pressures of work had been getting to me, at the time, and I needed a weekly release, to take the pressure off. I'd been drinking a lot, every day, even on the job, and looking back now I know I was an alcoholic back then—although I know that isn't an excuse for what we did. I was on medication too. I was a real mess. I don't think I was thinking straight. I was just surviving. I hardly even remembered what happened every week. It was all like a bad dream.'

'What about the videotapes?' asked Walker.

'Things escalated,' she said, shaking her head. 'He started to film what we did, said he wanted to watch it back when we couldn't be together. Said far worse things happened in vice, that at least *we* weren't hurting anyone. I was too far gone at this stage. I must have been brainwashed, or had just gone too far down the rabbit hole and couldn't get out. I couldn't understand why Sally kept participating, convinced myself that she'd been enjoying it as much as I had. I didn't drink as much one day, and realised that she was out of it too, completely wasted, just as much as I had been. I started to look around, watch Harry a little more closely. I saw him put something in one of Sally's drinks, so I demanded to know what it was. He told me it was a little GHB—liquid ecstasy. He'd been spiking her drinks—and maybe mine too, getting us completely out of it.'

'I see,' said Walker.

'In lower doses, it can increase feelings of euphoria, libido, relaxation, and lower inhibitions,' she said. 'I was drinking alcohol too, so the combination was probably quite powerful. In higher doses, it can also intoxicate, cause memory loss, lead to impaired judgement and risky behaviour. That's why it's been labelled as a "date rape drug". I believe he'd been spiking Sally's supper with this in large quantities before I arrived, prepping her.'

'So, why didn't you just give him up then? Turn him in?' asked Walker. 'He'd been drugging the both of you, getting you to engage in abhorrent sexual acts, and filming it. You were both victims.'

'He'd already recorded a couple of our sessions, on these,' she said, gently kicking the box of VHS tapes. 'It was around the time when people had started uploading porn on the Internet. The whole world would be able to see, and we'd never get it back. I'd never live it down, and it would affect Sally's whole life too. Plus, despite everything, I still liked him. No, I *loved* him, was completely obsessed. I can see that now. But I couldn't then. It was a raw, animal instinct that kept me going, but deep down, I knew it was wrong, and it ate me up. I was split, right down the middle, between hating him and loving him.'

'And then what happened?' asked Walker, wondering what her endgame was, whether she had anything up her sleeve, whether she might attempt to kill herself too like Harry had, once she'd got everything off her chest, used him as her Confessor.

'I told him it wasn't right, said we shouldn't involve her anymore, that I wanted him all to myself. He showed me the tapes—said if I told anyone, I'd be in a lot of trouble. Told me she wasn't sixteen after all, like he'd told me before, and that she was only thirteen. He'd lied. My mouth almost hit the floor with that, even after a few drinks. It was much worse than I'd thought. He said it was too late now, and that if I didn't carry on, he'd send a tape showing just me and her to the media. I'd be humiliated, finished. I'd lose my job, go to prison, most likely, lose my family, everything. It wasn't just that though. I can't really explain it. He had a real hold on me. It was like he owned me. I agreed it was too late, and I still, for reasons I can't explain, wanted him to be happy, to keep being with him, so I just drank more, numbed myself, and kept going. I felt like I had no way out. If I didn't keep doing it my life would be over. So, we made a new videotape every week, doing riskier and riskier things, more extreme acts. It just got so out of control. I didn't know what I was doing any more, didn't know right from wrong—kept trying to convince myself we were doing more good than bad. My moral compass was stamped on, broken. I'd stepped over a line and couldn't get back. I know how it looks. It seemed that he was giving Sally so much GHB that she never remembered a sodding thing. I felt like the only choice I had was to keep going. I even thought about suicide a time or two. I just made sure I was drunk enough not to care.'

'You participated in the sexual abuse of a child,' said Walker. 'And then when she grew up, you conspired to have her killed. Isn't that right? You ruined a person's life, and the lives of her family and friends. You should have put a stop to it, no matter what.'

'When your back's to the wall, DCI Walker, you'll do just about anything to keep your life,' she said. 'Especially when you have so much to lose.' She threw her arms up, gesturing to her house, her garden. 'Look, I did it for my daughter, so

CHAPTER FORTY-THREE

she might have a normal life. You have kids, right, so you'll know—we'll do almost anything for them.'

'Almost anything,' said Walker. 'But not that. Not if their lives are not in immediate danger.'

'I felt that it was, if everything came out. I'll come willingly,' said Chief Constable Harriet. 'Would you not put the handcuffs on in front of the neighbours, as a professional courtesy?'

'I guess I can do that,' said Walker. 'But if you try anything...'

'I won't try anything, Detective. You have my word,' she said.

Walker stopped. 'Did you put the frighteners on Gary Cooper, after you tried to kill him. Did you warn him off, somehow, make sure he didn't ID you?'

'We made a deal,' she said. 'He wouldn't give me up, and I'd help him out in prison, do him some favours.'

Walker had thought as much, but it was good to have it confirmed, have all the loose ends tied off for once.

'Sarah Harriet, I'm arresting you for the suspected murder of Kevin Lawson, for conspiracy to murder Sally Fielding, for the attempted murder of Gary Cooper, and the sexual abuse of a minor. You do not have to say anything, but it may harm your defence if you do not mention when questioned something which you later rely on in court. Anything you do say may be given in evidence,' said Walker.

'Bit late for that, isn't it, Detective?' she said with a wry smile. 'It's okay. I'll provide a full confession. It's time to tell the truth about all this, come clean. It's been eating me up inside.'

'And your daughter,' said Walker. 'What time is she due home?'

Sarah looked at her watch. 'In about three hours,' she said.

'You can make some calls down at the station then,' said Walker. 'Arrange for her pickup and care.'

Sarah began to cry dry tears, her lip quivering. 'I don't know how it came to this,' she said. 'The last twenty years have been a blur, almost like a bad dream, until recently. Ava is the only thing that has kept me going, the last few. I almost started drinking again, but couldn't—because of what I did, and knowing what that can lead to.'

'We really have to go now,' said Walker. 'If you wouldn't mind, Chief Constable.'

CHAPTER FORTY-FOUR

'Where is she?' asked DI Hogarth. They were all back at Blackpool Police HQ—Walker, DI Hogarth, DC Briggs, and DC Ainscough. It had become almost like home in the past few weeks, what with the Blackpool riots and serial killer case they had there, and now this nearby in Lytham.

'In a holding cell, of course,' said Walker. 'She's no longer our Chief Constable. She's a criminal who's going to be charged for multiple counts of murder and child abuse.'

'Well, I never saw that coming,' said DI Hogarth. 'Jesus. The press is gonna be all over this thing. We'll be a laughing stock. Worse than that—we'll lose the respect and trust of the general public. She's right screwed us over; our *great leader*.'

'Harry Potts was the real evil bastard here. She just went along with it, tried to protect herself and her daughter,' said Walker, surprised he was defending her after everything she'd done. It was though, Harry, who'd been the sexual pervert, the incestuous paedophile. He'd drugged her too, got her to do things she wouldn't normally have had she been in her right mind. She'd been intoxicated—a combination of alcohol and drugs. The problem was that when she'd found out, and realised what was happening, she didn't put a stop to it. That was her crime. She participated, for weeks and months, and then years later, having got away with it for so long, she helped to cover it all up by conspiring to murder Sally Fielding, by killing Kevin Lawson, and by attempting to kill the person who saw her and Harry Potts at the scene—his son, Gary Cooper. It was a messed-up situation, and she'd made some very bad decisions along the way, but Walker still believed she wasn't a bad person. She'd just got sucked into a quagmire and couldn't get out. She'd tried to survive, at the expense of others, and tried to give her daughter a good, normal life. She'd somehow convinced herself that what she was doing was for the best, the lesser of two evils. 'I'm sorry, I don't mean to defend her. I'm just saying that Harry was the worst of the two of them.'

'Why do you women always fall for these bad guys?' said DC Ainscough.

'*Us women?*' said DC Briggs. 'I'm sorry. What century are you from?'

'I just mean... I've seen it too many times on the force now—women who fall for these criminal types, get sucked into their madness, get themselves in trouble,' said DC Ainscough. 'I just don't get what they see in them. What's wrong with a good, reliable, caring chap?'

'What? Like you?' asked DC Briggs.

'Harry was one of us, at the time,' said Walker. 'A copper. She thought she was falling for a copper, not a bad guy. And by the time she found out, it was too late.'

'Utilitarianism has a lot to answer for,' said DC Ainscough.

'You... till... what?' said Walker, pretending he didn't know what it meant, but he really did, of course. 'That's a big word for such a young detective.'

CHAPTER FORTY-FOUR

'Utilitarianism,' said DC Ainscough. 'She probably thought much more good would be done by her staying out of prison and doing her job, getting criminals off the streets. She stopped many more crimes than she committed. There's no doubt about that. That's how she probably justified it to herself. That she was doing the greatest amount of good for the greatest number of people possible.'

'You're right,' said Walker, having already just had a similar thought himself, but he'd let him have it. 'She alluded to as much. Nice insight there, philosopher Ainscough.'

DC Ainscough sported a rare smile, usually being very serious. 'Thanks,' he said.

'Maybe that's why Jimmy Savile did so much charity work,' said Walker. 'To try to make up for his abhorrent crimes.'

'Wasn't that just a cover, so he could gain entry to all those hospitals,' said DC Briggs. 'What is wrong with these people? Are they just wired wrong.'

Walker shrugged and picked up one of the VHS cassette tapes from the box that they'd taken from Sarah Harriet's garden.

'You're not really going to watch all that shit, are you, Chief?' said DC Briggs. 'Can't you just leave it in the hands of the CPS now?'

'Afraid not,' said Walker. 'One of us is going to have to watch this lot, log it, document it as evidence. We can't just take the word of the suspect. If these were to be blank for some reason—if they'd degraded over time or something—then we might not have enough to prosecute, at least for that particular crime.'

'Once you've seen that stuff, sir, you can't ever *un-see* it. You do know that, right?' said DC Briggs.

'Don't worry. I've already seen my share of the unseeable, and I'm still standing. I'll be alright,' said Walker. 'I can handle it.'

'Are you talking about Rocky V?' said DI Hogarth, seemingly trying to lighten the mood. 'Now that was bloody unseeable.'

'DC Ainscough, could you see if there's a VHS video player somewhere, and a TV, so I can take a look at these?' asked Walker.

'I think there's one in the storage room,' said DI Hogarth. 'We kept it for viewing evidence just like this.'

'I'm sorry,' said DC Ainscough. 'I don't know how to set one of those up. It was before my time, really, all that VHS stuff, tapes as big as bricks and all that. I'm more a CD and DVD kind of guy.'

DI Hogarth got up, struggling to his feet. 'I'll do it,' he said. 'Done my time around those things. Should be easy.'

'Thanks,' said Walker, but he wasn't looking forward to his task one bit. It would be a difficult watch. These things—child abuse cases—always were.

* * *

Walker turned the tape off. He'd seen enough—enough to ID Harry Potts, Sarah Harriet, and Sally Fielding, all engaged in sexual acts together, drugged and incoherent. Harry was a monster. He'd known exactly what he was doing; the only one that did out of the three of them. Kevin Lawson, used as a pawn by Harry to kill his cousin, had been a different kind of beast, but a monster all the same. His first victim, a Cynthia

CHAPTER FORTY-FOUR

Roberts, had also now been found and identified nearby the other three bodies, taking his body count to four—that they knew of.

He bagged the tape, marked it as evidence against Sarah Harriet. She'd have called her daughter by now, told her what was happening—or, at least, some of it. The girl would hopefully be home with her father now, where she'd likely be staying for the foreseeable future. Her mum was not coming home, not anytime soon, anyhow.

Walker thought about his own daughter, how he might feel if she went through something like that, drugged and sexually abused by a family member, over a considerable period. And then, when she was old enough, and brave enough, to do something about it, her abusers had talked a serial killer into making her his next victim. It was just awful. If that was his daughter, he'd kill them all, and then probably himself too. So, it was probably a good thing that Kevin Lawson and Harry Potts were dead. That was one less thing for Sally Fielding's family to concern themselves with. But Sarah Harriet was still alive, and it was her that would be facing the music for all this. They'd need to be told, what was going on—Sally's family—and Walker wanted to be the one to tell them. It was only right it should come from him. He'd been charged with finding Sally's killer, after all, and that he had. Little did he know that her murderer would turn out to be one of their own—Sally's own sodding cousin, Harry Potts, with their very own Chief Constable, heading the operation, as his accomplice. It was mind blowing.

* * *

'Mr and Mrs Fielding?' said Walker. He was stood outside of Sally Fielding's parents' residence, a modest semi-detached affair, both stood in the porch. 'I'm Detective Walker, and my colleague DC Briggs. I'm so sorry for your loss. May we come in for a few minutes?'

They led Walker inside, followed by DC Briggs.

'Ken and Sheila,' said Ken, an extremely pale and unhealthy-looking man, his skin slightly grey. 'You can call us that, I mean. No need for formalities. Not after what you've done for us. Please, take a seat.' They'd been led to a dining room, and Walker and DC Briggs took the offer, got settled, as Ken and Shiela joined them.

'I'm here to tell you that we've found your daughter's murderer, and that Sally's body will now be released to the family so you can have a proper funeral,' said Walker.

Shiela broke down, and Ken held her hand on the table.

'Oh, that's great,' he said. 'Really great. Finally, we can put our Sally to rest.'

'I never thought you'd find her,' said Shiela, still crying. 'After all these years. I never thought she'd be found.'

'Well, we have found her,' said Walker. 'And those responsible will be held accountable.'

'Who was it?' asked Ken. 'Who bloody did this to her, our daughter, our sweet little girl?'

'This might come as a bit of a shock to you both,' said Walker. 'It's come as a bit of a shock to all of us, to be honest. But... I'm afraid there was more than one person involved in all this.'

'What?' said Sheila. 'What do you mean?'

'Do you remember when Harry used to babysit for Sally, when she was thirteen?' asked Walker.

'How do you know about that?' asked Shiela. 'That was

CHAPTER FORTY-FOUR

years ago. Long before she disappeared. What's that got to do with anything? *Seriously, what has that got to do with anything?*'

'Just listen to what they have to say,' said Ken, his face serious, his tone strict.

'I'm afraid we've recovered evidence that shows that Harry Potts sexually abused Sally, over a significant period of time,' said Walker.

'He did *what?*' said Shiela. 'I'll bloody kill him!'

'I'm afraid that will not be necessary,' said Walker. 'Harry Potts committed suicide when we tried to arrest him. He's dead.'

Ken breathed a sigh of relief. 'Well, good riddance,' he said.

'Who else was involved?' asked Shiela. 'You said there was more than one person. And what does this have to do with our Sally's death? Did Harry do it?'

'Harry was investigating a serial murderer called Kevin Lawson. He had something on him. And when Sally threatened to go to the police, tell them what Harry did to her, he used Kevin, got him to kill her,' said Walker.

'This is unbelievable,' said Ken, shaking his head.

'Well, actually, I'm afraid there's more,' said Walker. 'Harry had an accomplice.' Ken's eyes went a little wider as he was listening. 'Her name was Sarah Harriet. She'd been having an affair with Harry. He drugged both of them—Sally and Sarah—and they participated in sexual acts together, which he recorded.'

Shiela began to cry even more, unable to take it all in, overwhelming her.

'That's not all. I'm really sorry to tell you all of this. Sarah was our Chief Constable, who'd been heading the investigation. She's now in custody, being charged with conspiracy to murder, and the murder of Kevin Lawson.'

Shiela looked at Walker now, dead in the eyes. 'She killed him, the man who murdered our Sally?'

'She did,' said Walker. 'She thought he was going to turn them in, for the part they played, so she killed him.'

'Well, everyone involved is now either dead or in prison,' said Ken. 'So that's good enough for us, isn't it, Shiela?'

Shiela slowly nodded. 'I suppose so. I mean, thank you, Detective Walker. Sorry, I'm just shell-shocked with all of this. We're very grateful for what you've done, for bringing our Sally home, and finding justice for her. I'm just glad it's finally all over. It is all over, isn't it?'

'I'm sorry to put you through this. But I'm afraid not everyone involved has been put to justice yet,' said Walker, letting it settle for a second. He took out his phone, started to load a video up, ready for viewing.

'What?' said Shiela, confused, looking at her husband.

'We don't need to see any of this,' said Ken. 'We've had enough. We've been through more than anyone should.'

'Just... humour me,' said Walker. 'This is a video of one of the babysitting sessions between Sally and Harry. As you can see, this is yourselves, coming home, with a video still rolling. He must have hidden it, on a bookshelf, or something. You disappear, Shiela, carrying your sleeping daughter to her bed, no doubt, leaving Harry and you, Ken, alone. There's a brief discussion between the two of you, which I've transcribed here.' He took out a piece of A4 paper from his briefcase, gave it to Ken and Shiela, and kept a copy for himself. 'Can you see?'

The paper read:
Ken: How did it go?

CHAPTER FORTY-FOUR

Harry: Great. Here's a copy last week's tape, all edited for you.
Ken: Great. Keep 'em coming.
Harry: And the money?
Ken: Oh, yeah. Almost forgot.

'Can you see, on the video on my phone, Sheila, how your husband, Ken, gives Harry a pile of cash. This is not an amount that would be given for babysitting. This is for the tape he just gave him, one of the tapes that documents this abuse,' said Walker. 'These are pornographic tapes involving a minor.'

'This is...' said Ken, stuttering. 'This is not what it looks like, Shiela. They've twisted it. I didn't know anything about this. It was just a pirated film, probably "The Matrix" or something. We used to hand them around back then, share what we had.'

'Harry was making the films for you, wasn't he, Ken? And you were paying him well for it. There must have been several hundred pounds there.'

'Ken,' said Shiela, now out of her mind, it all being too much for her. 'You didn't, did you?'

'We're going to need to search your premises,' said Walker. 'Why don't you save us the trouble? Are we going to find some videos like the ones we already have?'

Ken shook his head, looking like he might run, or fight, but then his shoulders slumped forward in defeat, an action Walker had seen many times before. 'She was a bloody slut, was what she was,' he spat. 'You both are.' His face had changed now, his mask having fallen off, leaving behind something vile, something repugnant and dirty. He was like a different person.

'Ken Fielding, I'm arresting you for conspiring to sexually abuse a minor, in your daughter, Sally Fielding, and for recording illegal pornographic materials involving a minor. You do not have to say anything, but it may harm your defence if you do not mention when questioned something which you later rely on in court. Anything you do say may be given in evidence. Do you understand?' said Walker.

'Screw all of you,' said Ken. 'I did nothing, just watched a few vids, that's all. It's Harry that did it.'

Shiela took the opportunity to slap Ken, hard, in the face, and then proceeded to hit him in the body, over and over, until Walker and DC Briggs could get up and restrain her—although they weren't in much of a hurry to do so. With that done, Walker immediately put Ken in handcuffs, not wanting to take any further risks, after what Harry did to himself.

'Mrs Fielding, is there anyone I can call, to give you support, I mean?' said DC Briggs. 'I don't want to leave you here alone after all this.'

'Just... get him out of here,' she said. 'I want to be alone for a while.'

'We're going to have to search the premises now,' said DC Briggs. 'For evidence. Is there anyone you can stay with, for a short time?'

'Donna and Peter, next door. We're pretty close,' said Shiela, struggling to breathe properly. 'I could go over there for a while, if they're home, if you need me too. They should be. Their car is there.'

'Okay, then, Shiela,' said DC Briggs. 'We'll be taking your husband away now. Do you understand?'

'Yes, I understand,' she said, glaring at him, looking like she wanted to kill him. 'Good riddance. Bastard. I don't know who you are. You dirty, vile, horrible, *bastard!*'

CHAPTER FORTY-FIVE

'Could you pass the wine, Jon?' said DC Briggs. Her and Walker were off-duty now, having a meal together at The Elephant, an Indian restaurant in Chorley. 'It still feels weird, calling you "Jon", you know.'

Walker passed her the red wine, which she'd already finished a glass of during the starter of their meal—some poppadoms, a chutney tray, and a mixed meat starter. 'Take it easy, Shel. I don't want to have to carry you home.'

'What? You saying I'm fat?' she said, grinning. She liked having him on, winding him up a bit. It was part of their relationship dynamic, although Walker wasn't entirely sure what that relationship was anymore, or where it might be heading. They'd had lunch before, but never dinner. Dinner was an altogether different ball game, and with just the two of them, it felt almost romantic—especially since the waiter had placed some candles and a single flower on their table.

'Course not. But you know how my back is,' he said. He meant it wasn't good. She'd seen him hopping over fences and walls when they'd been in pursuit of a suspect—he was hardly in peak condition.

'I do indeed,' said Shel.

Walker looked at her. He wanted to say something. When

she'd been kidnapped, when her life was in danger, he didn't know what he was going to do if anything happened to her. He wasn't just worried about his colleague—he had feelings for her. He just wasn't entirely sure what those feelings were.

'Look, Shel. When you were... taken... I was really worried. Like, *really* worried,' said Walker.

'Yeah. So was I,' she said. '*Really* worried.'

'No. You don't understand. I've been concerned about colleagues before. But that wasn't like this. It wasn't like Hogarth or DC Ainscough were in danger. This was different. This was... *you*.'

'It was,' she said. 'What are you trying to say, Jon?'

'I don't know,' he said. 'I guess, in a roundabout way, I'm saying that I care about you.'

'I know that,' she said. 'I care about you too. Hey, you're not going to bloody propose, are you?' She was joking, of course: the candlelight, the meal, the music.

'Yeah, as if,' he said, brushing it off. 'Hey, we're just two work colleagues having a meal after a traumatic ordeal.'

'Who care about each other,' she said.

'Who care about each other,' he repeated. He raised a glass. 'To us.'

'To us?' she said.

He was confusing her. This wasn't his intention. He just wanted to spend a little time with her, away from work. 'To good friends,' he said, to clarify.

'To good friends,' she repeated, but she was speaking slowly, without much conviction or certainty.

She tucked into her food, face down, looking at the plate. 'I knew you'd save me,' she said, without looking up. 'I just knew it.'

CHAPTER FORTY-FIVE

They sat there in silence for a minute or two, just eating, taking in the ambiance. She took another gulp of her wine, then topped up her glass once more.

'I mean it. I'm not carrying you home,' said Walker.

She shrugged her shoulders. 'Well, I could always sleep at yours if push comes to shove, couldn't I?' Still not looking at him, focussing on the food, nonchalant.

Walker wasn't entirely sure what she meant by that, and he took a drink too, topped his own glass up. They were sharing a taxi, after all, so why not have another one?

They got eye contact, and he smiled at her, and she smiled back—there was a warmth to that smile, something more than just good friends, he was sure of it. But he wasn't sure if his feelings were rooted in his mentor relationship with her, or something of a more romantic nature. What he was sure of was that if it was just a silly schoolboy crush, he certainly didn't want to damage their professional relationship by indulging in that. It was too precious. Then again, if it were something deeper, he also didn't want to miss out on a chance of happiness. So, it was difficult. He was just about to say something, to really open up to her, take a chance, when his phone rang. It was his wife, Dawn—the woman who he was currently separated from, and had been for some time.

'Excuse me. I have to get this,' he said, taking the call. 'Hi Dawn. Yes, of course I could... okay. Sure. I'll see you soon then.' He hung up the phone. She wanted to see him. She hadn't asked him to come over for months, said there was something she wanted to talk about, about them. This was what he'd been waiting for. He'd almost given up hope, hence him having this meal with Shelly.

'That was Dawn,' he said to Shelly.

'Yeah. I got that,' she said.

'She wants me to come over. I should go, after this, I mean,' said Walker. 'It might be important.'

'Look, if you want to go now, that's—'

'No, no,' said Walker. 'We can finish the meal.'

'Jon, I know how much you want to get your family back together. You've been waiting for this for ages. Go,' she urged. 'It's alright.'

Walker thought about it, but not for too long.

'Thanks, Shel,' he said. 'You're right. I really should go. I really…'

'Just go, Chief,' she said.

And with that, Walker got up, put a few tenners on the table, and left The Elephant restaurant.

EPILOGUE

'Why didn't you take the promotion then, Chief?' asked DC Briggs.

She was referring to him being offered the position of Chief Constable at the Lancashire Constabulary, which would have made him head of the territory. It had been a political move, he'd guessed, aimed at appeasing the media and the public after the whole Sarah Harriet debacle. The media had a field day with it—their very own Chief Constable charged with one count of murder, one count of attempted murder, one count of conspiracy to murder, and one count of the sexual abuse of a minor. It would take a long time for the public to trust the police again, at least it would in Lancashire. He hadn't even been able to buy his team that meal he'd promised them when they finished, the one at the Beach Café, as it wouldn't have been a good look to be celebrating after closing this case—so he'd given them all an IOU. But since he'd been one of the few people coming out of the case with any credit, he'd been surprisingly offered the post of Chief Constable, which he'd promptly turned down.

'I didn't take the promotion because I don't like the politics of it all. I just want to catch the bad guys—even if those bad guys are one of us,' said Walker, eyes on the road, driving him and DC Briggs to Lancaster for their next assignment.

It had been months now since the arrest of Sarah Harriet, and a lengthy trial had ended with her being given a life sentence without any possibility of parole. She would die in prison, and most likely sooner rather than later since a lot of the inmates she'd be housed with had been put there by her in some way or another.

'I don't blame you for not taking it,' she said. 'I don't think I'd like it either—all that pressure. How's Dawn?'

She was asking about Walker's wife, who he'd now moved back in with, trying to give their marriage another go. It had all happened so quickly—the change of heart by his wife, handing him a lifeline, a way back into his family. He didn't entirely understand why she'd suddenly changed her mind, really, but he hadn't pushed her for a reason, just pleased to be given another chance. The timing of it had been odd though, just when he'd started to have some feelings for DC Briggs, while they'd gone out to dinner for the first time together. He still wasn't entirely sure what those feelings were, or what they meant. He wasn't good with feelings—they were so... difficult to grasp. What he did like, though, was evidence, something tangible he could get his hands on, derive theories from. And that was exactly what he was about to do. They'd been handed a new case on special assignment by the new Chief Constable—an older, well-experienced gentleman with a cleaner than clean record. He was just what the Constabulary needed, on paper at least. Walker had never worked with him before, though. He came from London somewhere, didn't seem exactly pleased to be stationed up north. Perhaps he'd been hoping for something better.

'Things are... Things are pretty good at home. I mean, not

great—it's a bit uncomfortable at times. But... it will take time, I guess,' said Walker. He was a bit uncomfortable at work too, now, as it happened, since they'd started to become close, after DC Briggs had almost died. He'd still rather be working with her than with someone else, though. He was sure things would get back to normal soon.

'Well, that's good,' said DC Briggs. 'Do tell her I said "Hello", won't you?'

There were a few seconds of silence, while Walker continued to drive up the M6 motorway towards Lancaster.

'So, what are we looking at, exactly? A woman found dead, you said. Any details?' asked DC Briggs. He'd not really gone over everything with her yet, as it had been a last-minute change of plan.

'Some woman, mid-thirties, found hung from the Gatehouse at Lancaster Castle,' said Walker. 'Someone apparently strung her up there somehow.'

'Wow. What's wrong with people these days. Anything else?' she asked.

'Yeah,' said Walker. 'They wrote "judged" next to the body with some paint, adding vandalism to their crime by defacing the castle walls.'

'That's not funny,' said DC Briggs.

Walker looked at her, then returned his gaze to the road. 'It wasn't meant to be,' he said. 'Anyway, with the history of that place, and all the witch-hunts that used to go on around there back in the day—you know, the Pendle witch trials—I think we've got some researching to do, just in case it's a little bit more than just some nutter.'

'Roger that, then, Chief. I suppose men have been persecuting women for centuries. I guess it would be a bit naïve to expect it to end today,' she said. 'I hope the Duty Officer has extended a wide perimeter on this one. The social media freaks will be having a field day with it if not.'

Walker sighed, gripping the steering wheel a tad firmer, and applying a little more pressure to the accelerator. 'This could be an interesting one, Detective. You'd better buckle up for the ride.'

'I'm already buckled in,' she said, and he caught her smiling.

'*That's* not funny, Constable,' he said.

She looked at him while he had his eyes firmly on the road.

'It wasn't meant to be,' she said.

They took Junction 33 and started to exit the motorway. They were almost there, but not quite. Not yet.

A Note From the Author

"Thanks so much for reading my book, *The Dunes*. I hope you enjoyed it. Please could you be so kind as to leave a **review** on Amazon? (Goodreads and Bookbub also appreciated) I read *every* review and they help new readers discover my books. In fact, they're invaluable for my career and the continued lives of DCI Walker and the gang. So… please, do it now before you forget! (and I'll keep writing)"

J.J. Richards

SIGN UP to my mailing list at **J-J-Richards.com** for news of new releases and more!

A LANCASHIRE DETECTIVE MYSTERY

THE CASTLE

When the Hunt Begins, You'd Better Be on the Right Side

J.J. RICHARDS

DCI Walker Crime Thrillers BOOK FIVE

Coming soon...

Printed in Dunstable, United Kingdom